The blade sliced air.

Adam veered quickly. But the tip of the rapier nicked his cheek; he could feel the blood.

He grabbed the shadow, knocked the blade from its grip—and stilled.

"Evie?"

She gasped. "Adam, is that you?"

"Evie, what the devil do you think you're doing?"

She was shaking. "I heard a noise. I thought . . ."

The panic, the fright in her voice was hard to miss. He relaxed his brutal hold, gathered the woman in his arms.

A heat filled him at the lithe body pressed in his embrace, so round and feminine—and scantily attired.

"Did I hurt you?" she said.

"It's just a scratch."

"Oh, Adam." She reached for his face, cupped his cheeks. Her fingers trembled as she moved them across his rough skin, wiping away the blood. "Forgive me."

His heart throbbed at the supple way she rubbed against him, her soft breasts brushing his chest as she stroked his jaw in tender regard.

It was more than Adam could bear. He dropped his head with a groan and took her sweet mouth into his own.

Other AVON ROMANCES

Coming Soon

And Don't Miss These
ROMANTIC TREASURES
from Avon Books

Too Dangerous To Desire

Alexandra Benedict

AVON

An Imprint of HarperCollinsPublishers

This is a work of fiction. Names, characters, places, and incidents are drawn from the author's imagination or are used fictitiously and are not to be construed as real. Any resemblance to actual events, locales, organizations, or persons, living or dead, is entirely coincidental.

AVON BOOKS
An Imprint of HarperCollins*Publishers*
10 East 53rd Street
New York, New York 10022-5299

Copyright © 2008 by Alexandra Benedikt
ISBN 978-0-06-117047-8
www.avonromance.com

First Avon Books paperback printing: August 2008

Avon Trademark Reg. U.S. Pat. Off. and in Other Countries, Marca Registrada, Hecho en U.S.A.
HarperCollins® is a registered trademark of HarperCollins Publishers.

Printed in the U.S.A.

10 9 8 7 6 5 4 3 2 1

For my readers

Too Dangerous To Desire

Prologue

The Sea, 1819

"I'll take that 'ere watch, nob, if you please."

Adam Westmore stared down the barrel of the gun and gritted, "I'd rather you shoot me."

The cheeky kid grinned, infuriating Adam even more. The indignity of it all! To be stripped of his most treasured possession by a dastardly brigand just out of swaddling clothes. Why, the kid couldn't be more than fifteen!

"Please, Adam." Teresa gripped her husband's arm in persuasion. "Give him the watch. I'll have the watchmaker fashion you another one as soon as we reach England."

"Aye, Adam," the cutthroat mimicked. "You'll get another lovely watch just as soon as you reach England." He stretched out his hand. "Now give me the bauble."

A surly Adam didn't budge.

Teresa hissed, "Adam, *please*."

At last the desperate plea of his wife convinced Adam to do as the pirate bade. With a disgruntled sigh, he handed the fob watch over to the buccaneer.

"Thank you kindly," the kid quipped.

Adam resisted the urge to flatten the impudent scamp's nose.

The young scalawag then had the audacity to present the fob watch to his captain as a gift, for it had apparently caught the black devil's eye.

Adam gnashed his teeth.

Amid the anxious whimpers of passengers and the grumbles of the crew, the pirate lot retreated across the deck of the *Hercules*, leaving the passengers frightened but unharmed.

One by one the pirates returned to their ship, positioned broadside, clutching gold and silver, whiskey and wine—and Adam's fob watch!

A rather rowdy cabin boy, perched in the ratlines high above Adam's head, suddenly cried, "Tell us your name, pirate capt'n!"

He was the last of the pirates to retreat—and the biggest of the brigand lot—with long black hair tied in a queue, eyes as blue as the sea, and a dark brow etched with a wicked grin. "Black Hawk."

And with that, the pirate captain bowed, thanked the passengers for their generous "gifts," and then climbed down the rope ladder, into the waiting rowboat.

As soon as every brigand was back aboard the pirate ship, the cannons aimed at the *Hercules* disappeared inside the dark portholes, and the schooner slowly sailed off.

Teresa clutched her breast and let out a noisy sigh. "Oh, thank heavens we're all safe!"

Adam slipped a protective arm around his wife's midriff. "Were you terribly frightened, my dear?"

"*Yes!*" She smacked his arm. "How could you quarrel with a pirate—over a watch?"

Adam scowled at the piratical schooner sailing away, still disgruntled to have lost the fob watch. "But it was a wedding gift from you, Tess!"

She humphed. "I'm going to retire to our cabin. I have a profound need to scream into a pillow."

Adam slumped his shoulders forward and watched his bride of two months skirt away in a huff. All right, so he had frightened her by resisting the pirate's demand. But, devil take it, the brigand was a kid still wet behind the ears. It was a humiliating business, to be robbed by a child. And of one's most beloved possession!

With a growl, Adam moved through the throng of still hysterical passengers, making his way to the cabin he and his wife shared. At least he still had his wedding ring. He fished the gold band from his pocket and slipped it back over his finger, content to have saved *one* valuable item.

Adam reached the cabin. He didn't bother to knock on the door, walked right inside the room—and found Teresa curled on the bed, crying.

"I'm sorry, Tess." He truly had not meant to panic her with his foolery. "This is not how I wanted our wedding tour to end."

A pillow sailed across the cabin space and smacked him in the chest.

He closed the door and sighed. "We should never have left Italy; we should have stayed on the peninsula another month."

"Don't say that." She sniffed. "Your mother needs our help. Don't you remember her letter?"

He did indeed remember the correspondence:

My dearest Adam,

I know how happy you and Tess are in Italy, but I must beg you both to return to England. Your brother is up to his wicked ways again. I have not seen him a fortnight, and the tales reaching my ears about his monstrous behavior do not bear repeating. Please come home. You are the only one who can help your brother. You know how he listens to you.

Faithfully yours,
Mother

"I don't know what to do anymore." Adam let out a heavy sigh of frustration, even failure. "I don't know how to save my brother."

Adam had tried over the years to drag his elder sibling away from the devastating debauchery that consumed his life. But his efforts, however promising at the start, always failed in the end.

Damian Westmore, the Duke of Wembury, dubbed the "Duke of Rogues" by his peers, was a villain through and through. He always returned to his familiar, sinful ways. Would he ever change? Adam wondered about that. And yet what else could Adam do? He could not give up on Damian. The duke was his brother.

"You will find the right words to say to your brother when the time is right," said Teresa, wiping the tears from her eyes. "You always do."

Adam smiled at his lovely wife. He walked across the room and gathered her in his arms.

"Oh Tess." He kissed the rest of her briny tears away. "What would I do without you?"

If only his brother could find such marital peace. If only the duke didn't rant and drink and wallow in darkness. It pained their mother to see Damian in so much distress. And it grieved Adam to see them both in such misery.

"You would perish at the hands of a pirate, that's what you would do," she quipped.

"You're right, my dear. I could never live without you." He kissed her softly. "Does this mean you forgive me for almost getting shot?"

She looked ready to protest, so he kissed her again—a little less softly this time.

She let out a dreamy sigh. "I suppose it does."

Adam awoke with a start.

A crashing boom echoed overhead; the ship dipped perilously.

"Good grief, what is it now?" Teresa cried. "More pirates?"

"I don't think so." Adam grabbed his wife by the midriff to keep her from rolling out of the bed. The pirate raid had happened hours ago, besides . . . "The pirates already took everything of value. There's no reason for them to return."

His bride secure, Adam scooted to the edge of the bed and gripped an overhead beam for support. The ship pitched violently then, sending him crashing into the opposite wall, smacking his head.

Teresa screamed and clutched the bed frame to keep from being tossed across the room.

Adam groaned, the pain in his head throbbing. Carefully he made his way to the other side of the cabin to collect his clothes.

"Stay here, Tess."

He snatched his trousers. A bit woozy, he grappled with the confounding apparel, his balance precarious at best. At last draped in decent attire, he slipped on his boots and quickly donned a shirt.

He bussed her brow. "I'll be back soon, luv."

"Don't go, Adam. Stay here with me."

She was shaking, and he rubbed her back in reassurance. "It'll be all right, Tess. We've hit choppy waters, is all. I'm just going topside to see if the crew needs any help. I'll be back in a minute."

She squeezed his wrist. "Be careful, Adam."

He nodded and left the cabin.

A grisly darkness filled the ship, the air brimming with moisture. Adam sloshed his way through the corridors, slowly filling with water.

The salty sea was spilling into the ship, the hatchway loose and ajar. Adam pushed through the deluge topside, blinded by the wicked spray and deathly darkness.

Choppy waters indeed. The wild tempest tossed the *Hercules* about like a rag doll. In the rough upheavals, Adam all but crashed backward down the hatchway. Arm swinging, he seized a thrashing rope for support and steadied his unsteady sea legs.

It was a sound English vessel; Adam had faith in its construction, its crew. The rig was built to withstand a brutal summer storm, surely. Besides, they were almost home. With each sizzle of lightning, he could see the distant shadow of shore. There was no need to panic, to fret about the safety of his beloved bride belowdecks.

Stifling the creeping alarm in his breast, Adam thought it wise to offer the tars his support. He wasn't a deft sailor, but if he could help in any way, he would.

Lightning flickered and spat. Adam spotted the rangy figure of the cabin boy, struggling with a stubborn brail. He was at the mercy of the lashing wind and combers, too weak to secure the loose rigging.

Adam pushed against the mighty gales. He wasn't a hefty man himself, but he had more strength and stamina than the weary cabin boy lobbing about in the wind.

"Let me, kid!" he shouted, and grabbed the coarse rope between his hands.

Adam and the boy yanked at the brail to keep the mainsail flat against the boom, while sailors secured the canvas.

A bright spark of lightning hit the mainmast.

Adam blinked; colorful spots bounced before his eyes. It took seconds to register the hollers, the fear. He glanced up, squinting, the rain stabbing his eyes . . . but the flames burned and dazzled against the gloomy black sky.

Fire.

It snaked down the mainmast, a blistering

glow. The heat, the surge of electrical charge too potent to be washed away by the flicks of rain.

It engulfed the canvas, the rope; slithered down the mainmast and licked at the deck.

Sailors swatted at the flames; a crack of thunder erupted overhead.

The sharp sights and stinging sounds, the thumping pain in his head from his earlier mishap with the wall, crowded Adam's befuddled mind, distracting him.

The wave hit, an icy slap against his every sense. He couldn't breathe, dragged away by the stinging numbness of the water, swallowed by the lashing waves.

Adam thrashed and screamed; the sea filled his lungs. He spat and gasped, breaking the surface, his eyes burning with salt and smoke.

The ship was ablaze, floating away. It heaved and plunged in the shifting surge.

"Oh God . . . *Tess!*"

He flapped his arms, but he was a poor swimmer. And the combers kept coming, pummeling him, pushing him deeper into the sea.

Adam struggled to keep afloat, to get to the ship—to Tess.

But in a matter of minutes, the charred wreckage slowly dipped . . . and dipped . . . and slipped beneath the dark and churning waters.

With a hoarse scream, Adam beat the waves,

trying to get to the whirlpool of ruin. But each defiant lash against the current only pushed him farther and farther away from the rubble.

"Tess!" he croaked, delirious with grief.

Something snagged on his ankle.

Death.

It beckoned him to the bottom of the sea—to Tess.

Spent, Adam surrendered to his sorrow; he stopped fighting the roiling waters.

But the weight at his feet shifted, rushed to the surface. Buoyant, the crate bobbed in the water and nestled against him.

Adam latched on to the wood and let out a sob.

Teresa was gone: his childhood playmate, his sweetheart, his bride! She had been with him his entire life. She *was* his life, his soul. She was the only good part of him . . . and *he* had snatched her away, the way he always snatched away everything good and true.

His brother: the Duke of Wembury.

The cumbersome grief in Adam's belly collapsed and burned like the wreckage of the *Hercules*. A deep and unmoving rancor for the ignoble duke, so selfish, so evil, consumed him.

He had cursed Adam, the duke. Cursed him to live a life in hell. Adam had dedicated years of his life to dragging his elder brother away from his wicked pursuits. And in the end, the fraternal goodwill had cost him his dearest Teresa. But for the duke's immorality, his debauchery, Adam and Tess would still be in Italy, enjoying their wedding tour, their married *life*.

Filled with the incoherent ramblings of a fever, Adam vowed, "I will kill you for this, brother."

Chapter 1

England, 1825

The gray sea churned softly.

Adam stared at the rolling waves and listened to the surge of water rush in with the tide, then slowly ebb away.

The beach was deserted, the sand cool and moist between his toes. He looked away from the swell of the water to the letter in his hands. It was from his mother, the epistle. She wrote to him often, bringing him tidings about his ancestral home, his family . . . what was left of his family.

"It's your fault she's gone." The rage billowed inside Adam. He shook with repressed agony and hatred. "I had to sail home to drag you from your filthy existence. I had to wallow in muck for most of my life, lugging you out of whorehouses and gaming hells—and I lost Tess because of it. You." Adam pointed to his brother with the knife, the blade trembling in his shaky hand.

"You've destroyed everything good in your life—and mine."

The steady rush of seawater slightly soothed Adam's tortured memory. He searched the horizon for further comfort.

But it was empty.

When would he stop looking out to sea for Tess?

She was gone, the vast and restless ocean her tomb. And yet he could not bear to part from her. He owned a small cottage by the seashore. He never strayed too far from the ocean—from Tess.

Thunder resounded in the distance; the waves churned with greater passion. A summer tempest was about to ignite. It was time he returned to the cottage to seek shelter indoors.

Adam stuffed the letter into his shirt pocket. He reached for his leggings and boots, had the soft linen and leather in his grip, when a peculiar figure intruded upon his barren and familiar surroundings.

He stared at the mountainous cliff some few hundred yards away.

It was a woman.

He could tell by the flicker of her skirt in the stormy breeze. She was alone atop the cliff; her long, dark hair loose and free in the mighty gale.

Adam watched her, curious. She brought her hands to her breasts as though in prayer . . . but not in prayer.

Her fingers moved toward her midriff, button by button. Soon she slipped out of the dress.

Adam lifted a brow.

Perhaps she was undressing for her lover? Adam should go before the other man arrived.

But something compelled him to stay and admire the woman's artful movements.

Piece by piece, she removed her clothing: shoes, shift, chemise. Stripped to the flesh, she approached the precipice.

Adam bristled.

The woman outstretched her hands; the pounding winds tried to push her back. But she let out a sorrowful sob—and threw herself off the cliff.

"No!"

Adam dropped his boots and sprinted across the beach. He jumped into the sea, the water chilling despite the warm summer air.

He did not feel the nip of the waves, though. Blood throbbed in his heart, driving him onward in a near bout of madness.

In deft strokes he swam toward the base of the cliff, desperate to get to the woman. He was more robust, a skilled swimmer. He had practiced every summer since his late wife's demise. He would not let the sea beat him down. Not again. Not the way it had on the night Tess had perished. He would not let the mysterious woman drown—the way Tess had drowned.

"Where are you?" Adam shouted, stroking across the water with fluidity.

But there was no sign of the woman.

The angry sea swelled. He gasped for breath and dove under the swirling waves.

It was dim beneath the surface: a soft, silvery light. Adam struggled against the current, kicking, searching. He touched rock, sand.

Where are you?

Adam groped along the rough seabed; there was nothing but sharp rock.

No! You have to be here!

He reached into the cold darkness—and grasped flesh.

Icy flesh.

Adam grabbed the lithe body and pressed it against him. He broke through the thrashing waves, thirsty for air.

The woman was limp, lifeless in his arms.

"Wake up!"

Her head lolled to the side.

Panicked, Adam started for shore, fighting the now battering storm, the hail of rain. He reached the beach and dropped to his knees, hugging the sea nymph in his arms.

"Wake up," he coaxed, shaking her softly. "Please wake up."

The rain spit hard.

Adam pushed the dark locks from her eyes.

Something flickered in the very depth of his soul. A familiar, yet long forgotten verve. A kinship with another being.

He touched her lips, blue from the frigid sea.

Warm breath.

Faint puffs of air, but she was alive.

Adam struggled to his feet and hurried back to his cottage.

The firelight flickered across the whitewashed cottage walls. A soft rain pattered overhead, the brunt of the storm over.

Adam observed the sea nymph from his wicker chair. She was asleep in his bed. He dared not fetch a physician and leave her unattended. He feared she'd recover while he was away and throw herself off the cliff once more. Instead he had built a small fire in the hearth to draw out the humidity in the air, and layered thick blankets over her to make her warm.

Wake up.

He willed her survival. He was determined to see her well. The sea would not claim another life; he was adamant.

Adam abandoned his seat and moved closer to

the bed. What hapless circumstance had urged her to try to take her own life? He couldn't fathom. The world was filled with so much tragedy. It would take very little to make an indigent lass desperate. One so wont to hardship might think there was peace in death. Adam had once believed that, too. But being near the sea had soothed his troubled thoughts, put them to sleep.

There was a scrap of linen saturating in a nearby dish. He picked up the cloth and wrung the water, mixed with a dash of brandy. With gentle taps, he cooled her brow.

So lovely, he thought.

Adam blinked. He had not considered a woman in such a way since the death of his wife. He was still faithful to Tess. He would always be faithful to Tess. That the sea nymph had inspired such a reflection disturbed him.

Adam placed the linen back in the bowl and returned to his seat. The vim in his blood surged, the same burst of energy that had gripped him on the beach. Again he sensed a bond with the castaway maiden. The demons of his past and the demons that had chased her to the cliff today united them in sorrow.

He watched her sleep. She had elfin features, soft and delicate. Aristocratic in length and symmetry. And that hair, such a shadowy shade of black, it sparkled blue in the light.

He would presume her a lady, but for her hands. Her hands were much too dry and rough to be those of a genteel-bred miss. She worked with her hands. In the soil? It would explain her apparel. Threadbare rags, really.

Adam had risked leaving her alone for a few minutes to collect her clothing from the precipice. The garments were stretched across furniture throughout the cottage, drying. Very poor quality garments, so she must be from a simple home. And yet that necklace.

Adam eyed the jewelry at her throat. It glowed in the firelight. It was the only thing she had not removed before she'd stepped off the cliff. It was a gold necklace with a heart-shaped pendant, the heart cast in two halves. The sort of piece intended to be broken: a half of the heart given to each wearer. She wore both halves, though. Together as one.

It was a very delicate ornament, designed with fine filigree. A work of art, really. Much too expensive for a woman of the soil. Was she a thief? Or did the necklace belong to her? If she was wealthy enough to afford it, why was she in such poor attire, and why did she have callused hands? Yet if it did not belong to her, if she had filched it, why had she tossed herself off the cliff? A thief would surely rejoice at such a precious spoil, not attempt suicide.

Adam was stumped. He would just have to ask the woman her identity as soon as she roused.

The bedcovers rustled.

Adam lifted his eyes to meet the sea nymph's—and stared.

Her eyes!

The rain had stopped, the storm clouds disbanding. Sunlight pierced the cottage windows through the pockets in the clouds, warming the room . . . lighting her eyes.

Adam had never seen such a striking pair: a heavy blue center surrounded by a soft gray ring. In the light the irises sparkled violet. He very nearly dropped headfirst into her bewitching eyes.

He whispered, "Hello."

Chapter 2

Evelyn Waye opened her eyes, confounded by her obscure surroundings. Her thoughts in disorder, she took a moment to reflect. But her only memory was a feeling: a feeling of cold, dark . . . water!

The image came sharp to her mind: heavy winds beat against her naked breast as she approached the precipice and outstretched her arms in search of freedom. Freedom from *him*.

A figure moved beside the window. A voice resounded.

"Hello," he said again. "My name is Adam."

Her heart fluttered. She looked from the table to the cupboard to the braided rug by the door. She should be dead. She should be at the bottom of the ocean. What was this place?

Adam slowly approached the bed. "Are you all right?"

She stiffened. He was big. The wide breadth of his shoulders blocked the light coming in through one of the small windows. She was too dizzy from her fall to see his features clearly, but she could sense the man's inquisitive gaze. She loathed that look. It always reminded her she was different, cursed.

Adam touched her brow. "Don't cry."

The gentle caress disarmed her. She flinched.

He quickly curled his fingers into his palm and retreated from the bed. "I won't hurt you."

She trembled, unconvinced. He was a man. Selfish. Cruel. He had stared at her with that *look*. He would hurt her just like . . . *him*.

A sob filled her sore lungs.

Adam appeared discomfited. "Are you in pain?"

Yes, she was in pain. She was alive! And that meant *he* was still out there, searching for her. She had not escaped him. She had not found freedom yet. And it was all Adam's doing. He had pulled her from the sea. She wanted to rail at him for his unwelcome gallantry: *You should have let me die!*

"Have you any broken bones?" said Adam.

Evelyn shifted under the warm covers, her muscles tender. But no part of her body throbbed with agony to indicate a fractured limb. Not that she voiced the sentiment aloud, too wary to do so.

"That's a very beautiful necklace," he said next.

The necklace!

Evelyn reached for her throat, searching for the pendant. Her palm quickly gripped the heart, the gold warming between her fingers.

Oh, thank God! She still had the necklace, if nothing else.

"What is your name?" he said softly.

Evelyn eyed the stranger with scrutiny. It was still too difficult for her to see him clearly, but she appraised the low and steady sound of his voice. It filled the small space with its commanding presence. And for some reason the deep timbre put her frazzled nerves to rest.

Yet she still ignored his question about her name. She didn't trust the man. Instead she looked around the room and noticed her garments draped across the furniture.

Adam guessed her intent. He reached out and touched the hem of her dress, stretched over a chair. "It's still damp. Are you sure you want to wear it?"

Evelyn continued to stare at the dress.

He sighed. "Why don't I step outside and give you some privacy?"

He moved away from the window and opened the door. He left the cottage and closed the barrier behind him.

Evelyn stared at the door, waiting to see if the stranger would come back inside the room. It would not surprise her if he did. Men were so disreputable, always looking to abuse a woman.

She had to get away. But how?

She eyed the window above her head. It faced the rear of the cottage. If Adam was still standing by the front door, she could crawl out the back and disappear . . . return to the cliff.

Evelyn dropped the covers and snatched her clothes from various spots around the room. The garments were still damp, as Adam had said, but she didn't care. She shimmied into the shift and chemise, the frock and boots, then clambered up onto the bed.

The window had no clasp. She lifted the pane of framed glass and stuck her head and shoulders through the opening. She was still a bit dizzy, but there was no reason for her to recuperate. She would do it right this time; she would end her life with no witnesses—and finally be free of *him*.

Evelyn's posterior was next—and she rolled out the window, feet over head. She landed in a patch of strawberries.

Having struck the ground with a hard thump, she blinked. But soon her wits returned and she scrambled to her feet.

She tiptoed around the cottage to avoid the stranger, then took off running.

A set of brawny limbs clinched her waist.

She let out a cry of vexation and thrashed.

"Hold still!" Adam barked. "I won't hurt you."

"Let me go!"

"So you can talk?" came the dry inquiry. "I was beginning to wonder."

Evelyn struck back with her fists, but she was too weak to do the big brute damage. Not that she could have done him much harm if she'd had all her strength; he was that heavily built.

"Be still, woman! I said I wouldn't hurt you."

"But *he* will!"

Adam set her on the ground. He maintained a firm hold on her waist, but turned her around to face him. "Who will hurt you?"

Evelyn opened her mouth to protest his jostling, but words deserted her. She was confronted by a set of strong features: sharp lines across a hard and masculine face. He had a straight nose and square jaw, dusted with the shadow of a beard. Firm lips came together to demonstrate his displeasure over her attempted flight.

He was virile. Robust. She was even more wary to be in his presence, for he emitted a thrumming energy, a potent strength that frightened her. The sort of strength that could hurt her, crush her if she wasn't careful.

A crisp, dark curl dropped over his eye.

Evelyn dismissed the anxiety in her belly for a moment, rapt by the stunning expression in his eyes. She delved deep into the set of blue pools, as sad as hers.

He was filled with grief, she reckoned. And she suddenly sensed a kindred spirit in the man.

Evelyn stilled in his embrace.

"That's better," he said. "Now who is going to hurt you?"

She pinched her lips.

Adam sighed. "No one will harm you. I promise."

She shook her head. "You can't make such a promise."

"I can," he said with curt confidence. "And I will. No one will trouble you here. I live at the edge of the world." He nodded toward the sea. "You are safe here."

Evelyn had not been safe in years. Thin hairs spiked on the back of her neck in trepidation. This stranger could not offer her sanctuary. Nothing could offer her that—but death.

"I want to go back to the cliff," she said.

Adam bristled, the straight cut of his jaw rigid. "You will *not* go back to the cliff. Do you hear me?" Stormy eyes pegged her. "I will protect you. You can live here with me. I won't tell anyone that you're here."

Evelyn took in a shaky breath. She didn't know what to do. To trust the stranger? She couldn't do that. She didn't dare. She trusted no one but herself. She had been alone for so long . . .

"Don't cry," Adam said softly, and touched the tear at her cheek. "Tell me your name?"

She sniffed. "Evelyn."

She would not tell him her last name. She feared he might recognize her; that he might still betray her. He was only a poor fisherman, but still, he might be familiar with her name. He might seek a reward for her return . . .

"You are safe with me, Evelyn."

She was unsure of his words. But his eyes. That look in his eyes was almost honest. It had been so long since she'd seen such an expression. Not since the last time she'd been with her beloved sister more than three years ago.

Evelyn glanced around the property, to the cottage first. It was a quaint home with a thatched roof. Ivy crawled and covered the rear of the shady abode.

Her eyes drifted to the rain barrel and rose bushes, the hollyhocks and sweet peas. There was a small garden to the north, trimmed with hedges, filled with cabbages, potatoes, onions, and parsnips. Pear and apple trees dotted the grounds. A woodshed in the rear was piled with chopped and neatly stacked logs, and laundry flapped in the breeze, stretched across a simple clothesline.

Her eyes returned to Adam. He maintained

the property. It was pretty. Peaceful, even. If he treated the trees and the flowers and the root vegetables with such care, maybe he wasn't like all the others?

"I can mend that." She pointed to the tear in his sleeve. "I can cook, too."

Evelyn didn't want charity. She would work for her board . . . for her life.

It appeared death would have to wait another day for her. At least one more day. She would accept the stranger's offer of help. There was just something about him—his eyes—that inspired her to take the chance.

Adam nodded. "Fair enough. But you must promise me one thing, Evelyn."

"Evie." She sniffed, then quietly said, "My sister used to call me Evie."

Adam's features softened, but his words stayed firm. "You must promise me, Evie, not to go near the cliff."

Evelyn took in a deep breath, a near gasp. There was so much pressure on her chest, as if she had not breathed in years.

Stay away from the cliff? From death? For today. Perhaps for tomorrow, too. If the stranger's words came true: that *he* would not find her here.

She nodded. "I promise."

Chapter 3

The potage bubbled in an iron pot over the fire: the only sound in an otherwise quiet cottage.

Adam hunkered beside the hearth and slowly stirred the thick soup. "Dinner should be ready soon."

Evelyn didn't respond. She was seated at the table, wrapped in a blanket and drinking a cup of coffee. She appeared lost to her thoughts. And with reason. She had craved death this morning. Now she was safe, alive. Much had happened to her in just a day.

"I can make drapes for you," she said.

He looked at the naked window. Is that what she had been thinking about all this time? How to neaten his home? Or perhaps she was assuring herself she could work for her board?

Adam picked up an iron ladle. "You should rest." He poured the broth into a wooden bowl and set it on the table in front of her. "Don't worry about the drapes."

"I can make you a new shirt, too."

She was looking out the window, not at him. He took her moment of reflection to gaze surreptitiously at her graceful figure. The firelight bounced off her dark locks; the tresses shimmered under the lambent glow. The dancing light enlivened her, and her presence in turn made the room so much more animated.

It struck Adam soundly, the energy stemming from her. He was more sensitive to her every artful movement, more alert to his own sense of self. For too long he had endured solitude. He was accustomed to the quiet stillness of life and the emptiness of aloneness. Evelyn's company disturbed him in a way he had not anticipated. How to even converse with her? He had not dined with a woman in years. The simple ritual seemed so strange to him now.

Adam joined her at the table with his own bowl of soup. "You don't have to make me clothes or drapes."

He lived a simple life, dressed in simple attire. He had no need for lavish waste. Ever since the death of his wife, he had forsaken the privileges of the *ton*. He did not belong to that glittering world anymore, for it offered him cold comfort.

He preferred the solitude of the beach, the gray waves and tempestuous skies.

He preferred to be close to Tess.

"You don't have to work for me," he said again. "I offered you my protection. You don't owe me anything in return." He touched her hand, limp on the table. "Evie?"

She didn't flinch at his touch this time. She looked away from the window, down at his hand clasping hers. She appeared dazed.

"Did you hear me, Evie?"

She shifted her eyes, those stunning—and broken—violet eyes.

Who is he? Adam wondered. *Who hurt you, Evie?*

A burning bitterness gripped him, an unmistakable desire to snap flesh and bone.

Was *he* her husband?

Adam glanced at Evelyn's fingers. No ring. She could have removed the bauble. But still, there was no mark or imprint where a ring might have been. So who was *he* then?

"I want to do it," she said. "I want to make you the drapes."

Her hand was warm beneath his touch. So warm and comforting. That he could feel anything at all, that he was not deeply asleep inside, disarmed him.

Adam let go of her hand. He picked up the spoon and tasted the soup.

"I'll go to town in the morning," he said. "I'll purchase some material for the drapes."

He didn't feel at ease with the arrangement. He had offered the woman his protection; it was neither right nor gentlemanly to accept compensation, even in terms of labor.

Yet what else could he do? She had vowed not to go near the cliff. If he reneged on his part of the bargain, if he did not allow her to perform some household chores, she might renege on her half, too.

Her lashes fluttered in wariness. "Town?"

"I won't tell anyone that you're living here," he assured her. "You are safe with me."

Again those violet eyes bewitched him. She looked at him as though he was a curious creature in a sideshow carnival. Did the idea of being safe, of trusting someone, really baffle her?

That dark rage still brewed in his belly. Whoever *he* was, he would not hurt Evelyn again. Adam would see to it.

She glanced around the sparsely furnished room. "How will you afford the material?"

Clearly she thought him just a little less destitute than herself. "I live off of a respectable family allowance."

"You're not a fisherman?"

"No, I'm not."

I'm not the man you think I am, Evie.

"Then why do you live so close to the sea?" she wondered.

He could feel her misgiving. She wanted, *needed* to know something more about him. He had offered to protect her. But why should she trust him?

"Six years ago my wife died at sea." He was careful to keep the inflection in his voice steady. Conversing about his late wife always disarmed him. "I feel close to Teresa here."

Although that was not the only reason he stayed so close to the sea. He had another, more dangerous, motive for keeping near the water. He refrained from commenting about it, though. No need to frighten his easily spooked houseguest.

Evelyn lowered her eyes to her soup.

"Have I upset you, Evie?"

She whispered, "I was thinking about my sister."

"Where is your sister?"

"She's dead." Evelyn clutched the pendant at her throat. "This is all I have left to feel close to her."

Slowly the woman's mysterious identity was being revealed. She was no thief. The necklace belonged to her; it was there in her haunting eyes, the great meaning it had for her. And more and more he was beginning to suspect she wasn't a woman of the soil, as he had first believed. Her hands might be calloused, but her speech was superb, the accent reared to be of quality.

However, there was still so much to learn about her. He wished to know it all—who was chasing her, for one—but a tentative trust was forming, and he didn't want to upset the delicate bond by intruding too deeply into her troubles and distressing her. He would just have to be patient. To wait for the right moment to make more subtle inquiries.

"How is the soup?" he asked.

"Good." She let go of the pendant and returned to her meal. "I can cook for you, too. And make jam." She looked sheepish. "I'm afraid I ruined your strawberry patch, though, when I landed in it."

He smiled. "It'll grow back."

Adam finished the soup and took the dish over to the dry sink. He dipped it into a bowl of cold water to rinse it.

"It's getting late," he said. "You should get some sleep."

He could hear her breath catch.

"I'm going to sleep outdoors tonight." He moved over to the dish rack and returned the wooden soup bowl. "It's a warm night, and I like sleeping under the stars."

Not true, but he wanted her to take the bed. She deserved to rest, to feel safe. And she wouldn't take the bed if she thought he wanted it. He understood enough about her to conclude she was loath to feel like a bother.

He headed for the chest at the foot of the bed. "I'll just gather a spare blanket."

She seemed a little perturbed by the sleeping arrangements. "I can sleep outside; I don't mind."

"Really, Evie, I much prefer the crickets and warm summer breeze. I never sleep indoors in the summer. It's better if you take the bed. No sense in it going to waste."

After a brief pause, she nodded. "All right, then."

As Adam opened the chest, a wealth of familiar items greeted him. The contents evoked memories: both pleasant and foul. He stared at the weaponry: swords . . . a knife.

"I think it's time your wicked ways come to an end, brother." Adam pushed the knife in deeper. "You've disgraced this family long enough."

He thrust aside the foul memory by thrusting aside the luminous blades, and reached for the more pleasant keepsakes.

Adam's heart quivered as he caressed the silver comb and mirror. With reverence, he placed the items, along with a bar of lemon soap, on the bed. "This is for you."

Evelyn eyed the toiletries warily. "I can't pay you."

"You don't have to pay me; it's a gift."

"I don't need anything," she was quick to assure him.

"Listen, Evie. I don't know if you realize how this works, but I've offered to protect you, and now it's my duty to see to all your needs." He removed a bundle of fabric from the chest, too. "There's some clothes for you here, as well."

"I can't wear your clothes."

"The pieces are not mine."

As he unraveled the garments, violet eyes circled. "Oh. The apparel belonged to your late wife."

"I keep a few of her things."

Most of Teresa's belongings had perished with her in the sea, but some had remained behind in England: accouterments she had not packed with her for their wedding tour.

"I have a dress," she said. "Truly, I don't need another one."

He looked at the rags she termed a dress and said, "It's settled, Evie. I must see to all your needs. And you need clothing."

She quit protesting at that.

"Take one or all of the frocks if you like. I don't know how many will fit you. Teresa was shorter in stature, but you are welcome to alter the garbs."

Evelyn appeared shy and lowered her head. "I cannot repay your kindness."

"Yes, you can." He smiled. "You can sew me some new drapes."

That must have put her at ease, for she, too, smiled then.

Chapter 4

"You're alive."

Damian Westmore, the Duke of Wembury, was bewildered. Adam could appreciate that; he should be dead. In a way, he was.

"Am I?" said Adam. "It doesn't feel like it."

He entered the duke's bedroom and yanked off his hood, the blade snug in his grip. Two years ago to the day, Tess had died at sea. And with her all joy and hope for the future. But tonight the notorious "Duke of Rogues" would bleed to make amends. Tonight Damian's dynasty of wickedness would come to an end.

Damian eyed the luminous blade in his brother's hand. It was clear he comprehended Adam's intent; he wasn't foxed and disoriented like his usual self.

A bloody miracle. It was also a boon. Adam did not want his sibling to have the comfort of an easy death in a hazy dream. Tess had had no such comfort. She had drowned in a fiery wreckage. She had screamed in fright before a cold, watery darkness had silenced her forever.

Adam shuddered, sweating at the morbid thought.

The duke was not alone. He quickly whisked the woman in his arms across the room, shoved her onto the balcony, then locked the glass doors—so Adam could not get to her.

Something twitched in Adam's belly. Jealousy. He was no fool. He could see the fear in Damian's eyes: fear for the woman. The same sick and twisting fear Adam had suffered whenever Tess had been frightened or hurt or unsure. The kind of fear born of love that urged a man to protect a woman with his breath, his blood, his very fists. That his sinful brother should have such a love, while Adam endured the misery of aloneness, was an injustice. A cruelty. And a disgrace to Tess's memory.

"I thought you had died at sea," said Damian, bemused.

"Oh, but I did." Adam kicked the bedroom door closed with the heel of his boot. "I died on the night Tess perished."

There was something different about the duke. A look of . . . grief? Even remorse?

Adam dismissed the sentiment. It was impossible. The duke was a selfish bastard. That he could mourn or feel pain was ridiculous, unworthy of consideration.

"Adam, where have you been?"

"In hell." Unhooking the clasp at his neck, Adam allowed the cloak to slip free. "All thanks to you."

Damian choked on his words. "Adam, please, tell me what happened?"

"Why? You don't give a damn."

"Please, Adam, tell me," he beseeched. "I have to know."

"Do you now?"

Adam spotted a pistol resting on the surface of the writing desk, and slowly maneuvered his way closer to the weapon. It was just like the duke to be so irresponsible: to leave a gun unsecured.

"Very well, then," said Adam. "A wretched storm hit, sinking the ship. I washed ashore on a little island off the coast of Wales, where a group of monks living in an isolated monastery looked after me. For more than a year I had no memory of who I was or where I had come from. And then one night, during a brutal storm, lightning hit the holy dwelling and my memory came back."

Adam picked up the gun. Armed with both pistol and blade, he resumed his steady advance on the duke. It was time to avenge Teresa.

"It's your fault she's gone." The rage billowed inside Adam. He shook with repressed agony and hatred. "I had to sail home to drag you from your filthy existence. I had to wallow in muck for most of my life, lugging you out of whorehouses and gaming hells—and I lost Tess because of it. You." Adam pointed to him with the knife, the blade trembling in his shaky hand. "You've destroyed everything good in your life—and mine. You're no better than Father."

Their father had been a wicked scoundrel, too. And

Damian had turned out to be just like the former duke, worse even.

The duke whispered, "I'm sorry, Adam."

Was that a tear in Damian's eye?

Adam blinked to dispel the thought. The "Duke of Rogues" shedding tears? Overwhelmed with repentance?

Horseshit!

The devil cannot reform his wicked ways. The devil deserved to die.

"Oh no." Adam shook his head vehemently. "That paltry and insincere gesture isn't going to absolve you of what you've done." The duke did not want to die, was all. A few tears might fool some simpleton into believing the duke's atonement sincere, but Adam was far too familiar with his brother's nefarious habits to believe such a deceit real.

He glanced at the glass balcony doors. Throughout the exchange with his kin, the woman had pounded on the doors, wrestled with the knob. Fearful. For the duke?

"She appears to care for you a great deal," said Adam. "And I suspect you care for her, too."

Damian's eyes darkened. "What are you going to do?"

"I'm going to set things right."

Adam paused. He was just a few feet away from his brother. Damian made no effort to run or even defend himself. He had lost this battle, and he knew it. Adam was armed. And he was strong. He was not the lean man he had been two years ago. The physical demands of monastic life had offered him an opportunity to build his strength. He was now as big as the duke. And he was a proficient assassin. He had spent the last year learning the art of death in preparation for this moment. There was nowhere for Damian to hide. No way for the duke to win the strife.

"In memory of Tess, I'm going to take your place as the next Duke of Wembury and put an end to the dynasty of misery you have wrought . . . or I was." Adam looked at the glass balcony doors, at the woman rattling the knob in a desperate attempt to get back inside the room. And save the duke? "But I've changed my mind. I think there's an even better way to make you pay for what you've done."

Adam lifted the gun and aimed it for the glass doors.

The woman stumbled back in surprise.

"No!"

The duke pounced on his brother, and both men crashed to the ground with a tremendous thump.

"You will not hurt her, Adam! She is as innocent as Tess. Your strife is with me!"

Adam stopped struggling. It was true. He had not come to take an innocent life, but a guilty one.

The pistol hit the rug with a muffled thud.

"You're right," said Adam.

With one piercing stroke, he stabbed the duke.

Damian gasped.

"I think it's time your wicked ways come to an end, brother." Adam pushed the knife in deeper. "You've disgraced this family long enough."

The woman on the balcony screamed.

Blood oozed over Adam's fingers.

The duke was on his knees. He grabbed Adam's shoulders, but Adam shrugged off his brother's grip and yanked the knife from his chest.

Adam stood. He lifted the blade high above his head, ready to take another stab at the duke.

But still Damian did not move. Prostrated at Adam's feet, the duke looked like the lost boy Adam remembered. The brother who had once cherished Adam in youth before their father had twisted his soul and made him a villain.

Something snagged on Adam's heart. A lost childhood memory. Two brothers sheltered together in the castle, in hiding from their cruel father, sharing boiled apples rolled in brown sugar and whispering about the adventures of Robinson Crusoe.

Adam trembled. "Why won't you fight me now?!"

Damian gripped the gash in his chest, blood seeping between his fingers, and croaked, "Because I love you."

Those words . . . Damian had never said those words to him. He was a black devil; he could not feel love, surely. He was a monster. He . . .

Adam closed his eyes. The tears came. Fresh and briny drops that soaked his cheeks, his soul like balm.

He dropped the blade. Grief overwhelmed him, pounded him. Grief for all he had lost: his wife . . . his brother.

Adam sunk to his knees, opposite Damian, and brushed his fingers roughly through his hair, the need for blood slowly ebbing away.

He suddenly grabbed Damian by the sides of the head and leaned in to whisper, "Why did it have to be like this?"

Why?

Why was Tess gone?

Why was his brother his enemy?

Adam pulled away from the wounded duke. A disturbing truth settled in his belly. It was not his brother's fault that Teresa had suffered a gruesome death—it was his. He had failed to save her from drowning.

The woman on the balcony kicked her foot through the glass doors, desperate to reach the wounded duke. She would take care of Damian. She would try to heal him. Adam had no strength left. Unfounded rage had consumed him. All of him. There was nothing left.

Adam picked up the knife and softly made his way to the bedroom door. His mother appeared, stunned. He touched her cheek. He had no words for her.

He was a broken man.

Evelyn breathed in the tart scent of lemon soap. She dipped the creamy bar into a bowl of water and rubbed it between her palms to work up a lather.

She yearned to be clean, and scrubbed her cheeks with the sweet citrus bubbles, thinking of Adam and his gift. It was such a lovely gift, the soap. She wanted to enjoy its fragrance and touch, to think no ill thoughts about the man who'd given it to her or his motives behind the gesture.

But a habit of mistrusting men was difficult to shake, and Evelyn was slightly apprehensive about Adam's generosity. She had to wonder: *Did he want something in return?*

He had given her gifts, too. Extravagant presents. But *he* had wanted something very precious in return: her soul.

Evelyn shivered and dismissed the creature from her mind. Her thoughts returned to Adam. He'd promised to protect her. But no man had ever offered her that before. Her father had failed to take care of her. *He* wanted to possess and abuse her. But Adam . . .

Evelyn rinsed her skin with cool water, then patted it dry with a small towel. She knew very little about Adam. So wary of strangers, why had she settled into his cottage with such ease?

She wasn't sure. She was baffled by her own choice to stay. But stay she would. For a time.

The small silver mirror sparkled under the warm firelight, the glass shiny and winking.

Evelyn stared at the hand-held mirror on the bed, another gift from Adam. Without sparing it another thought, she picked up the glass and turned it upside-down. She hated to see her own reflection.

Free from the mirror's disturbing call, she returned to the table. Under lamplight, she finished the last few stitches in the dress. The alteration complete, she lifted the lovely butter white frock to inspect her handiwork.

"I think it will fit."

To be sure, though, she shimmied out of her tattered clothes and stepped into the finely woven attire.

It was cool to the skin, the soft linen. She couldn't reach all the buttons in the back, so a few went unclasped. For the most part, though, the garb fit her well around the midriff.

She moved about the room, testing the garment's fluidity. It was a tad too short in the hem, but that didn't matter. It would suit her just fine around the cottage.

Evelyn stilled.

She listened for the noise once more.

Heartbeat drumming, she picked up a candle and slowly opened the door. She stepped outside. A sudden dread enveloped her; that *he* had found her. She waited for *him* to jump from the shadows and steal her away. But she soon realized her fear was unfounded. The noise was not the shuffle of feet, but a cry of distress.

With her hand shielding the flame, she moved around to the back of the cottage, searching for the cause of the sound.

As she neared the woodshed, the groaning surged in pitch.

Feet bare, she tiptoed closer to the shelter and peeked inside to see Adam lying on the ground—swatting at something in the air.

"Adam?"

He swatted some more.

Evelyn set the candle on the dirt and crouched at Adam's feet. She shook him by the ankle. "Wake up."

When he still swiped and punched, she gave his ankle a hard jerk.

Adam flinched.

Evelyn was quiet for a moment, then wondered, "Are you awake?"

He slowly shifted to sit, rubbing his eyes. "I think so . . . where am I?"

"In the shed. Come inside and take the bed. I will sleep outside."

"No," he croaked. "I'm fine."

"You're not fine. You don't like to sleep outside, admit it?"

He had forsaken the bed for her. Out of duty. But Evelyn didn't want to displace the man from the comforts of his own home. Clearly he didn't like being outside with the crickets, and she was determined to get him back indoors where he belonged.

She took him by the hand. "Come inside, Adam."

Evelyn gasped when he captured her wrist and gripped it tight. It was a strong hold. Unbreakable. And yet she did not shake or squirm. In Adam's strong hold, she did not feel a prisoner. She felt safe.

"It's all right, Evie," he whispered. "It was only a dream."

He let go of her wrist, the warmth of his fingers slipping from her flesh. She shivered at the loss of his touch.

Evelyn was baffled by her curious response to Adam. She had never yearned for a man's touch before. Never trembled at the loss.

She looked away, bashfulness overwhelming her. "What did you dream about?"

He stroked his dark and curly locks. "My brother."

She gazed back at him. "You have a brother?"

"I did."

Her heart cramped in sympathy, for she understood the dreadful loss of a cherished sibling. "I'm sorry. How did he die?"

Adam's eyes were heavy with sleep, but there

was also a hint of bewilderment in his somnolent gaze. Then a look of thoughtful reflection . . . and then a dark fire.

Another stirring shiver.

"That dress," he whispered.

She looked down at the garment. "I've upset you, haven't I? I will go inside and take off the dress."

"No, don't."

"But it reminds you of your late wife."

"You don't look anything like her," he said, a note of confusion in his voice. "Even in the dress."

Evelyn could almost feel him caress her, the strength and heat in his eyes was so great. And what's more, she didn't mind the stirring sensation.

"Go back to bed, Evie."

Flustered under his scorching stare, Evelyn scooped up the candle and quickly returned to the cottage.

Chapter 5

The steady chopping sound roused Adam from his deep and troubled slumber. His mind filled with nightmares about the past, he slowly sat up and rubbed his neck, the muscles stiff with discomfort.

Adam shifted to his feet and stretched. He approached the cottage, smoke rising from the short stacked chimney. The distracting thunks were coming from somewhere nearby. He rounded the structure to find . . .

Evelyn splitting wood.

She raised the axe high above her head—and paused. She glanced at him, and lowered the blade to her side. "Good morning."

Such lovely eyes, he reflected. The exertion of the chore had sparked a bright glow in her otherwise dreamy gaze.

She stood before him sure and steady, a well-honed grip on the axe. Her thick, dark hair was loose and flowing in the soft summer breeze, her breath deep and labored. Cheeks flushed, lips rosy red with blood, she looked vibrant . . . seductive.

His heartbeat quickened at the treacherous thought. He still loved his late wife. He would always love her. So how could he even think of another woman in such a way? A desperate woman under his protection?

"Good morning," he returned gruffly.

"Are you hungry? I've prepared breakfast."

Yes, food. That's what he needed to chase away the baffling sentiments. He was famished and groggy. No wonder his thoughts had blurred together like that.

She put the axe aside, and he followed her inside the cottage.

Adam stilled.

It looked . . . neat.

Hollyhocks in a jar of water brightened the table. There was a bowl of raspberries, too, making the air smell sweet. Porridge was boiling over a small fire in the hearth. The floors had been swept, lavender sprinkled across the planking to keep away the bugs. The bed was tidy, the linens folded and tucked tightly around the edges. Even the grimy rug under Adam's boots wasn't so grimy anymore, beat clean of dirt.

"I see you've been busy," he said.

"I always rise early to do chores . . . do you like it?"

She was watching him closely, eager to hear his opinion, he could tell.

"It's lovely." He smiled. "Thank you."

She offered him a small smile in return, a tender gesture that warmed his belly.

Only Tess's smile had warmed his belly in the past.

He closed his eyes.

The feelings aren't real! You need food in your belly and everything will be all right.

As Evelyn scooped the bubbling porridge into a wooden bowl, Adam sat down at the table. "I'll fetch the material for the drapes today. Is there anything else you need from town?"

"No, I have all that I need."

She placed the bowl of porridge between his hands. Adam reached for the spoon too soon. Before she had an opportunity to remove her hands from the dish, he brushed his fingers across hers.

A blue spark of static electricity snapped.

Evelyn gasped.

Adam was likewise startled. During his wedding tour in Italy, he'd heard about the late anatomist Luigi Galvani's attempt to animate corpses with electrical current. It had seemed fantastical to him at the time, but now, struck by Evelyn's bewitching touch, he wasn't so sure. She was stirring his long dormant senses back to life with each touch, each smile. Calling out to parts of him he had thought long dead.

Adam needed food.

He dipped into the bowl of porridge and tasted the freshly cooked fare. "Delicious."

Evelyn sat across from him. She said nothing about the sizzling touch, but her voice was shaky as she confessed, "It's an old recipe."

Adam maintained a steady interest in the meal. "You're a very good cook."

She appeared sheepish under the praise. "I had to learn. Our cook . . ."

Clearly timid to admit the truth, Evelyn stared at the table.

But Adam had already learned one important fact: she had once been able to afford a cook.

He let the quiet stretch for a minute before he coolly inquired, "What happened to your cook?"

"I don't know." She shrugged. "I haven't seen Mrs. MacFaden in years."

Adam swallowed another spoonful of the roasted oats. "Why?"

But Evelyn refused to reveal more.

He was not disheartened by her silence, though. Determined to learn more about the mysterious woman, he pressed on in another manner: "Tell me about your sister."

Evelyn blinked. "Ella?"

"A very beautiful name. Was she older or younger than you?"

"She was two years my senior."

"And how old are you?"

"Twenty."

He'd pegged her at about that age. "Did you get along with your sister?"

"Oh yes! Ella was my dearest friend."

The woman's expression brightened. Talking about her sister put a bloom in her cheeks, a bounce in her voice, making her even lovelier.

Eat your porridge!

Adam returned to the meal in discomfiture. "Ella gave you the handsome necklace, didn't she?"

Evelyn reached for the heart-shaped pendant at her throat. "Yes. She had two halves of a heart cast. She always wore one and I wore the other."

"And now you have both halves . . . because she is dead."

"Yes." Her joyful expression fell. "Ella died last year."

"How? Was she ill?"

"No." Evelyn caressed the gold pendant with methodical strokes. "*He* killed her."

Adam bristled. Hunger deserted him as the muscles in his belly clenched—and he imagined hacking *him* into a mountain of little pieces.

"He killed your sister?" Adam had never been

a vicious man in youth, but since the death of his wife, an interminable fury had gripped him for all things sinful. And the loathsome villain chasing after Evie smacked of sin incarnate. "But why?"

There was a firm rap at the door. "Capt'n?"

A spooked Evelyn darted across the room and hissed: "Who is that?"

Another set of loud taps.

Bewildered, Adam glanced from the door to Evelyn. "Don't be frightened. The man's a friend."

"Why does he call you Captain?"

But Evelyn didn't wait for an answer. She was already on the bed and crawling toward the window in distress.

"Evelyn, stop!"

Adam was too late to prevent her from wriggling her torso through the window. Only her posterior remained inside the house.

He was quick to grab hold of her before she tumbled out the window again. "Get back in here, Evie!"

More knocking. "Capt'n, wake up! I know you're home. I can see the smoke from the chimney."

"You promised me I'd be safe here, Adam; that no one would ever find me!"

"You are safe here," he gritted. "Now come inside before you break your neck!"

With his cheek pressed against her thigh, Adam pulled her roughly through the window.

The couple landed on the bed in a breathless tangle of limbs.

The cottage door opened. "Capt'n, I've news about—"

Lieutenant Eric Faraday eyed the rumpled appearances of the couple on the bed—in particular the comely Evelyn—before he gathered his wits and politely retreated. "Pardon, Capt'n."

The door closed again.

Adam sighed. He dropped his head back against the feather tick, still squeezing Evelyn by the waist to keep her from escaping through the window.

"Let me go, Adam!"

"Promise me you won't crawl out of the window again."

She struggled in his arms, the friction setting his skin afire. He quickly released her without the assurance, so perturbed by the familiar heat, the longing stemming through his thighs, his belly.

Evelyn scrambled off his lap and pressed her back against the wall. Her loose hair was striking, a billow of dark waves across her shoulders. Eyes like a goddess. Lips so damn kissable . . .

Adam bounded from the bed. "Lieutenant!"

"Aye, Capt'n?" resounded from the other side of the door.

Adam opened the door and glared at Eric Faraday. "Lieutenant, come inside. I'd like you to meet—"

But the cottage was deserted.

Adam growled. "That bloody minx."

"Capt'n?"

Adam marched outside. "Wait here, Lieutenant."

"Aye, Capt'n."

As he circled the cottage in search of Evelyn, Adam tamped the desire to rap the woman's knuckles so she never opened another window again.

A figure sprinted across the beach, heading for the sea.

The blood in Adam's veins turned to ice. He pounded down the grassy knoll and across the sand. "Evie!"

But Evelyn stopped short of the rising tide— and sat down.

He reached her, breathless. "I told you *not* to go near the water!"

"No, you told me not to go near the cliff. And I haven't."

"That's a paltry difference, and you know it." Adam dropped to his knees beside her, very tempted to rap the woman's knuckles, after all. "Why did you run off like that?"

"You promised me I'd be safe."

"You *are* safe. Lieutenant Faraday is a good man. I trust him."

"Well, *I* don't trust him."

Or you was on the tip of her lips.

Adam sighed. "Listen, Evie. I understand why you're so frightened of *him*; he murdered your sister. But he won't find you here."

Enchanted by the woman's handsome profile, Adam stroked the line of her jaw in tender regard. The delicate bone beneath his fingertip evoked a ruthless need inside him to protect her.

"Who is *he*, Evie? Why is he chasing you?"

Her lips quivered beneath his thumb. "I don't want to talk about him."

Adam dropped his arm. "Come back to the cottage then."

"No."

"Very well."

"Adam!"

Ignominiously, he carried her over his shoulder. "You're not going to sit beside the water."

"I won't drown!"

"No, you won't because you're going to stay away from the water." He set her down in the garden. "I don't suppose you'd like to crawl back inside through the window and meet our guest?"

She glared at him, flustered. "No!" She fingered the twisted hair away from her flushed cheeks before she snatched the axe beside the cottage wall. "If you'll excuse me. I have firewood to chop—Captain."

She had a tendency to shirk from confrontation, yet the fight in her eyes was unmistakable. Adam was pleased to see it—even if he was the cause of it. It offered him hope; that she was not so very passive, after all. That she would survive her troubles. And he would help her to do it.

"I'm not a captain, Evie."

She sliced the wood into kindling with unsettling precision. "I heard the lieutenant call you Captain."

"Well, I'm not a captain in the naval sense."

The wood split effortlessly. Evelyn picked up another log and placed it on the chopping block. "You said you weren't a fisherman."

"I don't hunt for fish in the sea."

"Then what do you hunt for?"

"Absolution."

She glanced at him askance. "I think it's best if you keep your secrets, Adam . . . and I keep mine."

Chapter 6

Lieutenant Eric Faraday eased himself into a seat, for a bullet to the hip had rendered him crippled and discharged from the navy.

"Good to see you with a woman, Capt'n . . . a very bonny woman."

Adam sighed. "I'm not *with* her, Lieutenant."

"Of course not, sir." The lieutenant shifted his leg. "My apologies for interrupting."

"No, you don't understand." There was only one lass in Adam's life: Tess. And he intended to remain faithful to her for the rest of his days. "She's my . . . ward."

"Your ward, sir?"

"Yes, my ward."

Evelyn wasn't really his ward, not in the legal sense. But she was under his protection, so the circumstance was similar.

"Didn't know you had a ward, sir."

"Well, I do." He fixed him with a pointed look. "And you're to keep quiet about her, Lieutenant."

"Aye, Capt'n."

Adam nodded curtly. "You have news?"

"I do, sir . . . we have him!"

A fire lighted in Adam's belly at the tempting thought, and he fisted his palms. "Are you sure, Lieutenant?"

"Aye, Capt'n."

After years of hiding, eluding capture, had the dastardly brigand surfaced at last? Adam intended to apprehend Black Hawk, the infamous leader of a roving band of buccaneers. The very buccaneers who'd pilfered from him a cherished fob watch six years ago!

There was scant chance Adam would recover the rifled watch. The pirates had surely sold the purloined booty. But Adam intended to see Black Hawk and the rest of the brigands hang for the foul deed—in memory of Tess.

"Where is he, Lieutenant? I'm tired of chasing shadows at sea."

The strife with his brother over, Adam now wanted pirate blood. For years he had hunted the waters in search of the notorious Black Hawk. But the dastardly cutthroat was elusive. A story surfaced on occasion, a sighting. No firm evidence to confirm his whereabouts, though.

Faraday lowered his voice. "The village is rife with tales of ghosts, moving about the terrain under darkness—leaving crates of whiskey and rum on the doorsteps of pubs! If the corsairs need to unload their pilfered goods, I say we buy the booty."

"How do you mean?"

"I've had to haggle with a scalawag close to the pirate leader, but I've managed to set up a meet between you and Black Hawk."

"When?"

"Tomorrow at midnight."

"How theatrical," said Adam dryly.

"Aye, Capt'n. The scoundrel Black Hawk does have a flair for the dramatic." The older man shifted his leg once more. "You're to pose as a merchant captain, searching for cheap spirits to bootleg on the side."

Adam mulled over the plan. A midnight gathering was perilous. Without a moon for guidance, he might easily lose his target in the blackness. Yet what other choice did he have?

"How's the ship, Lieutenant?"

"Tip-top, sir."

Adam might dislike an evening rendezvous, but he had come too far to risk allowing the devil to slip between his grasp. "I want you to ready the men, Faraday."

"Aye, Capt'n," he was quick to assent.

"Quietly, Lieutenant. I don't want gossip to stir and my target to vanish."

"You can trust me, Capt'n."

Adam did trust the proficient lieutenant. Injured during the continental war, thirty-eight-year-old Eric Faraday, along with many of his contemporaries, had lived like a vagabond for years. Dramatic cuts to military personnel after the war with Napoleon had reduced most officers to paupers, beggars in some instances.

Adam had found the lieutenant and many other former naval shipmen in bleak circumstances. For a generous income, a good two dozen had agreed to aid Adam in his endeavor. And after years of searching, Adam and the motley crew of sailors would see their mission complete.

Tomorrow.

At midnight.

Adam stretched his hand across the table. "You've done an excellent job, Lieutenant."

"Thank you, Capt'n."

Only Lieutenant Faraday was aware of Adam's true lineage. The rest of Adam's crew believed him a gentleman with his money and manners, but knew no more about him or the reason behind his pirate quest. Yet the tars were keen to follow their captain anywhere, so long as he provided them with a steady income and a chance to avenge Black Hawk's many victims.

Faraday limped toward the door. "I'll let you get back to your . . . ward, Capt'n."

"Lieutenant . . ."

"I'll fetch you before the meet, sir."

The door closed.

Adam dismissed the lieutenant's cheeky quip, and rubbed his palms across the length of his face. Fire danced beneath his feet, the impatient jig the result of years of fruitless searching for the infamous buccaneer.

I have you at last.

There was nothing to stand between Adam and the ruthless brigand—except for his "ward."

Adam looked out the window to spy the woman still chopping wood. What was he going to do with Evelyn while he went to apprehend Black Hawk? She spooked so easily. He needed to find some way to make her feel safe at the cottage while he was gone. But how?

"Bloody hell."

Evelyn dropped the axe with gusto. Her fingers burned with energy. She minced the wood into kindling, thinking about Adam.

He was not just a quiet cottager, mourning the loss of his wife. He was a captain. He was aggressive. He was a man—with secrets.

Had she really expected to find a safe haven with him? The man had a dual nature—all men did. She knew that, too. So why had she agreed to stay at the cottage with him?

"You're very proficient with an axe."

She paused, startled.

Adam stood beside the house with a shoulder braced against the wall. He watched her closely, his stone blue eyes friendly.

His eyes!

She remembered now; she had trusted the look of kindness in his eyes. That's why she'd agreed to stay at the cottage with him.

She wondered, "Where's the lieutenant?"

"He's gone."

Adam approached her slowly. Her bones tingled as the expression in his eyes turned smoldering—aggressive.

With care he grasped the axe and curled back her fingers before he took the tool from her grip.

She was bewitched by his robust touch. It singed her skin, firm strokes that swelled the blood in her veins and made her heart throb.

Adam tested the weight of the axe. "It's quite heavy." He observed her closely. "You don't look very fatigued, though."

She was baffled by her peculiar reaction to the man, overwhelmed even by the warm—yet un-familiar—sentiments gathering inside her. "I've chopped wood for years."

"You're strong, then?"

She gathered her brow. "I suppose so."

"Wait here."

Adam set the axe aside and disappeared inside the cottage. He returned shortly—armed with two blades.

Evelyn stared at the luminous steel, resplendent in the sunlight, and took an instinctive step back. "Where did you get the swords?"

"I keep the pair in the chest at the foot of the bed."

"Why?"

"Because I might need them one day."

He spoke with conviction, as though he was *sure* he would need them one day.

She shied away from the blade—and from Adam. "What are you going to do with the weapons?"

"I'm going to teach you how to dance—with a sword."

She looked at him, bewildered. "But why?"

"So you won't be afraid of *him* anymore."

Would such a day ever come? She had to admit, it was an appealing idea. But she cringed in the face of violence. How was she going to learn to fight?

"I can't, Adam."

"Take it." He lifted the blade higher. "You already possess the strength to wield it; you only lack the skill. Let me teach you to protect yourself."

She stared at the sword, tendrils of fright—and anticipation—wrapping around her spine.

You won't be afraid of him *anymore.*

This was her one chance to learn how to defend herself. And despite her misgiving, her distaste for violence, she wasn't ready to resign the opportunity just yet.

Evelyn complied; she took the sword.

"Good," he said. "Get a feel for the weapon in your hand."

She maneuvered it from side to side, testing the weight, the girth.

He eyed her movements closely. After a few minutes, he moved beside her. "Let us assume the position." He adjusted his form. "En garde."

Evelyn wondered where Adam had learned the art of swordplay, but her curiosity was stifled as she eyed his feet and mimicked the man's posture.

"No, not like that, Evie. Like this."

He moved his right foot forward again.

She did, too.

He cocked his left foot sideways.

She did, too—and wavered.

"Steady," he said.

Adam cupped her lower back to balance her. A thrilling warmth stabbed her spine and quickly spread throughout her body.

Evelyn was startled by the intensity of her response to the man's intimate touch. So startled, she very nearly dropped her sword.

"Stretch out your left arm, Evie. It will balance you."

Evelyn wondered about that, but obeyed her teacher. She lifted her left hand.

"A bit higher, Evie."

He nudged her elbow upward.

Another sharp prick of heat, making her arm tingle. Whatever was the matter with her? That baffling sentiment was stroking every nerve in her body again. It was difficult to concentrate on the lesson at hand when her limbs were shaky, her feet unsteady.

"Now spread your legs apart."

She bristled at the command. Yet another dewy warmth beset her . . . right between her legs.

She couldn't fathom the peculiar sensation. Blood rushed to her heart. A loud thumping resounded in her ears.

Woozy, Evelyn tried to obey Adam's command, but his rough voice and muscular touch and robust essence were making it hard for her to do so. And his words! She licked her dry lips. The man's words made her feel faint.

"Very good, Evie. Now bend your knees just a bit."

She was already shaky. If she tried to crouch, even a little, she might drop straight to the green.

Adam placed his palm on her shoulder and

pushed her down. She buckled—but didn't quite collapse altogether.

"There," he said. "Now for the footwork."

Evelyn swallowed a groan. She was quivering, sweating slightly. Her legs were light, unstable. She didn't think she could dance around with the blade.

There was an odd feeling creeping into her belly. A heat she had never known before. It alarmed her . . . intrigued her. She wanted it to disappear, yet she wanted to explore it a mite longer, too.

She closed her eyes and took in a deep breath to quell the conflicting emotions inside her. She was with Adam to learn how to fight, to defend herself. She must concentrate. Wayward thoughts only distracted her. She had a chance to protect herself from harm.

Take it!

"Are you ready, Evie?"

No!

"Yes," she whispered. "What do I do next?"

The blade quivered in the air.

Adam offered her a curious eye.

"I'm fine," she confirmed. "Please continue with the lesson."

Adam lifted his own sword to mirror her posture. "First we advance."

He stepped forward.

She moved quickly—too quickly—the energy inside her overwhelming, and lost her footing.

A thick arm circled her waist to stop her fall.

He was flush with her; she could feel his breath stir the hairs on her head—and bring her to life. Such potent life. She could smell him. Feel the sinewy muscles at his midriff move against her arm. The rapid knock of his heart beat against her shoulder, and she closed her eyes to better feel the rhythmic thumps, to match her own heart's tempo to his throbbing pulse.

"Not so fast," he said in her ear, the warmth of his breath making her shiver. "Take it slow."

He stepped away from her.

She almost cried out at the loss of his touch. For too long she had suffered in solitude. The brief connection with Adam, the bond of blood and bone reminded her how very much alone she was—and how very much she mourned the loss of companionship.

"Are you all right, Evie?"

She nodded, weakly. And to dismiss the ache in her belly, she resumed the first position. "How do I advance?"

"Observe."

She looked across at him, admired his sharp and masculine profile.

"Extend your right foot first, Evie."

Evelyn snapped her attention to his boots.

He demonstrated. "Then follow with your left foot."

She mimicked.

"Much better," he praised—and smiled.

Evelyn's heart pinched at the man's soft expression, so dashing.

"Next we retreat." He tapped his leg. "Move your left leg first this time, then your right."

He danced backward.

She followed suit.

"Well done, Evie."

She smiled in return. The admiration he offered filled a dark and lonely chasm in her soul. She wanted to do better, to improve.

"Now we lunge." He darted forward.

Evelyn mirrored his movement with ease. She had an abundance of energy inside her, and shooting outward with her body was a very convenient way to dispel some of that emotion.

Adam quirked a brow. "Impressive."

Evelyn shied under his praise.

"Let us tackle the blade work, shall we?" He brandished the sword. "To defend yourself, strike from side to side." He demonstrated. "Or in a circular motion."

Evelyn assumed the first position, then cut air.

"Good, but be sure to keep control of the blade." He gripped her wrist to steady her hand. "Like this."

There it was again: the stirrings in her heart, her belly. Why did his touch disarm her so?

Evelyn absorbed the warmth of his fingertips. She tried to absorb the lesson, too, but was having a deuced hard time listening to the instructions.

Adam moved to stand in front of her. "Now for the attack. Strike under your opponent's blade." He slowly demonstrated. "Or over."

She mimicked once more.

Adam assumed the first position. "En garde."

Evelyn carefully thrust forward. He parried.

"Good, Evie. Again."

Again she attacked. Again he protected himself.

"Now defend yourself," he said, "while I attack."

Adam slowly moved forward, giving her an opportunity to practice the foot and blade work.

For some time the couple exchanged tepid blows. But with each attack and parry, Evelyn grew more accustomed, more comfortable with the blade.

At length, Adam stilled. "Well done. Now I want you to attack me. Really attack me. Put all your strength into the blow."

She wavered. "But I'll hurt you."

"No, you won't. Trust me."

He assumed the first position.

Evelyn swallowed the knot in her throat. She took in a deep breath—and lashed out.

With a lightning-quick stroke, Adam parried the blow and knocked the blade right out of her hand.

She gaped.

"You have to learn how to *really* fight, Evie. In battle, your opponent will strike back with greater force than I did." He inclined his head toward the fallen blade. "Pick up the sword."

She retrieved the weapon.

"Attack me again," he said.

The man was a proficient swordsman, she realized. There was no reason to fear for his well-being. With less anxiety, she lunged again.

But once more, Adam deflected the blow with precision and disarmed her.

Again she wondered: *Where did he learn to fight like that?*

"Evie, you have to think of me as an enemy."

She picked up the sword, uncomfortable with the suggestion. She was already wary whenever she was near the man. What secrets did he keep? Why did his smile, his touch, shake her very senses? But to think of him as an enemy? It was too chilling, too real. *Was* he a foe?

"Evie, look at me."

She glanced up to find his expression determined.

"Think of me as *him*."

Her heart throbbed at the very idea, the wild beats booming in her ears. She shook her head with intrinsic revulsion. "No, I can't."

"It will help you to focus; give you reason to strike at me—hard."

"I don't want to think of you as *him*."

"Fight me." Adam advanced. "Fight me like you would him."

Startled, Evelyn raised her blade to parry the blow.

He lunged.

She deflected the next strike, too.

"Fight me, Evie!"

But a numbness beset her at the thought of *him*, made her legs and arms wooden. She stumbled backward, pressed against the cottage wall. She was cornered, Adam's blade aimed for her throat.

"I can't," she whispered.

The dark cloud of determination in Adam's eyes softened. He sighed. "I've pushed you too far, too soon, haven't I?"

He lowered the sword.

She dropped hers in shame. "I can't do this."

"Evie, wait!"

But Evelyn dashed from the garden, insensible to his entreaty.

She was never going to be free of *him*. Even the mere thought of *him* had made her cower, foiled all the progress she had made with Adam. She could never fight *him*, much less win. And she had been a fool to think otherwise.

Chapter 7

Evelyn picked at the blades of grass in a blind and lazy fashion.

"Evie?"

She stiffened at his approach, but did not turn around to confront him. Twisting the meadow grass around her finger, she snapped it from its root.

Adam hunkered beside her, blocking the sunlight, casting her in shadow.

"I didn't mean to upset you, Evie."

"I know," she said quietly.

She wasn't mad at Adam. She was angry with herself. Ashamed, too. *He* had such power over her, enough to render her weak and worthless. She resented *him* for it . . . but she feared him even more.

"Come back to the cottage," he said. "There's still more to learn about swordplay. I won't push you too hard this time."

She plucked another blade of grass. "I will never best *him*."

A firm finger tipped her chin upward. "You only think that because you're afraid. But you don't have to be afraid anymore."

She was met by a pair of striking blue eyes. Such a soft shade of blue, near gray. There was a softness in his countenance, too. Beneath the rugged features and hard expression, she sighted a mark of thoughtfulness—and was disarmed by the vision. So few had been kind to her over the years. Was Adam different?

"Tell me who *he* is, Evie?"

To quell the panic rising in her breast, she inhaled an unsteady breath. How could she trust Adam? He was still a stranger in so many ways.

And yet she was weary. Weary of keeping her troubles, her pain pressed deep inside. She was alone in the world. She had no one to turn to, no one to offer her a comforting hand.

Yet Adam offered one.

Dare she take it?

"*He* is my brother-in-law," she confessed.

Adam stilled. Something changed in his expression. A dramatic anger flared; she could tell. Not toward her, but toward *him*.

"And he murdered your sister? His wife?"

She struggled to keep back the tears. "Yes."

"But why?"

It chilled her to think about *him*, and she started to rock herself in comfort. "Because *he* likes to destroy everything which is good, everything which is beautiful."

"Ella?"

Evelyn inhaled a deep, salty-air breath. "Yes, my sister was very beautiful. She had hair like a night's sky, and eyes . . ."

"And eyes like yours?"

She nodded.

Adam stroked her knuckles in comfort. "And what does your brother-in-law want with you?"

But even the soothing ministration of his touch was not enough to calm the icy fright that danced in her heart and snatched her breath away at the thought of her fate if *he* ever found her.

Evelyn scrambled to her feet. "I have chores to do."

"Evie, wait!"

He reached out to stop her, but she was too quick for him; she sprinted back toward the cottage.

Adam took in a long breath to ease the rumble of rage in his belly. To murder one's own wife? It was beyond foul. Though he was not so naïve as to believe each husband cherished his wife the way he had honored Teresa, it still revolted him, boggled him, the abuse.

The distant shriek of gulls evoked a long

dormant memory. He could still hear the echo of his mother's cry—as Father thrashed her mercilessly.

Adam cut through the terrain with quick and angry strides, tamped the grisly reflection into the very bowel of his soul. He might shun such cruelty against a woman, but he was accustomed to it. Father had been a beast. A lifetime of hedonistic pursuits had put him into an early grave—and saved Mother from more misery. But had the former duke lived, Adam wondered if his mother, too, would be buried in a churchyard right now.

Adam returned to the cottage, a bundle of fabric tucked beneath his arm. He had been gone a good two hours. He should not have left Evelyn alone at the house, but the woman had insisted upon the material for the drapes. And he had already promised to purchase the fabric, so how could he avoid the trip into town?

Besides, it would do her good to be alone for a short while. He would not be beside her always— he had pirates to round up—so she had to learn to be comfortable with the cottage, to feel safe inside even when he wasn't around.

But he still hurried back to the seashore.

As Adam approached the dwelling, he heard the soft humming, the light splash of water.

Curious, he rounded the cottage—and stilled.

Evelyn rested on a wide wood stump, a bowl of water in her lap. She was dressed in only a chemise and dabbed at her skin with a moist towel.

Adam was unprepared to confront the woman in such a tantalizing lack of dress. True, she'd removed her clothes once before— in the course of drowning! He had overlooked the delicacy then. Now he had a moment to reflect, to observe her in the intimate act of bathing. And he was struck by the provocative sight.

She was blissful. With her eyes closed, she rubbed her neck, the line of her jaw. She moved the towel lower, to the tops of her breasts.

He had never noticed the deep swell of her breasts. But as she stroked the cleft of her bosom, he was privy to the lush round shapes, the delicious curves.

It was the shattered bowl, as Evelyn tossed it, that shattered Adam's reverie. He quickly turned around to offer her privacy.

"I'm sorry—"

"I didn't expect—"

The couple expressed sentiments simultaneously.

"I'm sorry," said Adam again. "I didn't mean to startle you."

She stammered, "I-I didn't expect you home so soon."

He heard her gather her clothes in a hurry. He now better understood why she had insisted he fetch the material for the drapes. The woman had wanted some time alone to see to her more personal needs. He was such an inconsiderate ass. He needed to offer her more privacy in the future.

Looking for some way to defuse the uncomfortable situation, he said in a casual manner: "I have the fabric for the drapes. I purchased a needle and thread. Shears, too."

She struggled with her dress; he could hear her fretful movements. "I'll get started on the stitching."

"There's no rush."

Adam set the linen and sewing implements aside. It was only then, as he twisted his body, that he noticed the stiffness in his muscles and joints. He searched for a distraction. Any distraction.

"Something smells good," he said.

She was covered in lemon soapsuds; the sweet citrus fragrance filled the air.

"In the house," he was quick to clarify.

"Oh, it's luncheon."

He started for the door. "Why don't I set the table."

Inside the cottage Adam sucked in a deep breath to chill the heat in his belly. But the alluring image of Evelyn's sultry figure was burned into his memory. And the more he thought about her, the more his own body burned.

He shouldn't feel this way.

Not for a woman under his protection.

Not for a woman not his wife.

Adam headed for the dish rack and removed two plates. He busied himself inside the house with the table arrangement. So engaged was he with his task, he didn't notice Evelyn standing in the doorway.

She was holding a handful of rubble. "I'm afraid the bowl is ruined."

Her soot black hair was moist and twisted around one shoulder. And her dress! It was clinging to her wet form, highlighting those tempting curves even more.

Adam looked away from her. "Don't worry about it." He crouched beside the hearth and inspected the bread pan. "The cornbread looks ready."

Evelyn placed the shattered pottery aside. "The potatoes smell ready, too."

As she worked around him to prepare the meal, Adam sensed the heat from the flames—and the heat from Evelyn, as well.

He had not lived with a woman for a long time. Her presence in the house was going to take getting used to, that was all. The feelings inside him would settle, retreat with familiarity and time.

But the memory of her sweet breasts . . .

For a man of eight-and-twenty years old he had poor self-control, he thought with disgust.

Adam was in the woman's way, so he stepped aside and took a seat next to the table. "Shall we continue with our lessons this afternoon?"

He had pressed her too hard in the morning. But he was still determined to teach her how to fight. The instruction would offer her confidence, keep her from jumping out of windows!

"Can we postpone the lesson for another day, Adam?"

She was hunched over the hearth with a ladle, scooping the boiling potatoes from the iron pot and placing them into a serving dish.

The very delicate arch of her backside quickly snagged his interest, and once more Adam had to tamp the inappropriate pleasure he found in admiring her.

He headed for the door. "I'll return shortly."

He captured her bewildered expression from the corner of his eye, but did not stop to explain his hasty departure.

He needed a good, cold dousing.

Chapter 8

It was a warm afternoon.

Evelyn grasped the soft blue fabric in her hands, cutting and stitching the material. She paused every so often to stare at the rhythmic swell of the water—her empty grave.

She should be at the bottom of the ocean right now, she reflected. Instead she was sitting on a grassy knoll, observing the waves and sandy beach, sewing drapes for Adam.

Adam.

Where was he? He had rushed off without a snippet of food. That had been a half hour ago. Was he all right?

But it was foolish for her to fret over him: a robust man who danced light with a sword. What danger could possibly befall him?

A figure darted through the garden, so quick Evelyn gasped and dropped her sewing. She searched the landscape once more, but the movement was gone.

He's found me!

Her pulse thumped loud in her ears; it washed away the steady sound of the rolling tide. She stumbled across the grassy knoll, treaded quietly along the beach.

Where was Adam?

With care she watched the cottage, the surrounding garden for more life. But only a fresh sea breeze teased the leaves and caressed the flowers. Otherwise the terrain appeared still, peaceful.

But Evelyn knew better. *He* was hiding somewhere. Skulking behind the woodshed. Or perhaps he had sneaked inside the house?

Each step shaky, she crossed the beach. She wanted to call out to Adam, but something strangled her voice, closed her throat.

Feet tangled, Evelyn tripped. Dazed, she stared at the pair of trousers twisted around her ankles.

Adam's trousers.

Quickly she tossed the article of clothing aside and bounced to her feet. She was sweating. Shaking. The sight of more clothes—a shirt, leggings, boots—crushed her spirit.

He had thrashed Adam.

The apparel was tossed across the sand in a wild fashion, ripped apart in the heat of a struggle. But where was Adam's body?

"Adam!" she croaked.

Her voice so raw and tight, she had to struggle to breathe.

Adam was gone.

She was alone.

With *him*.

Evelyn started to move toward the ocean, her only means of escape. She retreated into the salty water; she was already doused with tears and sweat.

She ignored the strong current and the bark of the sea ordering her back to the beach. Only the thought of evading *him* filled her mind.

Evelyn maintained her steady backward march into the ocean. She still trained her wide eyes on the distant cottage, searching for the devil. But he remained elusive.

I won't let you take me, she thought. *I won't suffer my sister's fate!*

Evelyn screamed as two thick arms circled her waist from behind and all but crushed her bones.

The sea roared, "What the hell do you think you're doing?"

Adam!

He hoisted her out of the water and climbed the steady ascent to land. He set her on the sand with unceremonious roughness before he grabbed her shoulders.

"Are you mad, Evie?!"

She gasped for breath, bemused. He was like a merman from the water, soaked and near nude. Only a set of drawers protected him from immodesty.

But Evelyn was too overcome with delight at the sight of him to notice the man's lack of attire. "You're alive."

"Of course, I'm alive." Adam's stone blue eyes pierced her with a hard stare. "Why the devil would I be dead?"

"You'd disappeared." She couldn't see him very well through her tears, and blinked to clear away the moisture. "I saw your clothes tossed everywhere."

"I went for a swim."

"But I thought *he* had killed you."

He cupped her cheeks in a firm hold. "Why would you think that?"

"Because he's *here*!"

Adam bristled. "Where?"

"I don't know; he's hiding somewhere. But I saw him dash through the garden a minute ago."

"Wait here."

Adam started for the cottage.

She grabbed him by the forearm. "You can't go back there! He'll kill you!"

In a moment of panic, she didn't think Adam

might actually defeat *him*. All she could think about was being alone—again—if anything happened to Adam.

"Don't worry about me." He pressed a finger against her nose. "And *don't* wade in the water again."

Evelyn watched him bound across the beach. As he neared the cottage, he hunkered and moved across the terrain with more stealth before he vanished behind a cluster of bushes.

She dropped to her knees, muscles weak. Her heart thumped wildly, every beat a sharp pang. She pressed her fingers to her lips to keep the sobs away.

And then the crushing pressure squeezing her breast lifted.

Adam appeared. He sauntered across the beach with a confident gait . . . a stray dog at his heels.

At first Evelyn didn't understand the appearance of the animal, her mind still gripped with images of *him*. But as Adam and the beast approached, her thoughts scrambled and formed a new conclusion: she had witnessed the *dog* dart across the garden.

Evelyn dropped her head in bewilderment. Was it right to laugh at her own folly? Or should she weep? She did both.

The lost mutt was spooked by her cries and choking laughter, and soon wandered off again. But Adam maintained a steady advance.

With the threat to her person no more, Evelyn took a moment to reflect upon the movement of muscle heading straight for her. With little attire to cloak his masculine form, Adam was like his namesake coming from the garden in glorious virtue.

Evelyn wiped the tears from her eyes. She had never observed a man in an improper way. The impulse to do so had never crossed her mind. In truth, she had done her best to avoid the male sex for most of her life.

And yet she was struck by Adam's virility. Her heart beat at a swift tempo, though the panic in her breast was gone. It beat now for another, more sensuous, reason.

Adam dropped to his knees in front of her and took her cheeks between the large palms of his hands. "You *are* mad, aren't you, woman?"

"No, I thought . . ."

Words deserted her. The energy, the sinewy strength thrumming through him was potent and easy to feel, and it stirred her senses and scrambled her wits.

"I know what you thought, Evie."

He leaned in.

The proximity to his lips was intoxicating; she could not take her eyes off his sensual mouth.

"But if you ever go near the water again, I'll drown you myself."

Hardly the comforting words she had expected to hear from him. But then again, she had noticed he had a tendency to become irate whenever she neared the ocean.

Adam set off to collect his scattered clothing.

Bemused, Evelyn tried to gather her own scattered senses, to sort out the peculiar loss she was suffering at his separation. But her eyes, her thoughts shifted to Adam once more.

He snatched his trousers from the beach and stepped into the pair with a jerking movement. She might have been alarmed by his clear vexation, if she wasn't so distracted by the sight of his sturdy legs.

A shameful inclination to press her fingers over his strapping limbs consumed her. A sudden desire to know him more intimately possessed her. She beat back the alarming and inexplicable passions, tried to put her thoughts to right. But when he next stretched his thick arms above his head, the muscles across his chest and belly elongating, and yanked the shirt over his midriff, she couldn't prevent the breath of disappointment at seeing him covered from passing between her lips.

Briskly he returned to her side and tugged at her arm. "Let's go."

She was still flustered and a bit shaky after admiring him dress, but she scrambled to her feet. "Where are we going?"

He dragged her. "To the cliff."

Chapter 9

A balmy breeze teased Evelyn's skin, as she took in the salty tang of ocean air. "Why are we here?"

"Because this is where I first spotted you."

Adam stood beside her on the cliff in rumpled attire. He had hauled her up the mountain so quickly, he hadn't the opportunity to tuck in his shirt. The hardy hike had also put a deep glow in his already bronzed skin and a pulsing life in his eyes.

Her heart pulsed, too: the effect of being so close to him. Why did he shake her senses so?

Together they overlooked the vast and restless ocean.

"You were more afraid of *him* than death two days ago." With a firm hand, Adam tipped her chin upward. "Are you going to run to the sea every time you see a shadow or hear a knock at the door?"

She turned away from him, a great upheaval in her soul. "You don't understand, Adam."

"Then make me understand."

He stood behind her, all brawn. It was so easy for him to confront his troubles, she thought. He had a hammer for a fist and could crush his adversary with little effort. She didn't even have the strength of mind to defeat *him* in her nightmares.

"You can ease your fears, Evie."

She was restless like the ocean. "How?"

"Admit them aloud; they won't have such power over you then."

"It sounds too simple."

He squeezed her shoulder. "It's a start."

The man's comforting caress made her shiver with inexplicable delight. She was still baffled by her peculiar response to his often innocent touch.

But she was also encouraged by it.

"I don't know where to begin," she said. The past few years of her life had been a whirlwind of confusion. She was strapped for words.

"Start at the beginning," he said in a low voice. "Where are your parents?"

With a heavy breath, she sorted through her chaotic thoughts to admit: "My mother is dead."

"And your father?"

"After my mother's demise, Father took to his

room. He rarely ventured out, he was so cheerless." She reached for the pendant at her throat and twisted her fingers around the gold heart. "He started to drink."

Evelyn remembered the inebriated hollers of madness every night, the foxed footsteps of a grief-filled husband, trolling the house in search of a wife's lost ghost.

"He started to gamble, too," she said.

And then life turned really bleak. The comforts Evelyn and her sister, Ella, had grown accustomed to started to vanish, one by one, the deeper their father descended into debt.

"It wasn't long before we had very little left. A leaky roof, really."

"And you had to let the servants go?" he guessed. "Like your cook, Mrs. MacFaden?"

"Father could not afford to pay her anymore. Ella and I tended to household chores after that."

"So that's why you can cook?"

"And sew."

"And chop wood?"

Evelyn shrugged. "Someone had to do it."

Adam stepped forward, meeting her gaze. "You lived a comfortable life before your mother died and your father took to gambling, didn't you?"

She drew solace from the look of understanding in his eyes. "Yes, but Father didn't want to live in poverty anymore."

"Did he stop gambling?"

"No . . . he sold Ella."

Adam took in a sharp breath. "He did *what*?"

Evelyn swallowed the sob slowly forming in her throat. "Father met a rich foreigner who liked unique beauty."

"*Him?*"

She nodded. "He offered to pay off Father's gaming debt in return for Ella's hand in marriage."

"Who is *he*, Evie? Tell me his name."

It was like summoning a curse, his name. But she gathered her valor and whispered: "Vadik."

For a moment she believed Vadik might appear, but she soon dismissed the wild thought as ridiculous fancy. Yet still her fingers trembled.

"Vadik took Ella to his home on the continent. I last saw my sister on her wedding day, three years ago."

"Did she write?"

"Sometimes . . . but she had to sneak the letters to the post. Vadik did not want her to communicate with me or our father. Not that our father cared about Ella. Only I cared."

"Your father continued to drink?"

"And gamble. He pretended Ella was happily wed and never mentioned her name again." A sharp cramp seized Evelyn's heart. "Ella's letters were so gloomy. She was in such pain."

The tears spilled at last.

"And there was nothing I could do to help her," she sobbed. "I had no money to travel abroad and sneak a visit with her. Father never offered me a coin; he'd gambled most of it away a second time. And there was no one I could ask for help. I had no other family or friends. After my mother died and my father turned wild, all respectable company deserted us. I was alone."

Adam wiped the dampness from her cheeks with the pads of his thumbs.

Why *did* his touch bring her such comfort? Ella's letters had been so grisly. A man's touch was supposed to be foul . . . but Adam's was not.

She took in a shaky breath and swallowed the last of her tears. "Vadik mistreated Ella in a very vile way. But Ella still protected me; she informed me of his character and warned me to avoid him should anything happen to her."

"And something did happen?"

"Her last letter was a good-bye; she feared for her life. She mailed me her half of the heart and counseled me to be brave, to run away if I had to. But I was to stay away from *him* at all cost."

"What does Vadik want with you?"

The crashing surf below matched the flurry of thoughts in her head. "He wants me to replace his late wife."

Adam's jaw hardened. "He wants to *marry* you?"

"Yes," she whispered, voice quivering.

After a respectable period of mourning had passed, a letter had arrived from Vadik. In it he'd announced he was coming to England for a friendly visit. But Evelyn knew the real reason for his trip to the island. Ella had cautioned her about the man's *obsession* with beauty.

"That's why I ran away," she said. "That's why I came here to the cliff."

"I understand, Evie."

"I *don't* want to be with him, Adam. I *don't* want to endure what my sister endured. Her letters . . . they were so ghastly."

He stepped even closer to her. She was over-whelmed by the strength he possessed—the strength she very much lacked.

"You're safe from him here, Evie."

But she wasn't so sure about that. "Vadik is rich and powerful, with many servants to do his bidding. Henchmen, really. I live but ten miles from here; I know they're looking for me right now. I don't think I will ever be safe."

"Did you leave a note, confessing your intention to drown in the sea?"

"No."

"Then don't panic. If the henchmen are looking for you, there are many miles to cover in many directions. You *are* safe."

She gazed into his soulful eyes, so determined. What fuelled his dogged assurances? His confidence? What provoked his passion so?

"What about your father?" said Adam. "He might be a drunkard, but surely he will not let *another* daughter die at the hands of a villain?"

A choking laugh. "Father is always searching for more money so he can gamble. He already consented to the betrothal with Vadik. We are to celebrate our engagement tomorrow night."

The depth of anger in Adam's voice was staggering. "But he murdered your sister!"

"No one believes Vadik killed her. It was purported she had died in a riding accident. But I know the truth. Only I read Ella's letters."

Adam approached the precipice in clear agitation. "He's your brother-in-law, though. He cannot lawfully wed you."

"In England, no. But there's no such law prohibiting the union in his home country. We're to announce our engagement in England, then sail to the continent for the wedding."

"That's *not* going to happen."

Evelyn wanted to believe him, but . . . "I can't hide here forever."

She was not his kin. He had no real obligation toward her. True, he had promised to protect her, but he had made the rash vow in the emotional aftermath of their first stormy encounter. He wasn't going to give her shelter forever. She had already intruded upon his life, and one day she would have to leave, allow him to return to his comfortable existence.

Adam was quiet for an unpleasant moment before he said, "You're right; you can't stay here forever."

Her heart pinched.

"I'm a widower. And you belong with a proper chaperone." He returned to her side, his gaze thoughtful. "You deserve a fitting home. A place where you can live in comfort and security."

She expected him to say that. She didn't expect the crushing sensation in her breast, though. She didn't understand it, either.

"But we don't have to think about that right now," he assured her. "You are safe from Vadik here. And while you are here, I want you to learn how to fight."

Evelyn wasn't so sure she *could* learn. "Ella always took care of me." She let out a sigh, lighter in her heart for having confessed her ordeal. "I miss my sister so much. I feel lost without her."

"I understand."

"Do you? Do you feel lost without your brother?"

Adam looked back out to sea. The sun's crimson rays caressed his tanned skin, his woeful eyes.

Evelyn could sense the deep turmoil in his soul. It pained him to think about his dead brother. She wanted to ask him more about his sibling, but she sensed he wasn't ready to confess his heartache yet.

"Yes, I feel lost," he admitted quietly. He looked back at her with those piercing blue eyes. "Come. Let's return to the cottage."

Chapter 10

It was a moonless night.

Adam folded his hands behind his head and reclined across the sand. He stared at the bright stars and listened to the smooth swell of the water lapping against the shore.

What was he going to do with Evelyn?

He had attended to her immediate needs: food, shelter, and clothing. However, he had not devised a plan for her future welfare. She couldn't live with him forever. It was improper. He needed to find her a secluded, more suitable, home. A chaperone, too. Perhaps even a husband? Now *that* would definitively put an end to Vadik's wedding plans. But Adam was no matchmaker. He hadn't the social graces to orchestrate a courtship.

There was so much he still wanted to do for Evelyn . . . so what if he didn't survive the night? What would happen to her then?

A soft light beamed in the distance.

Adam watched the glowing speck brighten, unperturbed. The tin lantern soon cast a soft sparkle over the dark beach.

"Evening, Capt'n."

Lieutenant Eric Faraday limped across the sandy turf.

"Good evening, Lieutenant."

Adam rose to his feet and dusted the sand from his clothes.

"It's a beautiful night for a pirate raid, isn't it, sir?"

Adam glanced back at the cottage, a short distance away. Lamplight flickered in the window; a shadow moved inside the house. "Yes, a beautiful night for a raid."

"Is something the matter, Capt'n?"

Yes. Evelyn. Adam had sworn to shelter the young woman. But what if something happened to him tonight? Who would protect her?

A morbid thought came to mind. Adam imagined Evelyn brutalized, suffering under Vadik's hand. The savage vision burned his blood. He desired to crush the villain's throat. But he would settle for keeping Evelyn far from his reach instead.

And yet Adam had also vowed to apprehend Black Hawk. It was a rotten truth, but to honor one duty he had to be remiss in another.

Adam stalked away. He was very much aware of the obligation upon his shoulders. He had made a sacred promise to capture the brigand in memory of Tess. And he loathed to break his vow. To fail Tess. To disappoint the loyal men who had served him so faithfully.

But what about Evelyn? What about the vow he had made to *her*?

Adam circled a small spot on the beach, mulling over the situation. At length, he wondered, "Is the crew ready?"

"Armed and ready, Capt'n."

A well-prepared crew. A loyal lieutenant. Adam need not fear failing his "ward" by getting hurt and leaving her without a guardian. And he need not neglect his duty to Teresa, either. He would capture the pirate captain *and* return to safeguard Evelyn.

He was adamant.

"Then tonight we apprehend Black Hawk, Lieutenant . . . but there's something I must do first."

A knock at the door.

The needle was poised to poke through the fabric when Evelyn stilled.

Another rap. "Evie?"

She let out a short sigh. For just a moment, she'd thought . . .

No, she would not reflect on *him* anymore. Not tonight. She would think about more pleasant things instead, like her sister.

And Adam.

Flustered, she said, "Come in."

Adam popped his head inside. "Still working on the drapes?"

He was rugged and handsome, and her heart thumped with more vigor at the sight of him. The low timbre of his voice made her shiver with pleasure, too. "I've one panel complete. I'll have the other ready shortly."

Adam stepped inside the cottage. In the dimness he seemed to fill the small space, his burly figure awash in lamplight.

Again she admired him. But only for a moment before she wondered: *Why is he here so late?*

A shiver of trepidation. "Is something the matter, Adam?"

"I have to leave."

She dropped the stitching in her lap. She was breathless. "You're leaving me?"

"It's only for a short time: a matter of business."

Her thoughts quieted to hear he was not abandoning her. "What sort of business?"

"Captain's business." After a short pause he offered: "I made a vow a long time ago . . . to my late wife. And tonight I have the opportunity to fulfill my vow."

To honor one's wife? She was unfamiliar with the sentiment. It should please her to hear Adam's assertion, though; it proved he was not like the cruel Vadik.

And yet it did not please her. Not entirely. To realize the promise to his late wife, Adam would have to leave her . . . alone.

"Will you be all right for a few hours, Evie?"

She gripped the stitching tight. Without Adam nearby, she was by herself in the world. *He* might jump from the shadows and steal her away.

But she was not Adam's keeper. She had no right to meddle in his affairs. He had been kind enough to let her stay in his home. She could not implore him to remain with her, however much she wanted to, and forsake the pledge he had made to his late wife. She had trespassed on his kindness enough.

"Yes, I'll be fine," she said, voice soft and shaky. She had endured the morning without him . . . but she'd had myriad chores to keep her active—and the daylight to chase away the shadows.

He scratched the back of his head in clear discomfiture. "There's another matter I need to discuss with you."

He moved across the room to the chest at the foot of the bed. She watched him closely as he lifted the lid and rummaged through the contents before he surfaced with a small jar.

Even in the soft lamplight, Evelyn recognized the banknotes.

"This is for you, Evie . . . in case I don't return."

She dropped the stitching on the table and jumped from her seat. "You *are* deserting me!"

"No!"

He set the jar aside and approached her.

She gasped as a firm set of hands pinched her arms and caged her tight. An equally firm pair of eyes imprisoned her, deep blue in the shadows.

"I intend to return," he said with a hard passion. "The money is just a precaution."

She was hungry for the man's intimate touch; it offset the panic in her breast. But she soon gathered her thoughts to demand, "A precaution for what?"

"In case I slip and crack my head on a rock."

He was funning with her. He wasn't the clumsy sort. He wanted to keep her in ignorance; he wanted to avoid talking about the true nature of his business. But she could see the sincerity, the gravity in his expression.

"It's dangerous business, isn't it?"

He admitted with a light shrug: "A little."

The muscles in her chest cramped, pinched her lungs. "What are you going to do?"

"I can't tell you."

"Why?"

Because I don't want to worry you even more. It was there in his piercing stare, the answer.

"Don't fret, Evie." He cupped her cheeks to emphasize, "You'll be all right."

But she was more worried about him. Why did he have to risk his life to honor his late wife?

"I'll be back soon," he said. "You're safe here, you know?"

She nodded wordlessly, swallowed the rising alarm in her breast.

Adam eyed her closely. "You'll stay away from the water?"

"Yes."

"Good." He headed for the door. He offered her one more heartening look before he whispered, "Good night, Evie."

She stared at the closed door.

Her feet twitched.

She wanted to run after him. She remained still instead.

Go to sleep.

Good idea. Sleep would while away the time until Adam returned . . . if he returned.

She hurried across the room to ignore the dark thoughts, ordered the clutter of thread and fabric. Once the cottage was put to right, she carefully divested the pretty dress Adam had gifted her and draped it over a chair.

Evelyn then picked up the lamp on the table and carried it over to the bedside. She crawled into bed, but did not extinguish the flame.

Warm under the woolly covers, she closed her eyes and envisioned a cheerful thought: her sister. But then the gruesome memory of her sister's death intruded upon her reflection, and Evelyn started to quiver, thinking of *him* and what he had done to her kin.

Evelyn opened her eyes. She was alone. The shadows in the room flickered under the lambent light. Her eyes darted from one dark silhouette to another, the pressure on her breast smarting.

The covers twisted.

Evelyn hopped off the feather tick and crossed the room. She opened the sturdy sea chest at the foot of the bed and picked up the rapier. Then once more under the sheets, she cradled the sword against her chest and prayed.

Chapter 11

Raven's Cross: a patch of rocky coastline. Adam and Lieutenant Faraday waited at the meet point. The notorious Black Hawk and brigand crew had yet to arrive. It was late, near midnight. But for the dim glow of lamplight, dark as pitch, too. If the pirates were approaching, Adam couldn't see them. Yet he wasn't worried. He trusted the two dozen armed shadows scattered across the hilltop, waiting for the signal to advance. His crew had never failed him in the past.

Still, if anything happened to him tonight, Evelyn would be without protection. He had offered her funds in case of a mishap; he was confident she would not be destitute. But she would still be alone—and frightened.

"Your weapon, Capt'n."

Adam stared ahead, insensible to the lieutenant's words.

"Capt'n?"

A nudge.

"What?" said Adam.

Faraday handed him the pistol. "Your weapon, sir."

"Oh . . . thank you, Lieutenant."

Adam tucked the gun behind his back.

"Is something the matter, Capt'n?"

"No."

But Adam's curt response did not silence the lieutenant. "It's your ward, isn't it, sir?"

Adam glanced sidelong at his trusted mate. "Why do you think that?"

"It's my job to be suspicious."

He snorted. "I thought it was your job to hunt pirates?"

Faraday shifted his weight from one leg to the other. "That, too."

There was a brief lull in the exchange before Adam said, "Should anything happen to me, Faraday . . ."

The lieutenant was quick to assert: "In the event of a calamity, I'd be honored to care for your ward."

"Thank you, Lieutenant."

More at ease, Adam fixed his thoughts to the matter at hand—arresting a notorious band of buccaneers. He had waited four long years for this moment. He should be savoring the anticipation of victory. Instead he was anxious to apprehend the brigands and head home.

There was a murmur of voices in the distance.

Adam girded himself for the confrontation.

"Do you have the blunt, Lieutenant?"

Coins jingled. "Aye, Capt'n."

Splendid. The stage was set for a spurious smuggling, for Adam and Faraday had to confirm the pirates' identities before announcing the signal to the crew. They had only one opportunity to accomplish their goal. No sense wasting it on a premature attack.

The figures advanced.

Adam counted six, maybe eight heads; it was difficult to see in the darkness.

Faraday lifted the tin lantern. "Who goes there?"

The shadows stilled.

One stepped forward.

The lieutenant squinted. "Is that you, Black Hawk?"

The shadow remained quiet about the matter of identity. "Do you have the blunt?"

Faraday rattled the gold coins.

"Well, toss it over," demanded the shadow.

The lieutenant shifted the tin lantern to illuminate Adam's features. "Capt'n here wants to do business with Black Hawk. Are you the pirate leader?"

There was a pause, then whispering.

"There's been a change in plans," said the shadow. "The capt'n will have to do business with me."

Adam hardened.

"And *who* are you?" snapped Faraday.

"The man you'll be doing business with."

The shadow's cheeky irreverence was intolerable. Adam wanted to yank his impertinent tongue out and dispense with the whole blasted proceeding. But he remained silent and still.

The lieutenant reiterated: "Where is Black Hawk?"

"Black Hawk doesn't want to get involved with such petty business and risk his identity revealed."

Adam glanced at Faraday in silent communication.

"I'm afraid we won't be doing business together then." The lieutenant raised his voice to carry over the crashing waves. "My capt'n here wants to be sure Black Hawk gets his money."

"Black Hawk *will* get the money."

"Not if a scalawag like yourself pockets the coin."

The shadow snorted. "The pirate leader would have my head!"

"Aye, he'd be mighty piqued," acquiesced Faraday. "But if you claimed my capt'n here reneged on the agreement, took the cargo, and disappeared, it'd be *his* head in peril."

"I'm not going to swindle Black Hawk!"

"How do we know that? We don't even know who *you* are! My capt'n doesn't want a misunderstanding with the pirate leader. We either do business with Black Hawk or the meet is over."

There was another round of whispering among the mysterious group of men. Soon, though, another shadow approached.

"Then let's do business."

Adam eyed the figure masked by darkness, listened to the baritone voice. Was it Black Hawk? He couldn't be sure. It had been so many years.

Faraday lifted the tin lantern, prepared to drop it and give the signal.

Adam raised his hand to stop the lieutenant. "Not yet," he whispered. He had to be certain it was the pirate lord. If the tars stormed the beach now, it would betray their true identities. And the *real* Black Hawk would lift tail and run.

"Are you Black Hawk?" said Adam.

The figure was still, black in shadow. "Aye."

Adam took in a sharp breath, a mixture of fury for the dishonorable brigand and cheer to be rid of him in his breast. "Come forward with the cargo."

But two other shadows hauled the crate of rum instead.

Adam cursed under his breath. He eyed the flasks. "They look to be in good order."

"The blunt," said Black Hawk.

Adam nodded to Faraday.

The lieutenant tossed the purse.

Black Hawk captured the coins. He opened the satchel, lifted a piece of gold to his lips, and bit.

The pirate leader laughed. "Good doing business with you, Capt'n."

Footsteps retreated.

"Capt'n," whispered Faraday, eager to drop the lamp. "Shall I give the signal?"

"Wait, Lieutenant." Then Adam shouted, "Shall we shake hands, Black Hawk?"

The pirate leader paused.

Adam had to see his face; he had to be sure it was Black Hawk.

After a moment of quiet, the shadow shrugged. "Why not?"

Black Hawk approached.

Adam did, too.

Faraday readied the lantern.

"Perhaps we will meet again, Capt'n."

The pirate stretched out his hand, stepped into the dim light . . .

Adam seized his wrist, recovered the pistol from his back, and aimed it at the man's head.

An uproar followed, the band of rogues advancing.

"Don't move," Adam ordered the shadows, "or I'll shoot him!"

"Capt'n!" Faraday cried.

"It's not him, Lieutenant!" Adam cocked the pistol, pointed it right between the charlatan's eyes. "Who are you?"

"Black Hawk."

"Horseshit!" Adam barked. "Who are you really?"

Adam was livid. He had chased the dastardly buccaneer for almost four years. He had ventured away from Evelyn to apprehend the brigand at last. And he had found a *fraud* in the pirate leader's place!

"Where is Black Hawk?" Adam pressed the pistol to the impostor's brow. "Tell me."

"I am—"

"Don't lie to me," growled Adam. "I know what he looks like. I had the misfortune to be divested of my personal possessions by the rogue pirate and his crew, so *don't* sham me!"

The trickster hesitated, clearly at a disadvantage. After a few stressful seconds, he sighed. "Very well. I'm not the pirate leader."

"I know *that*," Adam gritted. "Who are you?"

"The name's Hagley."

Adam eyed the miscreant. "Where is Black Hawk?"

"Dead."

Adam sucked in a sharp breath at the stinging news. He was too late. The pirate rogue was already gone. "Did you kill him?"

"No."

"Then how do you know he's dead?"

Hagley shrugged. "Well, there are stories—"

"Damn the stories!" cried Adam.

The corsair was like a ghost. Some whispered he had sailed away to hunt distant waters. Others believed him dead and trolling the nether regions of the earth. Adam believed neither tale. Black Hawk was an accomplished cutthroat. He was just good at hiding.

"*Why* do you think he's dead, Hagley?"

"Well, he must be dead. Otherwise where has he been all these years?"

Where indeed?

"And you've decided to take the villain's place, is that it?" said Adam.

The scoundrel grinned. "Aye. It's not easy to become the most feared buccaneer on the high seas. I figured, if the pirate leader don't need it no more, why shouldn't I take the title?"

Adam shouted another obscenity, turned on his heels, and stalked away.

"Don't you want your cargo, Capt'n?" Hagley shouted.

"Keep it!"

Faraday fell in step beside Adam, limping. "Capt'n, what are we going to do now?"

"It's over, Lieutenant." He tucked the pistol back inside his trousers. "We lost our target. Go into the hills and tell the men to stand down, return to the ship."

"Aye, Capt'n." Faraday lifted the lantern. "Where are you going?"

"Home!"

An hour later, Adam was back at the cottage. It was well after midnight, but he was too riled up to sleep. He peeked inside the cottage through a window to see Evelyn resting in bed before he stalked the garden in lanky strides, deep in thought.

"Blast it!"

He had failed Tess. Again! Failed to capture the dastardly brigand as he had vowed.

It boiled Adam's innards to think the *real* Black Hawk was still on the loose. Where was the mangy devil?

Adam kicked a garden stone and sent it into a nearby tree.

He didn't believe for one moment the infamous pirate was dead. Where was the body? Surely the carcass of the notorious buccaneer was a prize worthy of public display?

But if he had perished in battle? Then where

was the ship and crew responsible for the pirate's demise? It would be a victory worthy of celebration.

No. Black Hawk was a gifted cutthroat. He had ravished the sea for years. The villain was just hiding, resting. He would surface again.

There was too much notoriety surrounding the ill-famed pirate leader. Enough to hang him if he made a reckless mistake. A brief surcease in piracy offered the corsair a chance to escape the law's wrath. The navy might give up the pursuit, think the rogue dead—just as that charlatan Hagley believed. No one wanted to hound a ghost at sea. And all Black Hawk had to do was quietly enjoy the fruits of his spoils for a few years, and steer clear of trouble.

But Adam wasn't going to give up the pursuit. Ever.

He would see Black Hawk and the rest of the pirates on the gallows if he had to dedicate the remainder of his life to the chore of chasing the devil.

The blade sliced air.

Adam veered quickly. The tip of the rapier nicked his cheek, though; he could feel the blood.

He grabbed the shadow, knocked the blade from its grip—and stilled.

"Evie?"

She gasped. "Adam, is that you?"

"Evie, what the devil do you think you're doing?"

She was shaking. "I heard a voice, a noise. I thought . . ."

The panic, the fright in her speech were hard to miss. He relaxed his brutal hold, gathered the woman into his arms.

A heat filled him at the firm body in his embrace, so round and feminine—and scantily attired. He stroked her bare arms. She was in a shift: a light and fluffy and meager shift.

Voice strangled, he said, "It's all right."

"I'm so sorry, Adam."

"Don't be."

"But I could have killed you!"

He shushed her, stroked the long locks of her hair in comfort. "I'm proud of you."

"For what?"

"For taking care of yourself."

"But I made a miserable mistake!"

"You didn't know it was me." He inhaled the tangy scent of lemon soap, let it fill his senses. "You *can* protect yourself, don't you see?"

"Did I hurt you?"

"It's just a scratch."

"Oh, Adam." She reached for his face, cupped his cheeks. Her fingers trembled as she brushed them across his rough skin, wiping away the blood. "Forgive me."

He was rapt by her tender touch. "There's nothing to forgive. I was a reckless fool to storm back here and startle you. I apologize."

She pressed her thumb to his cheek to stave off the light flow of blood. Her other hand whisked across his other cheek, searching, exploring.

"Why *did* you storm back here?" she said. "What happened?"

He could feel her timidity as she caressed him, her curiosity, too. She moved her fingers down the side of his face—and he let her do it.

He closed his eyes, took in the rich waft of citrus fragrance. His heart throbbed at the supple way she rubbed against him, her soft breasts brushing his chest as she stroked his jaw in avid appraisal.

"I failed," he said, his voice a rasp. "I failed to fulfill my vow."

"I don't understand."

How he ached for a woman's touch! It rumbled deep inside him, the forgotten need. And Evelyn's feminine fingertips ignited that burning desire in the very depths of his lonely soul.

"I can't explain, Evie."

In a feather stroke, she swept her fingers across his lips.

It was more than Adam could bear. He dropped his head with a groan and took her sweet mouth into his own.

* * *

Evelyn was overwhelmed. A blast of sensation coursed through her blood, her bones, stunning her. She stilled in Adam's hot and hard embrace, let his mouth move over hers in fervid strokes.

The muscles in her breast tightened. A pulse thumped loud in her ears, drowning out the stormy swell of the sea, the chirping night critters.

So lonely for so long, she felt the intimate touch and taste of him fill her with strength and heat, and she greedily devoured the balm he offered with a kiss.

A kiss.

It was not the gruesome experience her sister had talked about in her letters . . . It was thrilling. Invigorating. She opened her mouth for more, gasped when he slipped his moist tongue across her upper lip, licking her, caressing her.

Again his mouth moved hard across hers. Tendrils of warmth wrapped around her loins, a pulsing heat—a wetness—invading her nether region in the most sensuous way. It alarmed her . . . excited her.

Evelyn hugged him, afraid to lose the wonderful closeness she shared with him. He didn't protest. He slipped his hand into the thick tresses of her hair to direct the tempo of the kiss, to keep it spirited and strong.

Evelyn pinched his shoulder, his neck in a return embrace. She was lost in the zeal of the fiery kiss. The heady passion was like a spell, charming her.

"Oh, Evie."

Adam's hand moved across the curve of her spine, making her shiver—and ache. She ached in the most wondrous way at his artful touch, his rugged words.

His hand slipped down her arching back, lower and lower. She quivered at the feel of stalwart fingers against her backside, kneading the supple flesh of her posterior.

But when he pressed her closer to his midriff, and she sensed the hard prick of his manhood, she tensed.

The spell broke.

Her hesitation, her resistance must have been palpable. Adam quickly let go of her lips, removed his hands from her flesh as if she had burned him.

Bemused, Evelyn blinked a few times, searching for clarity, her wits.

But all she could hear was Adam's rough breath, a sensuous reminder of the scorching kiss they had shared—and that she had craved.

"Go back inside the cottage, Evie."

Sound advice.

Evelyn didn't quarrel with the man. He was still a formidable figure in the shadows, one with a magical touch. She might find herself in his embrace once more.

She didn't mind the thought.

She *should*.

Evelyn lifted the hem of her shift and skirted away. Once inside the shelter of the cottage, she curled under the comforting covers of the bed and willed her wild heart to beat at a steadier pace.

She was so confused. The kiss, so delightful, had offered her a moment of bliss. A moment to forget her troubles and connect with another soul in a way she had never connected before.

But Adam was a man. If she found herself tangled together with him in a sinful way, he would hurt her. The way *he* had hurt her sister.

Evelyn still remembered the frightful letters Ella had written, warning her about the marriage bed and what transpired between the sexes. She didn't want to have *that* kind of an experience.

But the kiss?

Evelyn touched her swollen lips in memory. She would cherish the kiss.

Always.

She closed her eyes and tried to sleep . . . but a nagging thought intruded upon her dreamy reflections. *Why* had Adam kissed her?

He had offered to protect her. But was it all a scheme? Did he secretly want to abuse and take advantage of her like all the others?

Evelyn had struggled hard to escape the tyranny of her father, the wickedness of Vadik. Was she now under another man's autocratic hold? Adam did have a tantalizing pull over her—more so after the kiss!

Evelyn lifted her fist to her lips in quiet distress.

How was she going to learn the truth?

Chapter 12

Adam couldn't sleep. He walked along the beach, listening to the soft and lyrical swell of the tide. He stroked his ring finger, searching for the wedding band.

But it was not there.

He looked down at his empty hand. He had lost the gold band at sea—on the night Tess had perished.

Adam stopped rubbing his finger and closed his eyes. He reflected upon his wedding six years ago: a majestic occasion. It'd been the happiest day of his life. Even his scandalous brother, the Duke of Wembury, had arrived sober to the ceremony. With his family, the *ton* at large in attendance, he had vowed to forever honor his beloved Teresa.

But tonight he had broken his promise to be faithful to Tess; he had kissed another woman.

Evelyn.

Adam opened his eyes and blinked to clear the

watery image of Evelyn from his mind. She had touched a lonely place in his soul, stirring him. A carnal place, too, for the memory of her plump lips and tender touch scorched his blood even now.

And the guilt was overwhelming.

Adam bowed his head in shame. He had enjoyed the kiss, so much so that he ached deep inside to taste Evelyn again. And that she'd offered him her lips without protest, that she had kissed him with an equally frantic desire, revived him from his ascetic existence. Even the thrill of chasing Black Hawk did not match the balmy sweetness of Evelyn's mouth against his.

He had betrayed Tess.

There was an odd odor in the air.

Adam sniffed the sea breeze. It smelled like . . . smoke.

He swiftly sprinted across the beach, scaled the grassy knoll—and chilled.

The cottage was on *fire*!

"Evie!"

Adam bounded toward the abode, pounding across the grass in long and desperate strides.

Thick smoke curled and wafted through the humid night air as the fire quickly spread, the wood structure an inferno.

Adam rounded the front of the blazing cottage. As he neared the door, he heard the scuffle, the choking cries.

A devil had Evelyn in a tangle of limbs. He was dragging her through the smoke, his meaty forearm pinned under her chin.

Adam snapped.

He grabbed the brute with savage energy, and cracked him right between the eyes. The oaf slumped to the ground unconscious.

A weak Evelyn dropped to the dirt, too. Adam knelt beside her, cradled her in his arms.

"Evie!"

She sputtered and coughed wildly, and he let out a shout of relief to hear her muddled cries.

She was still alive!

The woman's tears stained his wrist; her lips parted in a silent wail. After a few strangled gasps, she let out a wretched sob, so heartfelt, it pierced Adam's soul.

But Adam had no time to comfort a distraught Evelyn further. Two more devils moved through the smoke just then, wicked apparitions aglow in the firelight.

Filled with a rabid desire to protect the woman in his arms, Adam reached for the pistol still tucked behind his back. He aimed. But the villain pounced, knocked the gun clear out of his grip.

The other fiend snatched Evelyn.

She screamed, "Adam!"

Adam roared amid the chaos, struggled with the zealous scoundrel keeping him from Evelyn.

The man was a formidable brute. He pinched Adam's elbows behind his back, forcing the arms to dislocate at the shoulders.

Adam girded against the pain, thrust all his strength, his power forward to counterbalance the devil's debilitating hold.

He had to get to Evie!

Sweat burned in Adam's eyes, the heat from the flaming cottage intense. He couldn't see Evelyn anymore, but he could hear her hollers. They ripped him in two, her frantic cries.

"Evie!" Adam shouted. "Fight him!"

One *more* villain approached. Outnumbered, Adam was crushed beneath the load of two bodies, his breath scarce, his arms weak and numb. A hard stab of knuckles to the lower back sparked in Adam a devastating spasm, crippling him for a moment, making him faint.

The gun.

Adam could see the pistol, the metal luminous under the raging glow of fire. Trapped under a heap of bodies, the confusion great, he managed to maneuver an arm and recover the weapon.

A shot rang out.

One fiend yelped and rolled backward, clutching the bleeding wound at his shoulder.

Adam aimed for the other villain, but he missed, the pistol knocked from his hand again. Still, the interruption afforded Adam an opportunity to gather his wits and strike at the rogue sitting on top of him.

A solid jab to the nose cracked the devil's bone. He sputtered, the blood oozing from his nostrils.

Adam shoved the brute away. Unfettered from the clinging devils, he dashed into the darkness, away from the suffocating smoke, and toward the spot he had last seen Evelyn being dragged away.

"Evie!"

But she was gone.

Frenzied, Adam shouted her name once more.

But only the splinter of wood and the lash of flames as the cottage crumbled were heard.

"Adam!"

Adam whirled around and spotted a group of spooked and tethered horses.

And then he saw Evelyn.

A henchman was struggling to haul her across one of the mounts.

Adam rushed toward the grappling couple. Dizzy, his body cramped, he didn't care that he was in poor condition to engage in fisticuffs. He grabbed the villain and dragged him from the horse. Evelyn tumbled, too, shrieking.

But a swift punch to the jaw didn't even daze the fiend. He in turn knocked Adam to the ground and straddled him before he reached for Adam's throat. The devil squeezed, sucking the breath from Adam's lungs.

Adam could feel the blackness encroaching.

At the sound of Evelyn's cries and rasping cough, Adam gathered his remaining strength and aimed for the one part of the villain exposed to him.

He shot his fist right at the man's cock.

The scoundrel seized.

One more knock across the head with his fist, and Adam had rendered the devil insensible.

"Evie." Adam gasped and massaged his tender throat. "Are you all right?"

She was wheezing.

Bright spots dotted Adam's eyes, for he, too, was gasping for air. He crawled over to Evelyn, reached out for her . . .

Adam opened his eyes and peered into the darkness, the shadows in the room taking shape.

Where was he?

He lifted his head to better explore his surroundings, but the spasms in his skull pressed him to keep still.

He was dizzy and weak. Blood dripped from the wound at his temple into his eye, blinding him for a moment. He blinked to brush away the moisture.

What had happened?

He was drained of energy. He tried to move, but something cold and heavy prevented him . . .

Adam was stripped to his trousers, chained—and hanging.

He clenched his teeth to gird against the intolerable abuse. He was suspended from a beam, wrists bound in shackles. His toes touched the ground, but the sharp stinging in his shoulders had him gasping for air.

His memories a blur, Adam concentrated on the ghostly sights and sounds storming his weary brain. Flashes of light, screams filled his head. Heat scorched his skin.

There had been a fire . . . at the cottage . . . and a fight . . . Evie!

"Evie."

Adam rasped the name, his smoke-stained lungs burned and dry. Fresh torment pumped through his blood, making him restless, eager to find Evelyn.

"Evie is not here."

The rough voice came from the shadows.

Once more Adam lifted his head, dismissed the spastic pulsing to explore the blackness. "Who are you?"

"I am Dmitri."

The shadow shifted.

Adam focused his watery gaze on the moving darkness, but his vision was a blur; he could not make out the villain's face in the dim light.

"Where is Evelyn?"

Another bout of vertigo brushed over Adam, and he lowered his head to release some of the biting pressure. He had to stay awake. He had to find out what had happened to Evie.

"Evelyn is with my master," said Dmitri.

The nausea in Adam's belly churned. Evie was with *him*!

Brutal images raged through Adam's already tortured mind: images of Vadik ravishing, then killing Evelyn.

The grief in Adam's heart ballooned . . . the rabid fury, too. He flexed his muscles and thrashed despite the pounding pulses in his head, hoping to break free of the beam.

"Do you wish to leave?" said Dmitri, his voice heavy with an unfamiliar accent. "Are you dissatisfied with my hospitality? Let me see if I can make you more comfortable."

Adam stilled.

The shadow moved across the room. A low-burning fire dwindled in the hearth . . . or was it a forge? Adam's vision was still a blur.

"You caused us a considerable amount of trouble tonight," said Dmitri.

Us? The henchmen?

"Not nearly enough," gritted Adam.

The shadow laughed. He pumped the bellows, feeding the hungry flames now bursting with life.

Dmitri approached again, a radiant red iron poker in his grip. "My master is a curious man. He would like to know what transpired between you and his fiancée."

Adam could better see the villain's face as his eyes adjusted to the faint light—and he recognized the devil as the henchman who had strangled Evelyn.

Adam spit in the fiend's face.

The villain was unperturbed. He wiped his brow and resumed his narrative with cool composure. "You are a violent man, Adam." He lifted his eyes, resplendent under the glow of the steaming iron poker. "It is your name, is it not? It is what she called you?"

Adam recollected Evelyn's panicked screams for help. Sweat poured down his back, the burning desire to reach her—save her—consuming him.

The hot iron poker hovered a short distance from Adam's moist chest. So close, he could feel the heat radiate and blister his skin.

"I have three comrades nursing wounds," said Dmitri.

Adam noted the bruise swelling between the villain's eyes, the spot where he'd cracked him. "Pity I didn't do you more damage."

The devil rolled the iron poker across the expanse of Adam's breast. The fiery metal never touched his flesh—but it came perilously near.

"I'm afraid I might have to do you more damage if you do not cooperate," said Dmitri.

"Then I suppose I have you to thank for this gash in my head?"

"No, that was my comrade's doing . . . but you do have me to thank for this."

Adam roared at the sweltering contact between his flesh and the burning iron.

The scoundrel whispered, "That was just a tap."

Nausea and dizziness overwhelmed Adam. For a moment, he believed he would black out. But after a few steady breaths, he regained his wits and maintained his senses.

Teeth gnashing, Adam growled, "I thought you were supposed to make me more comfortable?"

"Did I say that?" The villain moved the poker steadily across Adam's chest, a hairbreadth away. "Forgive me. I intended to make *myself* more comfortable . . . and it gives me great comfort to cause you pain."

Adam didn't doubt the man's words. His thoughts returned to Evelyn. What horrors she must be suffering! Grief filled him, suffocating him even more. His desire to save the woman was thwarted by chains and a pusillanimous devil!

The hate inside Adam twisted and burrowed its way into every pocket of his soul, darkening him, bleeding him of goodwill. If he could just wriggle one hand free, he would crush the devil's throat—and take pleasure in doing it.

"Shall we begin?" said Dmitri. "My master is a very impatient man."

"Fuck your master."

Adam let out another howl. Steam sizzled from the blistering wound at his nipple, the stench of burning flesh ghastly.

"I think you should show my master a little more respect," the devil warned. "Now tell me, is the woman still untouched?"

Adam was mute. One wrong word, and he might inadvertently put Evelyn in even greater harm.

Another tap of the hot iron poker.

Adam seized and clenched his teeth to refrain from shouting.

"Try to be a little more obliging," said Dmitri. "My master does not want to take a whore for his wife. As a man, you can understand a husband's desire to take a pure and innocent woman to his marriage bed. My master only wishes to know if his fiancée is still such a woman."

Adam girded against the abuse, speechless. So that's what the bloody "master" really wanted to know?

Dmitri tsked. "I see I will have to be a little more persuasive."

The scorching iron dragged across Adam's ribs, making him howl. The room was spinning. He could not get his eyes to focus. Darkness was coming to snatch him away again.

"There are other, more invasive ways to prove her innocence, you know? My master prefers I interrogate you, but if you continue to be stubborn, I can always examine her quim—"

"She's innocent," gritted Adam. He had not touched her in that way, and since she lived a sheltered life, he suspected no one else had touched her, either.

But he had kissed her. And right then the sweet memory of their kiss eased the torment in his soul.

"Good. My master will be pleased to hear that."

Adam resisted the urge to curse his master again. He had learned one blissful truth. Evelyn was still alive! And untouched, it seemed. Her fiendish fiancé intended to marry her before he consummated the union—and then murder her like his first wife.

Adam searched his weary brain, thinking about Evelyn's harrowing plight. When was her betrothal to Vadik scheduled to be celebrated? Tomorrow night? Or tonight? Was it morning already? But then the couple were to head for the mainland to be married. If he could just break free, there was still time to snatch her from Vadik's monstrous hold.

But he was chained—and hanging.

Blast it all to hell!

A door opened.

A robust figure stepped inside the room and stormed, "What in bleedin' hell is going on in here?"

Adam gathered what was left of his strength, and seized the moment of distraction to kick his legs into the air and knock Dmitri into the opposite wall.

There was a distinct thunk as the villain smacked his head against a hard surface and dropped to the floor.

Very nearly drained of life himself, Adam whispered roughly, "Get me down!"

But the mysterious figure in the doorway didn't budge. "Who are you? What are you doing in my shop?"

With the door ajar, Adam had an opportunity to better explore his surroundings. And it was clear to him then he was inside a blacksmith shop: the perfect place to gather information, for it had a wide variety of torture devices—and it was nowhere near Evelyn.

"Unlock me!"

The other man was unmoved by the curt command, though. "I think I'd better fetch the magistrate."

"Wait!" Adam had to remember he was not a captain aboard ship, barking orders. He lowered his voice and rasped with more civility, "My name is Adam."

The blacksmith pointed to the body on the ground. "And who's he?"

"The devil."

The heinous charge gave the burly smith pause. "I still think I should summon the magistrate."

"You have to let me go!"

"How do I know *you're* not the devil?"

"You don't!" He sighed. "But I'm asking you to trust me."

Clearly cross, the other man looked ready to protest, but he must have sensed it a wasted effort, for he grumbled something unintelligible before he raided a chest of tools for the key. "I'll break your teeth if you misbehave."

Adam fully believed the robust smith.

The man unlocked the shackles.

Adam's arms dropped, and he groaned at the inflammation in his shoulders. He sat down on the ground with a loud grunt. His thoughts went round and round in his head; the room moved, too. He had to breathe deep and hard to keep from fainting. There was still Evelyn to find. He had to stay awake for her sake.

"Thank you," said Adam.

The man humphed in return. "You know, I have an order to make a dozen shackles for the local gaol." He closely examined his handiwork. "If you damaged this one, you're paying for it."

Adam rubbed his bruised wrists and stood.

Vertigo brushed over him. But he quickly regained his balance and staggered toward the door, the sunlight guiding him.

"Wait a minute!" The blacksmith pointed toward the floor. "What the devil am I supposed to do with *him*?"

Adam glanced at Dmitri's carcass. The man was still alive, breathing. But Adam had no time to waste on the brute anymore. It was fruitless to wait for Dmitri to rouse, he reasoned. The devil would never betray Evelyn's whereabouts, even under duress. Adam suspected the fiend was accustomed to doling out pain—and taking it when necessary. He was just too loyal to his bloody master; Adam needed greater help.

"Toss him into the forge," suggested Adam before he dropped to his knees, crippled by the throbbing pulses in his head.

"Don't *you* faint, too," the blacksmith ordered,

as he crouched beside him. "What *did* the two of you quarrel about?"

"A woman."

The man snorted. "It's always about a woman."

"Where am I?" said Adam.

"Abbey Mills in Colchester."

Adam remembered the name of the small town. It wasn't too far from . . .

"Do you know the Duke of Wembury?"

The blacksmith looked at him as if he were daft. "Aye, I do. We *all* here know about the Duke of Wembury."

"Can you take me to him?"

The other man cursed. "You're just determined to ruin my day, aren't you?"

Chapter 13

The castle.

It stood like a fortress, a mountain of hard, gray stone. Two lofty towers flanked the impressive keep, the spire rooftops invisible under the blinding light of the morning sun.

Adam stumbled toward the familiar entranceway, each step a methodical effort. The blacksmith had refused to escort him straight to the door, for fear of the master within. And so Adam had to make his way to the castle alone.

The crippling anguish in his arms, the blistering wounds burned into his breast had ceased to stir pain. He was numb. Intent on only one objective: to get to the duke and seek help for Evelyn.

Adam approached the polished mahogany, skimmed his fingers across the ornate wood carving in the door, searching for the handle. He still could not see very well; color and light blurred together in his eyes. But the castle was his childhood home, and he remembered every aspect of it well.

The latch was easy to find. Adam pushed open the door and stepped inside the main hall, quiet and cavernous. He closed the heavy barrier, the boom echoing throughout the large space.

Once he was safe inside the keep, the support in his legs buckled. With great effort, he tried to keep his battered body erect, but the vertigo threatening to snatch away his waking thoughts finally took hold of him, and he dropped to the ground in silence.

Adam opened his eyes.

He was inside the duke's study. It didn't look like the gloomy haven Adam remembered it to be. The windows, unmasked from heavy drapery, were bedecked in soft and diaphanous sheers. Sunlight streaked into the room and touched the ancient tomes on the bookshelves. And the smell. The musty smell so reminiscent of their father was gone, replaced by the tang of spirits and wood polish.

Adam was sprawled across the lounge. A figure hovered above him. He recognized Jenkins, the butler. The old man dabbed a scented napkin over his brow, burning the wound at his temple.

Adam grimaced.

"Your Grace," said Jenkins. "His Lordship is awake."

Adam took in a loud breath through his nose.

The stark and familiar clip-clop of boots resounded as the duke circled the study desk. A formidable figure, he stopped a short distance away from the furniture—and waited.

Adam exhaled a noisy breath. A great storm filled him. He had not seen the duke in four years, not since the night he had stabbed the man.

"Jenkins, I wish to speak with my brother alone."

"Yes, Your Grace."

The butler bowed and quietly vacated the room.

Adam observed his kin. He didn't know what to say to his brother, their last meet so dark and bloody. A heavy sentiment anchored in his belly, a sense of shame for what he had done so many years ago.

"You look like shit," said Damian.

Adam glanced down at his breast to find the wounds dressed, his chest wrapped in bandages. "I feel like shit, too."

Damian crossed the room. He picked up a decanter and filled it with a generous amount of spirits. "Here." He approached the lounge. "Drink this."

Adam accepted the glass. He regarded his elder brother with unease. It was there between them, the unspoken memory of their last encounter.

The brutal images stormed Adam's weary brain. He relived the attack: the feel of warm blood on his hands, the grief in his belly, the anguish in his soul.

He shuddered. Words deserted him. He could not bring himself to mention that ill-fated night, to speak of their fraternal strife. He could not find the right sentiment to express his shame.

The duke rounded the study desk again and paused beside the window. "I was beginning to wonder if I would ever see you again."

Adam downed the brandy with greed. It burned his innards like fire. But it sparked the ailing life within him, too. "I had not planned to return."

The duke looked from the landscape to his brother. The admission seemed to displease him. Adam couldn't imagine why, though. Not after what he had done to the man.

Fortunately the duke had survived the savage attack. He was married now with a daughter. No more the "Duke of Rogues," according to Mother's letters. Damian had found peace with his wife, Mirabelle: the very peace Adam had once wished for him.

But there was no peace for Adam. Or forgiveness. So why intrude upon the couple's newfound happiness? And he would have remained estranged . . . but for Evelyn.

The duke must have realized Adam's discomfiture, for he returned his attention to the window, the bright light caressing him. "Then why are you here?"

Adam stilled the fierce thump of his heart. "I need your help, Damian."

"I can see that."

Adam slowly shifted his weight and winced. He set the empty glass aside and grabbed his head, groggy with fatigue. He stilled, willing the dizziness away.

The vertigo under control, Adam said, "There is a woman . . . Evelyn . . . she is in danger."

Damian looked away from the landscape. "What sort of danger?"

"She is kidnapped and imprisoned against her will."

The duke appeared stumped. "Why do you seek my help? Why don't you report the kidnapping to the authorities?"

"Because you are the 'Duke of Rogues.'"

The duke's eyes narrowed . . . and glowed. "I am the former 'Duke of Rogues.'"

Yes, the duke had changed. Not in years, but in spirit. Adam could see the light in the man's eyes: a light long lost under their father's cruel hand. But now that light was restored. Thanks to the duchess and the couple's child, Adam had learned.

"Men still fear you," said Adam.

"Men fear the law, too."

"Not all men." The thought of *him* stirred the bile in Adam's belly. "Not the devil holding Evelyn hostage."

"Do you care for the woman?"

Adam was disarmed by the blunt query—and the almost hopeful note in his brother's voice. "I offered to protect her. There is nothing more between us."

"I see." The duke clasped his hands behind his back. "Protect her from whom?"

"Her fiancé."

Damian lifted a black brow. "Now I *really* see. I'm afraid I can't help you, Adam."

"You don't understand, Damian."

"I think I do. You've set your heart on a woman who belongs to another man, and from the look of your battered bones, her fiancé does not approve of your attachment."

"I have not set my heart on her!" Adam punched the settee. "My heart still belongs to Teresa, and it *always* will!"

In response to the outburst, Damian was quiet. He appeared grieved by the allusion to Teresa. Adam sensed a twinge in his heart, too. But he had not come to lament about the past.

"Damian, Evelyn will die if I don't do something."

"Die?"

"Her fiancé is a fiend. He already murdered her sister; he will murder her, too!"

"Are you sure?"

Adam pointed to his bandaged torso. "Look at what he had done to me."

The duke said dryly, "I would do the same if you tried to steal my wife."

"It's not like that, Damian. I *have* to steal Evelyn away. How can I leave her with a man like Father?"

Something flickered in the duke's eyes, a memory perhaps. He appeared more perturbed. "Tell me what happened."

Adam recounted the dreadful tale, every detail.

"Her father sold her?" said the duke. "To the man who murdered her sister?"

The darkness in Damian's eyes was akin to a black flame. Adam sensed the paternal rage in him, the disbelief that a father could do such a thing to a child.

"*Now* do you understand why I have to save her?" said Adam.

The duke slowly nodded. "Where is she?"

"I don't know." He sighed. "We were separated after the kidnapping."

"Who is her fiancé?"

"I don't know that, either."

"Well, what *do* you know?"

"That her fiancé is rich and powerful, and he keeps a band of loyal henchmen around to do his every bidding."

Damian snorted. "He does sound like Father."

The former Duke of Wembury had housed a castle full of nefarious devils, too. Men to guard their mother and ensure she didn't escape the keep. Men to torment him and Damian.

Adam said, "Will you help me?"

It was palpable, the energy between them. Once they were brothers, close friends even, but there was now a distance, an unfamiliarity to their bond. Adam had a desire to dispel the strangeness between them . . . yet it was a wistful wish. He had stabbed the duke. It was an unforgivable act. Adam's desire for repentance and reconciliation was his alone. The duke surely did not give one whit about him anymore.

"I suppose I must help you," said Damian.

Adam had been prepared to beg the duke for assistance. He had not anticipated the man's ready accord. But perhaps Damian's paternal instinct had been riled? Evelyn was a woman lost, without a caring father. Her predicament might have inspired the duke to acquiesce, for it wasn't brotherly fondness that had stirred him into action. Adam was certain about that. Still he whispered, "Thank you."

Damian eyed his brother with curiosity. After a brief pause, he said, "Do you remember anything else about Evelyn? Her surname?"

"I don't know her true identity; she didn't tell me."

"How did the two of you meet?"

"I saved her from drowning," Adam recounted, reflecting upon that stormy summer day by the seashore. "She tried to end her life."

"I believe I understand the woman," said the duke. "Her fiancé doesn't sound like a prince."

"I know." Adam brushed his fingers through his mussed hair. "He's a devil. And she's with him right now! How do we find her?"

"I can write to my solicitor. Ask him to make some inquiries in Town. Perhaps we can—"

"No, it will take too long." Adam bowed his head and grabbed his throbbing temples. "The couple will celebrate their engagement tonight before setting sail for the mainland. I will lose her forever, then."

"Well, what else do you remember?"

Still a bit woozy, Adam rubbed his aching brow. He was forgetting something, he could sense it. "Her fiancé is a foreigner."

"What else?"

"He likes beautiful women."

"Keep thinking. We need something more tangible. "

"Shit," Adam hissed, and pressed his palms into his burning eyes. "I know I'm forgetting something . . . Vadik!"

"What?"

"Her fiancé's name."

Damian stared, bewildered.

"What's the matter, Damian? Surely we can find the couple now. There must be an announcement in the paper, something to indicate the engagement party."

Damian circled his desk and shuffled through the clutter of papers.

"What are you doing, Damian?"

But the duke did not respond. He searched sheet after sheet, sparing each a brief glance before eyeing another one. At length he picked up a card and paused.

"Damian?"

The duke approached and handed Adam the card. "I think you should read this."

Adam blinked, willing his eyes to focus. Soon the words sharpened and he scanned the elegant script:

*The Earl of Bewley requests the presence of
their Graces,
The Duke and Duchess of Wembury
At the engagement ball of his daughter. . .*

"Lady Evelyn Waye," Adam whispered. Blood thumped harder in his head. "My Evie?"

He was privy to the fact that she had once been comfortable in life, but he'd never suspected her a member of the peerage. It simply had not occurred to him that society would allow a lady to fall so deep into ignominy, even with a dishonorable father. How could no one offer her assistance?

"Read on," said Damian.

Bemused, Adam gathered his wits and scanned the invitation again. ". . . engagement ball . . . Lady Evelyn Waye . . . her fiancé . . . Prince Vadik of Moravia." Adam blinked. "Vadik *is* a prince?"

"A very powerful one, too," said Damian.

Adam struggled to maintain his composure. There was a buzzing sound in his ears, making it hard to concentrate. "How so?"

"I don't suppose you've been following the political climate of late?"

Quietly he said, "No, I've been otherwise engaged these last few years." *Chasing pirates.* "What's happening abroad?"

"Greece is revolting against the Ottoman Turks. The empire is in danger of collapsing, and without the sultan to hold back Russia, Tsar Alexander will advance on the Balkans."

"Where does Vadik fit into all this?"

"He is the younger brother of King Tavo of Moravia, who formed an alliance with England. Moravia will stand against Russia should the Ottoman Empire fall. Moravia is an important ally, Adam. Our king himself will be in attendance at the engagement ball to show his support for the Moravian monarchy." Damian crouched to better eye his brother. "To steal Prince Vadik's bride will be akin to treason. We can't go after Evelyn."

Adam stared at his brother. The rush of blood to his brain made the buzzing sound in his ears even louder. "I understand."

"Do you?"

He nodded. "Give me the location of the ball."

The duke sighed and snatched the invitation from his brother's hand. "I see you do *not* understand the gravity of the situation."

"You have a wife and child, Damian. You cannot commit treason and lose your head. But I have no one, nothing to lose. I will go after Evelyn alone."

The duke stalked back over to the desk and dropped the card on the table. "It's not that simple, Adam."

"It is," he said with confidence. "I promised to protect Evelyn, and I will."

"You might lose your life."

"So be it. But if I don't go after Evelyn, she will surely lose hers."

Damian took in another taxing breath. "There will be guards, you know? How do you intend to get inside the house without an invitation?"

"I'll sneak inside."

"And if you're caught?"

Adam stood—and wavered—dizziness blinding him again. "It's a risk I have to take."

The duke approached him and with very little effort knocked him back across the lounge. "You're not going anywhere; you need to rest."

"I'm fine," Adam gritted.

"The devil you are." The duke pointed to his scarred and bandaged torso. "You have burn marks across your chest and a crack in your head. You won't be much good to Evelyn if you collapse at Vadik's door. Besides, you can't save the girl alone."

Rankled, Adam demanded, "Then what do you suggest I do?"

"I suggest you attend the ball . . . with me."

Adam softened his ornery disposition. "I can't ask you to come with me, Damian. The risk is too great to a man in your position."

"Don't remind me," he growled, and returned to the study desk. "But I won't see you hang."

Adam's pulse ticked faster at the unexpected assertion. Why would Damian care whether he lived or died?

Because I love you.

Damian's words, uttered four years ago during their last grisly encounter, echoed in Adam's head.

But he dismissed the sentimental memory. Four years was a long time for a temper to fester —and for brotherly regard to turn to brotherly rage.

So why *did* Damian care?

Perhaps he was thinking of their mother? He might want to spare her the distress of losing a son. It was a far more likely explanation than the absurd notion that the duke was worried about him.

Adam put aside his confusion to inquire, "What about your wife? The invitation includes her. It might appear suspicious if you bring along your brother instead of the duchess."

"The duchess cannot attend the ball; she is in confinement."

Adam's thoughts whirled, danced together in a mad rush. The duchess was expecting another child?

"I didn't intend to attend the ball myself," said Damian. "Without Belle by my side, I can't abide such dull affairs."

The cramp in Adam's heart took his breath away, the ache for someone at *his* side almost crippling.

"But you can't do this alone," said the duke. "You will never get inside the well-guarded house without me. Besides, I am the former 'Duke of Rogues,' am I not? No one will dare to question me—or my choice of companions."

Adam blinked to dispel the longing in his breast. "Companions?"

"We cannot storm the dwelling without help."

At the thought of a siege, Lieutenant Eric Faraday came to mind. "I know a good man, Damian. A naval shipman. Many sailors, in truth. Loyal men—"

The duke lifted a hand to silence him. "Even disguised sailors wearing fine breeches will appear out of place in mannerism; we will quickly be discovered. Besides, there is no time to round up the sailors. The ball is set to begin in a matter of hours. I'm afraid we need more timely—and professional—help. And as much as it pains me to do this . . ."

Damian moved to the door and opened it. "Jenkins."

The butler quickly appeared; he must have been waiting just outside the room. "Yes, Your Grace?"

"Please fetch my brothers-in-law and escort them to the study."

Chapter 14

Adam observed the duke and noted the man's scowl. "Your brothers-in-law?"

"Yes," said Damian darkly. "Four maddening men who insist on making my life miserable. Punishment for marrying their sister, you know?"

In truth, Adam wasn't privy to the antagonism of in-laws. His late wife an only child, he had shirked the merging of two headstrong families.

"They're here at the castle," said the duke. "They want to be present for the birthing, so you can imagine the rows we have over my wife's welfare."

"Then why have you summoned them to the study?"

"Because we need their help."

"I see." Adam ignored the dreadful ache in his head to inquire, "And will they help us?"

"Yes—once I deign to ask for assistance. It will give them great pleasure to hear me admit I need their support."

Adam was dubious about such an alliance. "Is there no goodwill between you?"

"My in-laws believe I should be shot." Damian tweaked a cuff link. "What do you think?"

"I think I should go to the ball alone."

"No," said the duke in a simple yet emphatic manner. "You will not."

There was an autocratic air to the succinct command. The duke was accustomed to giving orders and being obeyed . . . but there was something more in his countenance. A regard for Adam's well-being?

Impossible.

And yet that look in his eyes . . .

The thunder of approaching footfalls persuaded both men to glance toward the door.

"Adam, I should warn you about something."

"What is it?"

But the duke had no opportunity to explain.

Without so much as a ceremonious knock, the study door burst open, and four towering brutes with soot black hair and piercing blue eyes swaggered into the room.

"I hear we've been summoned," said the biggest of the lot. "What the devil do you want, *Your Grace*?"

As if someone had picked up an hourglass and turned it upside-down, Adam was transported back through time. He stood aboard the *Hercules*, disgruntled, observing a band of brigands retreat across the ship's deck—with his fob watch!

Adam eyed the fob watch dangling from the big brute's vest pocket.

Black Hawk!

Adam saw red.

He lunged off the furniture, his injuries dismissed by the blinding effect of savage rage. He knocked the pirate captain off his feet and pounded on him with his fists.

"You son of a bitch!" cried Adam.

There was an instant uproar.

Between the scuffle of arms and legs, and the duke's autocratic voice getting into the mix of things, Adam was lost to the chaos of the moment. He swiped at Black Hawk with nary a thought to the added harm he was doing to his already battered bones.

Adam could feel the hard pinch in his arm. Someone was tugging him away from the fray. Quickly he grabbed the fob watch from Black Hawk before he was pulled through the tangle of hands and feet and thrust up against the wall.

The duke pinned his forearm under Adam's chin.

Gasping, Adam struggled against his brother with wild resolve. "Your in-laws are *pirates*?"

"A travesty, I know," the duke said dryly.

Black Hawk was back on his feet. He righted

his rumpled clothes, wiped his lip, slightly swelling, and glared at Adam with murderous intent.

"Is this why you summoned us, Damian?" the pirate captain growled. "For a bloody row?"

"No!" said the duke before he pinned his steel blue eyes on his brother, and whispered, "I know you're angry, Adam, but think of Evelyn."

Adam sobered. His heart still beat at a swift canter, but he resisted the impulse to snap the corsair's neck.

"Then why *did* you send for us?" gritted Black Hawk.

"Aye, Damian, what the devil's going on?"

Adam eyed the other pirate. He had matured in six years, his boyish features and youthful structure more developed, but he smacked of the same irksome smugness that had riled Adam all those years ago. "*You* filched the watch from me, you bloody cutthroat."

The scamp beamed with pride at the appellation "cutthroat." "I thought you looked familiar."

Adam was gripped by a profound urge to flatten the scalawag's nose.

"My brother and I need your help," said the duke.

"Brother?" echoed Black Hawk.

Adam shouted, "Like hell!"

He struggled against the duke in opposition. Adam was *not* going to trust a bunch of wily buccaneers to rescue Evelyn. The dishonorable brutes would foil everything.

The duke pressed his brother back against the wall. "Think about it, Adam. Who better to defeat the prince than a band of scheming cutthroats?"

Black Hawk returned dryly, "I'm flattered you think so highly of us."

But Adam loathed the idea—however reasonable—with every drop of blood in his veins. For four frustrating years he had hunted the corsairs, seeking justice for their dastardly raid. How was he to overlook their foul habits? Even *trust* the scoundrels?

"But they're pirates, Damian!"

"Retired pirates," said the duke. "With a duchess for a sister, they can't enjoy the spoils of the sea anymore."

"A bloody shame, too," quipped the youngest brigand, disheartened.

Retired? At the height of their infamy? To protect their sister?

"Horseshit," said Adam.

"It's true," said the duke. "The brothers are merchant sailors now . . . but I suspect they can be tempted to return to their wicked ways for tonight."

Black Hawk lifted a dark brow. "And how do you intend to tempt us, Damian?"

"With a challenge," said the duke. He eased

his hold across his brother's chest, and looked at him with stern warning not to engage in fisticuffs again.

"What sort of challenge?" said the young upstart.

"And what's this about a prince?" inquired another brigand.

The duke explained: "There is a royal ball tonight. Prince Vadik of Moravia is engaged to marry Lady Evelyn Waye. But the prince is a villain; he is forcing the young lady to wed against her will."

Black Hawk growled, "And why do *you* care about the woman, Damian?"

The implication was clear: *Betray our sister and you're dead*. But Adam quickly put the misconception to rest. "She's *my* woman."

The pirate captain shifted his gaze. "Yours?"

The duke arched a questioning brow, too.

As the fight drained from his blood, Adam was more and more aware of the pain wracking his body, and he rested against the wall for support. "Yes, mine."

Evelyn wasn't really his woman; he didn't think of her in that regard. But he suspected the roving band of cutthroats were men who followed their primal instincts. They would never understand the idea of an honored vow. But there was nothing more primal than to protect one's woman from harm. The pirates would understand *that* sentiment—and keep their hands off Evelyn.

It burned Adam's blood to think he might be beholden to the wretched brigands. But Damian was right. Who better to best the brutal Prince Vadik than an equally brutal band of bandits?

However, Adam intended to make it clear to the corsairs Evelyn was *not* to be touched. One look into her enchanting violet eyes, and he suspected the buccaneers might be bewitched. If he claimed the woman as his now, he'd avert that from happening later.

"We have to save Evelyn," said the duke.

Black Hawk narrowed his eyes on the man. "We do?"

The duke said stiffly, "I'm asking you to help us."

"No 'please'?"

"Please," gritted Damian.

That seemed to satisfy the pirate captain, for humor danced in his cold blue eyes. "Very well."

The young scamp whooped. "We're going to steal a royal bride!"

It was then Adam realized he didn't know any of the would-be heroes by name. The duke must have realized it, too, for he made the introductions: "Adam, I'd like you to formally meet our allies." He inclined his head toward Black Hawk, who appeared to be near forty years of age. "Captain

James Hawkins." Flanking the captain was . . . "William." The duke next nodded toward a rather surly-looking devil. "Edmund." And then to the youngest of the lot. "Quincy."

So that was the young scalawag's name? Adam still harbored a deep grudge against the scamp for stealing his fob watch . . . and gifting it to Black Hawk. Why *had* the pirate captain kept the bauble all these years? Why hadn't he sold it along with the rest of the spoils?

"Tell us more about the prince, the ball," said Black Hawk . . . James Hawkins.

Adam would never grow accustomed to the pirate lord's name. The brigand would always be the infamous Black Hawk in his mind.

And to think the notorious villain was going to help him save Evelyn!

Adam moved away from the wall and returned to the lounge, the pulsing in his head, the throbbing in his arms making him woozy.

The duke related the essential details about the prince and the henchmen, and then plotted with the brigands about the siege. Adam could only listen to the unfolding scheme, his aching skull preventing him from contributing to the plan.

At length the prelude to the abduction had been set.

"Then we agree," said the duke. "I will ask the royal bride to dance."

"Be sure to inform her about our plan," from the pirate captain. "We don't want her to cause a ruckus and resist us when we take her from the house."

"Right." A curt nod of the duke's head. "I'll ask her to feign faintness and then escort her off the dance floor."

"Take her outside for a breath of air," said Quincy.

"And if the prince's henchmen thwart you, Damian?" wondered William.

"Break their noses," suggested the belligerent Edmund.

"William has a point," said the duke. "How will I avoid the henchmen?"

"Leave them to us," said Black Hawk. "Just get the woman out of the public's eye."

"Then what?" from the duke.

"Adam will steal her away. He'll keep clear of the guests—and the henchmen—to assure he isn't recognized."

The duke was thoughtful. "Sounds like a solid plan."

"But you must return to the ball," said Black Hawk. "The prince will suspect you had a hand in the abduction if you, too, disappear."

The duke nodded. "I will stay then."

"We will all stay," said Black Hawk. "Only Adam will return to the castle with the woman."

"Then let's get ready for the ball." The duke turned toward his brother. "Are you prepared, Adam?"

Adam slowly lifted off the lounge. "Yes, I'm ready."

"You're bleeding," said Quincy.

Adam glanced down at his bandaged chest to note the blood seeping through the linen. "I'm fine."

The men looked unconvinced.

"Perhaps you should remain behind," suggested William. He appeared to be the most level-headed of the group.

"No," said Adam. "I have to go."

"We can steal the bride without you," offered the duke. "She will be the center of attention and easy to spot."

"No!" Adam clutched his midriff, rife with pain. "I *have* to go."

"Adam—"

"You don't understand, Damian. Evelyn is terrified of the prince. She will be even more spooked if a horde of strange men try to whisk her away. She won't believe you're trying to help her. But she will believe you if she sees *me*."

The pirates still looked troubled. It was a gamble to bring along an injured collaborator. If Adam failed and their scheme was exposed, they might all lose their heads.

But Adam would not fail.

He would will his injuries away when the time to rescue Evelyn approached. He had suffered great hardship before and survived. He would again.

"We'll need weapons," said William. "Should anything go wrong."

"And fancy robes," quipped Quincy.

The duke approached his brother. "Let's get some food into you first, then dress your wounds again. I'll give you a coat and a pair of trousers for the ball."

Adam looked at his brother, grateful.

"Head out," ordered Black Hawk.

The pirates moved toward the door.

"And nobody tell Belle about our plan or she'll want to come with us," said Quincy.

"Agreed," the men said in unison; the duke, too.

It looked as if Mirabelle, the Duchess of Wembury, would not be apprised of the situation. Although Adam didn't believe a woman in the way of childbearing would want to come along, anyway.

As the pirates filed out of the study, Adam whispered to his brother, "Are you sure we can trust them, Damian?"

"No," returned the duke. "But what choice do we have?"

Adam wasn't mollified. "They're pirates! Fine breeches won't be able to hide their boorish manners."

"The Hawkins brothers have attended a ball or two since retiring from piracy. The *ton* is willing to overlook their "merchant" ways because of their connection to me. In truth, the younger brothers are considered quite a catch."

Adam grimaced at the thought of some unsuspecting debutante setting her cap for a buccaneer.

"It's still a great risk to bring them along, Damian."

"It would be an even greater risk if we left them behind."

True.

Blast it!

Chapter 15

The ball was in full swing.

Adam stood off to the side, discreet. With a glass of champagne in his hand, he observed the more than five hundred guests making merry in the grand ballroom.

It was a sumptuous event, filled with the crème de la crème of society. The house itself was akin to a palace, fitted with marble flooring resplendent under brilliant candlelight. So much lavishness. And it all belonged to the Moravian throne: a grand state dwelling for visiting royals or diplomats. The perfect setting to host a regal engagement ball.

The burns at his breast blistering, Adam girded against the pulsing pain and glanced across the heads of so many familiar lords and ladies, searching for Evelyn.

But he had yet to find her.

He skimmed his eyes over the crowd again. King George IV was in attendance; the monarch was easy to spot with so many courtiers vying for his attention. Adam went on to spy his brother at the other end of the room, socializing with a group of acquaintances. Next he eyed Black Hawk, lurking in the shadows. The pirate captain maintained a steady watch over the horde of guests, too. Every so often, though, he signaled to his brothers with a simple blink or nod to carry on with the scheme.

The rest of the pirates were scattered across the ballroom. Quincy and Edmund, the two youngest brigands, were dancing. It was a sight indeed, for the buccaneers had mastered the waltz. William, the second eldest of the lot—as Adam had later learned—stood near the threshold in cordial conversation with a group of adoring ladies.

It was really rather incredulous, the spectacle of four pirates mingling with the *ton*. Well, three. Black Hawk maintained a social distance. He apparently frightened the lofty ladies, ogre that he was. But then again, the other pirates weren't really mingling, either. Adam observed each brigand silently return the captain's signal. Even with their easy grins, it was clear the men were hard at work to find Evelyn.

But where was she?

Adam's heart pounded in sync with the swift music. A cold chill gripped his throat, like a hand squeezing the breath from his lungs.

Had the devil Prince Vadik harmed Evelyn already? Beat her to death in a blind rage? A punishment for deserting him?

It stirred an even greater welter of pain than the burns, the thought of Evelyn in agony . . . dead.

Adam stomped the ballooning grief in his gut. The duke was approaching, and he smoothed his features into a bland smile to maintain the ruse.

"Where is she, Adam?"

The duke stopped a short distance away from his brother. He appeared comfortable in manner, but Adam sensed the restless energy stemming from him. Or was it Adam's own restless energy bouncing off the duke?

"I don't know where she is," said Adam, and took a swig of champagne to soothe the fire in his belly. "She should be here, though."

"I met her father, the Earl of Bewley."

Adam hardened to hear the other scoundrel's name. "Where is he?"

The duke gestured with his head across the room. "Over there. By the window."

Adam spied the old man standing off to one side. He briefly lifted his bloodshot eyes to communicate with a passing guest, but then quickly returned to his stoic posture.

The earl was dead, soulless. It was apparent in his manner, his quiet and vacant expression. Addicted to drink and coin and whatever other vices befall a man, he was a mere shell, void of energy or life. No wonder he had sold another daughter. The man had no wits left to reason with. No heart to break.

The duke eyed the throng. "What does Evelyn look like again?"

Snapped from his reverie, Adam returned, "She isn't here, Damian. Believe me."

"Are you sure?"

"Do you see the crowd engaged in pleasantries? If Evelyn was in the room, every eye would be trained on her."

The duke lifted a sooty brow. "Is she so beautiful?"

"Yes. Why else is the prince so determined to have her?"

"Well, then I suppose we must wait for the royal bride to make her fashionably late appearance."

Adam did not voice the dreadful sentiment aloud, that Evelyn might not be making an appearance—ever. He refused to think about the ghastly possibility that she was dead. In truth, he couldn't stomach it.

"I'm sure she's fine," assured the duke.

Adam glanced at his brother, so astute. But he did not respond. The music had stopped, the crowd's attention snagged by His Royal Highness, King George.

"I wish to offer a toast." His Majesty lifted a sparkling glass. "To our dear ally and good friend, Prince Vadik of Moravia, and his lovely bride, Lady Evelyn Waye. Many blessings upon both of you."

A chorus of applause, the crescendo making Adam's head pound. He stretched his neck to peer over plumes and stacked coiffures, looking for Evelyn.

Where are you?

A gentleman approached the king. Adam loathed the stranger on sight. There was something about his methodical gait and prissy manner that provoked dislike.

"Thank you, Your Highness."

Vadik!

"I am honored by your sincere felicitations." The prince smiled. "I regret my fiancée is unwell and unable to attend the festive gathering, but I humbly accept your well wishes and return your blessing tenfold."

Unwell!

Adam thundered across the ballroom. A darkness filled him, goaded him to wend through the dense crowd with maddening purpose. He heard the distant command to stop, but he refused to listen to the duke.

Adam pinned his eyes on the devil, Prince

Vadik. A handsome man with golden curls and a smooth and easy smile.

Adam bunched his fists and moved closer . . . closer . . .

"Good evening, Your Highness."

The duke suddenly sidestepped his brother, blocking him from the prince and the king.

Adam glared at the back of Damian's head. His fingers twitched and burned to trounce the dastardly prince, to snap his despicable neck and hang his carcass from the highest bell tower to rot.

King George returned the greeting with a respectful, "Your Grace."

"My brother and I would like to wish Your Highness health and happiness."

His Majesty eyed Adam with a curious stare. "My lord, you have returned?"

His Royal Highness tactfully neglected to mention, *From the dead*.

Adam swallowed the black bile in his throat and stepped out of his brother's shadow. "I have indeed, Your Majesty."

It was like nails driven into the soles of his feet, the unbearable proximity to *him*. The notorious devil keeping Evelyn hostage was only four short feet away. All Adam had to do was reach out and grab the fiend, rip the skin from his back.

But Adam was impotent to do as he desired. He stood with steely resolve instead—glaring at the fiend.

"My brother and I would also like to wish Prince Vadik our warm congratulations."

Once he was no more the center of attention, King George found favor with another eager courtier desperate for his attention.

The prince approached the Duke of Wembury and held out his hand in deference. "Your Grace, I am delighted to meet you."

"The pleasure is mine."

The men shook hands.

"I have heard much about you." Vadik stepped closer to the duke and whispered, "I believe you and I are very much alike, Your Grace."

Damian bristled. "How do you mean?"

But Prince Vadik only smiled and refrained from further comment. He turned his dark green eyes to Adam.

"Good evening, my lord."

The prince extended his hand.

Adam envisioned hacking off the extremity. He pondered the thrilling idea for a brief moment before he gathered his composure and returned the greeting.

Their hands touched.

The prince offered a firm handshake . . . but Adam wasn't so cordial. He gripped the scoundrel's palm with savage force, crushed his fingers.

Something flickered in Vadik's emerald eyes.

Pleasure.

Adam quickly released his hold, perturbed. The villain had enjoyed the brief spurt of pain. And the idea of giving *him* any sort of delight made Adam's gut twist with nausea.

The duke intervened with a disheartened remark: "We regret to hear your fiancée is indisposed, Prince Vadik."

Vadik's gaze lingered upon Adam before he returned, "I, too, mourn the loss of her company."

Mourn the loss!

Adam was dizzy with grief, the wounds at his chest bleeding again. He could feel the blood seeping through the bandages, and placed a hand over his taut midriff to stave off the flow. But it did little good. His veins flexed in stiff alarm; the blood pumped through the wounds. The dark suit he wore covered the stains, but there was nothing to cover the bereavement in his eyes.

Was Evelyn dead?

Was he too late to save her?

Had he failed *again* to rescue a woman he had vowed to protect?

"And where is your wife, Your Grace?" Vadik's smile turned amorous. "I understand she is a great beauty."

The duke's features darkened. Adam recognized that rabid look, so reminiscent of their father.

Slowly Damian said, "The duchess is also indisposed, I'm afraid."

"Pity. I had hoped to dance with her tonight."

"Not tonight." The duke muttered under his breath so only Adam could hear: "Or any other night."

The brothers eyed each other. Both were eager to get out of the prince's presence.

The duke bobbed his head. "We bid you good evening, Prince Vadik."

"Good evening, Your Grace." Eyes set on Adam once more, the prince said, "Good evening, my lord."

Adam offered a brisk nod before he retreated with his brother.

The air stifling and hot, Adam was sweating. He battled nausea, too, the sickness in his belly compounded by the ravenous way Prince Vadik had caressed him with his eyes.

Adam prayed Evelyn was still alive. He had to get to her; he had to save her from Vadik's wicked hold.

Once a safe lead behind the ignoble prince, Adam and Damian clustered together to keep the other guests from eavesdropping.

"That lecherous son of a bitch!"

The outburst from Damian.

Adam was too pensive to express the heavy sentiments inside him, so dark and stormy. He gripped his midriff again, the pulsing wounds biting.

"Adam, are you all right?"

He gritted, "I'm fine."

A daunting figure approached.

"What the hell do you two think you're doing?" Black Hawk growled, "It was *not* part of the plan to communicate with the prince!"

"The plan has changed," said a discontented Damian. "Evelyn isn't here."

The pirate captain scowled. "Are you sure?"

"She's 'unwell' and cannot attend the ball."

"Shit!"

"She *is* here," insisted Adam, gripped with an idea. "She is under guard, though."

"How do you know?" from the pirate captain.

Adam spied the rabble. Hope burst into his breast. Evelyn was alive! She had to be because . . . "The henchmen are missing."

"So?"

"So Vadik won't leave her unchaperoned for fear she might run away again. We have to search the house for her."

It was the first real indication he'd had that Evelyn was still alive. If the henchmen were absent from the ball, they had to be guarding her!

Filled with renewed energy, Adam started for the door.

A firm hand gripped his arm.

"Wait," ordered the pirate captain. "We can't just troll through the bloody house without arousing suspicion."

"There isn't going to *be* anybody in the house," said Adam. "Every guest is already gathered in the ballroom."

"And the servants?"

Adam pointed to the scalawag Quincy dancing across the room. "Do you see how he smiles at his dance partner? Just make him smile like that at the maids."

The captain said dryly, "I'm afraid his charm won't work on the footmen."

"Then do what your other brother, Edmund, suggested: Break their noses!"

Black Hawk gnashed his teeth, evidently disgruntled by the unplanned turn of events. "Wait here," he ordered Adam. "We can't all leave the ballroom at the same time."

The pirate captain turned on his heels and positioned himself in view of his brothers. One by one he made eye contact with each sibling, indicating a shift in tactics.

William slipped out of the ballroom first. He politely excused himself from the amiable company surrounding him. Edmund was next to go, followed by Quincy. The young scamp kissed the gloved hand of his sweetheart before he discreetly strolled off the polished marble dance floor.

Adam and Black Hawk departed together, leaving the duke behind. Damian was charged with the duty of distracting the prince should the royal villain attempt to quit the ballroom too soon. Prince Vadik was clearly captivated by the "Duke of Rogues," considered him a kindred spirit. And while Damian might loathe the undertaking, it was a necessary component to their new plan.

Now to find Evelyn.

"Why is the west wing forbidden?"

Adam eyed the scoundrel Quincy from a dark corner with unease, but he soon realized the young scalawag was a proficient flirt, for he had the maid blushing and giggling in a matter of moments, her chores forgotten.

Adam should resent the brigand's mendaciousness, but in truth he was grateful for Quincy's charm. It was a bloody uncomfortable admission to make, but with the wounds at his breast sapping his energy, Adam needed the cunning pirates to assist him with the rescue.

"I can't say, sir," said the maid in a bashful manner.

Quincy smiled. He pressed his lips to the girl's ear and murmured a few choice words.

She colored and whispered back.

Quincy gave her a sound kiss on the lips.

She gasped . . . then giggled . . . then quickly skirted back to her duties.

Adam eyed the cocky kid as he swaggered back down the passageway and slunk into the shadows.

"Well?" growled the pirate captain. "Did you learn anything useful?"

"Aye," said Quincy. "The west wing is the prince's private quarters. The staff is under orders *not* to disturb his rooms."

"Then let's go to the west wing," said Black Hawk.

Adam followed behind the buccaneers, clutching his bleeding midriff. He was careful not to reveal his pain. The pirate captain might order him to return to the ballroom, and he was determined *not* to do that. If Evelyn spotted four strange brutes coming for her, she'd head for the nearest window. Adam was sure.

At length the group of men paused in another unfamiliar nook of the house.

Black Hawk motioned for Adam to step forward.

"The henchmen?"

Adam spied around the corner—and gnashed his teeth. "Yes, the henchmen."

Four slaves to the prince's every wicked whim.

One had an arm in a sling: the beast Adam had shot. Another had visible bruising across the face. Even Dmitri was there, the cursed devil!

The savages circled a particular door like stone sentries, drawing Adam's attention. He eyed the wood barrier with hope and longing. Evelyn had to be inside the room!

"Let's go," whispered Adam.

The pirate captain pushed him against the wall. "Stay here, Adam."

"Like hell—"

"Stay out of the way until we crush them." Black Hawk eyed him with dark intent. "The henchmen will recognize you and sound an alarm; you'll foil everything."

He would foil everything?

"Besides, you're in no condition to get involved," said Black Hawk.

Adam bristled. Could he trust the brigands to restrain the henchmen alone? Every fiber in his being screamed, *No!* But every fiber cried out in agony, too. The weakness in his head, his breast confirmed the pirate captain was right. Insightful, too. He had observed Adam's failing condition, but he hadn't ordered him back to the ballroom. Adam should be grateful for that, he supposed. He offered a curt nod of accord—even if it was against his better judgment.

Satisfied with Adam's compliance, Black Hawk

turned to his brothers and said in a low voice, "Ready the pistols . . . and ruffle your cravats."

The men obeyed without question, feeling for the weapons concealed behind their backs and tugging at their neck cloths.

Adam, however, was curious to know how ruffled cravats were going to help them defeat the devils . . .

The pirates emerged from the shadows—inebriated at that.

Footfalls staggering, voices slurred, the pirate lot approached the henchmen under the guise of foxed and disoriented guests.

Adam observed the entire charade from his vantage point, begrudgingly pleased to have the brigands as allies.

"Stop!" ordered a henchman. "You're not supposed to be here."

"Here?" Edmund echoed and twirled on his heels. "Where is here?"

"Here is there," rhymed Quincy.

Edmund grouched, "There is where?"

William scratched his head. "I thought there was here?"

The henchman growled an oath at the annoyance and approached the brigands. "*There* is the ballroom and it's *where* you should be right now."

Adam blinked.

It was lightning-quick, the assault. All four henchmen hit the woolen runner, stunned. Two clocked over the head with pistols, one rendered senseless with a solid jab right between the eyes, and another knocked against the wall with enough force to shake the paintings.

Adam emerged from behind the corner and briskly stalked toward the door the villains had been guarding. Palm sweating, he reached for the handle with eager resolve.

"Wait." Black Hawk lifted a hand to prevent him from opening the barrier. "There might be more sentries inside."

The pirate captain aimed his pistol at the door and slowly lifted the latch. After a quick glance around the bedchamber, he pulled back the weapon.

Adam kicked open the door and walked into the room. Heart throbbing, he cried, "Evie?"

It was a large chamber, fit for a princess. A floral motif on the wall. Frilly curtains and embroidered bed lace. Furniture upholstered in pink. Wood whitewashed to glow like ivory. It smacked of high-end, feminine charm. There was even a small round table beside the fireplace, set for an intimate dinner with dishes and flowers and a bottle of wine.

But there was no Evelyn.

Adam's heart dropped. "Where is she?"

Quincy moved toward the bed and flipped back the covers.

No Evelyn.

Edmund headed toward the wardrobe and tossed back the doors.

Still no Evelyn.

William peeked into one of the adjoining salons.

Empty.

Black Hawk peered behind the curtains.

Nothing.

The blood in Adam's veins burned. "Where *is* she?"

Thump . . . thump.

The men stilled and listened.

Thump . . . thump.

The baffled pirates moved about the room, looking for the source of the noise. They tossed aside furniture, pressed their ears to the walls.

"What the devil?"

Adam spied Quincy with his ear against the ornate headboard. "What is it, kid?"

Quincy said, "I think the sound is coming from the bed."

Adam rushed over to the structure and pushed Quincy aside. He placed his ear against the wood and listened.

Thump . . . thump.

The noise *was* coming from the bed . . . under the bed.

Adam dropped to his knees and fumbled under the bed frame. The pirates quickly gathered around the structure and reached into the darkness, too.

Fingers hit wood.

Adam wrestled with the smooth surface, but he could not grab a sound hold of it. At length he shouted, "Push!"

At one end of the bedside, the pirates pushed. At the other end, Adam yanked.

The coffin appeared.

Chapter 16

Powerless.

Evelyn was powerless to move, to see, even to breathe. The stale air in the coffin was making her light-headed. She sputtered and coughed, screamed silent screams.

There was a kerfuffle, a distant mesh of voices. She kicked against her tomb.

Let me out!

She choked on her tears. The smell of blood—her blood—filled her lungs as she scraped and pounded on the wood, her flesh raw and tattered from the abuse.

Please let me out!

Icy fingers of fright gripped her heart and squeezed. She gasped for air, the tiny carved notch in the coffin lid her only means of survival.

More racket, shouts.

A lock snapped.

The coffin opened.

Fresh cool air . . . blinding candlelight . . . freedom.

Evelyn cried out. She reared up with such swiftness, the blood rushed to her toes, making her dizzy and faint.

A set of strong arms crushed her, offered her the strength she had lost.

"I've got you, Evie."

A voice.

It was familiar, comforting. She couldn't see the man; she was blind with tears, but she cleaved to him the moment he gathered her into his embrace and lifted her from the tomb.

She was soaked with sweat, her pulse ringing in her ears like thunder. It was hard to breathe, each gasp a desperate pant.

"Calm down, Evie."

But she couldn't. Her heart beat wildly. Her blood rushed through her body at a mad pace. She couldn't relax her muscles, so stiff and rigid with terror. She was cramped and in pain, confused.

Evelyn could feel the bed beneath her aching limbs, the feather tick soft and warm.

"Take a deep breath, Evie."

That voice again!

The man rubbed her cheek, bussed the crown of her head. She could feel his other large hand stroke her damp and shivering spine, the ministrations soothing.

He whispered something. She couldn't understand the words, but the sound of his voice, the tenderness of his touch were enough to still the rampant thumps of her heart.

At length she focused, blinked away the tears. She lifted her head, buried in the man's chest, and glanced up to look at him.

Adam.

Her heart shuddered.

He rubbed the dampness from her cheeks with his palms, his eyes trained on her with such fiery purpose. He whispered, "It's over."

She believed him. The darkness in her breast, the suffocating chill were ebbing away.

"Thank . . ." She croaked. The air was stale in the coffin, so her throat was dry. Wounded, too.

Adam cupped her chin and gently tilted her head back to examine the injury at her neck: blooming marks left behind by the henchmen's deft grip as he'd dragged her from the cottage.

Under candlelight the bruising must look horrendous. The grim expression across Adam's face indicated it was ghastly.

In light wisps, he stroked the sore spot at her throat, his eyes a burning sea of blue. "Don't speak," he murmured. "Let your throat heal."

Evelyn was trapped by the dark fire in Adam's

eyes, the ginger touch of his thumb and forefinger, the comforting timbre of his low voice.

She blinked, stunned by the bewitching effect he had on her. For a moment, he had made her forget about her miserable ordeal. But just for a moment. The truth of her frightful predicament blustered its way to the center of her thoughts, quashing the brief, warm sentiment she had had of Adam.

"We have to get you out of here, Evie."

We?

Evelyn peeked over her shoulder, stunned. There were four devils surrounding the bed. Four very handsome devils, even with their rumpled attire and mussed hair. She could tell they were devils; she sensed it intrinsically.

And they were staring at her with that *look*.

Evelyn quickly turned her head to shield her eyes.

"It's all right," said Adam. "They won't hurt you, I promise."

But she still trembled. The other men looked so villainous. There was something in their eyes, an aura of brutality.

"Drink this."

One of the devils approached the bed, a bottle in his hand. He was young and dashing in a form-fitting ensemble. He offered her the wine, encouraged her to take it with a soft smile. But Evelyn wasn't fooled by the charming gesture and refused the refreshment.

At length Adam took the bottle and popped the cork. "Drink, Evie."

The inviting smell of fermented grapes was too heady for her to resist. Even with so many pairs of eyes staring at her, she accepted the spirits and ravenously drank to douse her parched and aching throat.

"Can you walk?" said Adam.

Revived by the cool tonic, she slowly eased off the bed with confidence.

But her legs buckled.

Adam grabbed her, snuggled her against his chest. "I'll carry you."

He took the bottle from her hand and put it aside. But when he stretched down to gather her in his arms, a sharp expression of agony crossed his face.

She quickly recovered her voice to demand, "Adam, are you all right?"

He looked pale, battered with fatigue.

Another devil stepped forward then, the biggest and most intimidating of the four. "I'll carry her."

Evelyn shied away from the man.

"No," said Adam. "I'll take her."

"You can hardly carry yourself," returned the

devil. "We have to get out of here before we're discovered."

"I can walk," Evelyn was quick to assert. She eyed Adam once more to impart, "Really, I can. I was just a little dizzy before. But I'm fine now."

Adam looked unconvinced.

But Evelyn didn't want to cause him even more discomfort. He appeared to be in great distress. And she certainly didn't want to be in the arms of that other sinister-looking devil. She would find the strength to escape the house. Already her energy was returning, the crisp, clean air a rich stimulus.

"Fine," said the black devil. "Let's move."

The men headed for the door, neatening their clothes and hair.

Evelyn eyed the lot warily. Was Adam friends with the forbidding brood?

But now was not the right time to voice her curiosity. She couldn't even inquire about Adam's ailing health. Or how he had found her. She had to concentrate on the flight at hand.

Adam put his arm around her waist and encouraged her toward the door.

Evelyn was very ready to leave the ghastly place behind. Her steps more determined, quicker, she moved alongside Adam with ever growing resolve and vigor.

She paused in the doorway and stared at the unconscious henchmen sprawled across the floor.

The recollection hit her soundly: four brutish fiends cramming her into the coffin, insensible to her screams.

Adam tugged at her sleeve. "Ignore them."

Evelyn took his arm and swiftly followed the rest of the party, banishing the gruesome memory from her mind.

She lifted her skirts—decadent layers of ivory glacé silk *he* had forced her to wear—and skulked through the lavish passageways, careful to avoid detection.

As they neared the ballroom, the music and twitter of guests grew lively.

Evelyn's heart twisted with dread: dread that *he* would find her and prevent her from leaving the palatial house . . . order her interred within the coffin once more.

She started to tremble at the thought and captured the heart-shaped pendant at her throat, searching for comfort.

But Adam squeezed her hand tight, reminding her she was not alone—and sending warm shivers darting down her spine.

She eyed him askance. There was something different about Adam. The manner in which he presented himself had changed. There was more formality in his gait, his clothing. Even his sooty hair, sometimes wild with curls, was combed in a neat fashion.

He looked like a peer. It made sense, though; he had to dress like one to attend the ball—how *had* he found her?—but he also behaved like a gentleman. He moved through the house with ease, as if he had strolled the passageways of similar abodes in the past. It wasn't true, of course. The man lived a very simple life by the sea . . . yet he acted with comfortable confidence, even amid so much pomp and presentation—except for the occasional grimace that crossed his face.

The party came to a stop.

The big devil stepped away from the band and approached Adam. "We part here. Take her back to the castle. We'll follow you shortly."

The castle?

Evelyn watched the brood head back toward the ballroom. The younger devil offered her another charming smile—and a wink—in passing.

She quickly lowered her head to avoid the flirtation.

A low growl stemmed from Adam before he tugged at her hand. "Let's go, Evie."

The couple absconded through another quiet corridor, then sneaked through a dark and secluded exit into the warm summer night.

Chapter 17

Evelyn was free.

The buzz of night critters, the light whisper of a breeze had never sounded so lyrical. Her eyes swelled with moisture at the sight of a flurry of fireflies, dancing to the soft swell of the music drifting from the house. And the stars! The stars had never appeared so bright, so alive with pulsing light.

She restrained her joy, though. She and Adam still had to traipse through the well-hewn grounds unnoticed before she truly distanced herself from *him*.

Evelyn moved in quick strides across the green before Adam steered her beneath the shelter of an oak tree. Breathless, he needed a moment to rest.

She eyed him warily. "What's the matter?"

He pressed his back against the tree and grabbed his midriff in support. "Nothing's the matter. I'm fine."

"You're in pain."

She examined the wide breadth of his torso, stared at the formal evening wear hiding his discomfort. She wished she could see past the layers of clothes to the grief that lay beneath.

"They hurt you, didn't they?" she said. "The henchmen?"

A vivid memory filled her head: the henchmen burning his home, thrashing his body. She was sick with grief at the thought of what Adam had endured—and all because of her.

"I'll live," he said softly.

He tried to make light of the matter, discourage her from fretting. But he'd failed in the endeavor.

Guilt overwhelmed her. Adam was in agony because of her, brutalized because he had tried to help her.

Gripped with a burning desire to heal the man's wounds, she reached out for him. "What did they do to you?"

But he seized her wrist, preventing the ministration. "Don't trouble yourself with my condition."

"Adam, let me help you."

"No." He was winded. "It's my job to help you."

She chewed on her bottom lip. Adam was such a hefty man, filled with robust strength. Yet he was suffering. The torture he had endured must have been brutal.

Wild images of cruelty stormed her weary brain. She shuddered at the morbid thoughts, tamped the wretched guilt in her belly. There would be time aplenty to make amends. First she had to make sure Adam was safe. He had escorted her thus far; now she had to see him to a restful haven.

"Here." She positioned herself next to him. "Take my shoulder."

Adam glanced at her sidelong. The shade of leaves covered his features, but she sensed his mulish expression.

"Don't be stubborn." She curled her arm around his lower spine in encouragement. "Let me help you."

At length he resigned to her entreaty with a loud sigh and slipped a thick arm around her shoulders, hugging her for support.

It was an intimate embrace, stirring feelings of warmth. To discourage the frantic flutters of her heart, she moved the discourse to another pressing matter:

"How did you find me?"

The couple treaded carefully across the lawn, a pair of shadows among so many.

"I had a little help," he said tersely.

"From the men at the ball?"

"That's right."

His succinct responses indicated ill-will between him and his friends . . . Or were the frightening devils his friends?

She wondered, "Are the men your comrades?"

He let out a soft, choking laugh. "My worst enemies, in truth."

"But—"

"There isn't time to discuss the matter now. I have to get you away from here." He guided her toward the procession of fine-crafted town coaches. "This way, Evie."

She dug in her heels. "No, we can't!"

"Trust me."

Trust him to steal a town coach? "Why can't we make our way toward the woods?"

"No, we have to get to the . . ."

"The castle? What castle, Adam?"

"You'll be safe there."

"Where *is* there?"

He stopped beside a regal vehicle, the family crest brilliant under flickering torchlight, and opened the door for her. "Get inside."

The driver didn't even protest their raid. Was he asleep? Didn't he realize he was being burgled?

At her lengthy hesitation, Adam very unceremoniously cupped her posterior and nudged her inside the compartment.

Flustered, Evelyn quickly scooted to the far end of the cushioned squabs and gathered her skirts. She expected Adam to take the seat opposite her, but he settled beside her instead, the heady musk of him filling her lungs like a divine perfume.

Adam knocked on the roof. "Drive."

The vehicle departed the queue and slowly rolled down the pebbled road.

Evelyn's heart was in her throat. "I can't believe we just appropriated a carriage!"

"We didn't steal it, Evie."

"The devil we didn't!"

"It belongs to my brother."

She gathered her brow. "You mean it *belonged* to your brother?"

He was silent.

Slowly she asked, "Adam, is your brother still alive?"

"You assumed the man was dead, and I let you believe it."

Evelyn gasped. "But why?"

The man tensed. She heard the audible shift in his breathing pattern, too. A deeper and heavier rhythm.

"I quarreled with my brother four years ago. After the row, we parted. In a way I did lose him."

It baffled her, the fraternal strife. She had never quarreled with her sister. She didn't even know what it felt like to be angry with Ella. "And now you've borrowed the man's carriage?"

"I needed his help to find you, Evie. He, too, is at the ball."

"Who is your brother?"

He paused, then said, "The Duke of Wembury."

Evelyn's eyes widened. "The 'Duke of Rogues'?"

He offered her a mordant smile. "I see my brother's reputation precedes him."

Evelyn's heart, her blood raced. *This* was Adam's idea of protection? To take her from the hands of one villain and deliver her into the hands of another? The "Duke of Rogues" was an infamous scoundrel. The worst reprobate in England! How was she supposed to be safe behind *his* walls?

"No!" She moved away from Adam and settled against the opposite squabs. "I won't go to the duke's castle."

Evelyn's thoughts whirled. It dawned on her that Adam was no ordinary man living off "a respectable family allowance," as he'd termed it. He was the brother of a duke!

And that meant Adam was also a member of the peerage. No wonder he had appeared so comfortable inside the royal house. He was used to living in a castle! And that's how Adam had found her, too: through his brother. The duke had been invited to the ball; she remembered seeing his name on the guest list before she had run away from home—and into Adam's arms.

Adam maintained a firm fix on her with his eyes. "The duke won't hurt you, Evie. He's not like that anymore. He has a wife and a child now."

Rot! The duke had married four years ago, it was widespread truth, but Evelyn wasn't a fool to think wedded life had changed the infamous villain. A husband's right to abuse his wife was common law. She understood that better than any lovelorn girl about to make the wedding march. And she was *not* going to put herself at the mercy of such a man.

"No, Adam. I won't reside with another devil!"

"He's not a devil." Adam said firmly, "And you must stay at the castle. You'll be safe there. I will be with you."

But even that assurance did not offer her comfort. The more Adam confessed his past, the more she wondered if perhaps he was secretly *like* his ignoble kin. After all, how could one brother grow up to be the "Duke of Rogues" and the other not?

"Let me go, Adam."

"Go where?"

"I don't know. Anywhere. I can—"

"No!"

She bit her bottom lip to hold her tongue.

He sighed. "I'm sorry, Evie. I didn't mean to be so curt."

She inhaled a steady breath before asserting, "I can make my own way in the world."

"How?"

"I can work in a household as a cook or a house-keeper or a governess. But I won't live with the duke or . . ."

Her thoughts returned to the sinister-looking devils who'd assisted Adam in her rescue.

"Who are the other men, Adam? The ones who helped you?"

"They're the duke's brothers-in-law."

"You said they were your enemies."

"They are."

"Why?"

He sounded disgruntled. "We had a disagree-ment—over a watch."

"A watch?" It didn't sound like the sort of thing one had a disagreement over, but Evelyn wasn't bothered by the pettiness. She was more per-turbed by the mounting number of houseguests in the castle. "The duke's brothers-in-law are going to be at the keep, too? Aren't they?"

She remembered the big devil's order: *Take her back to the castle. We'll follow you shortly.*

She shivered at the thought of sharing a haven with *them*, too. "I don't want to be near them, Adam. They're so . . . so . . ."

"Brutish?"

"Yes, brutish. And sinister. They remind me of . . ."

"Pirates?"

"Yes, pirates—" Evelyn blinked. "They're *pirates*!"

That did it. Evelyn reached for the door.

Adam wrested her hand from the latch and hauled her into his lap. "I'm afraid you'll break your neck if you try to jump at this speed."

She glanced out the window to observe the quick movement of darting shadows. The thought of physical injury had not occurred to her. The only thought troubling her was the revelation that she was going to live with a band of rogues and pirates!

"*That's* why you're a captain, isn't it, Adam? You've been chasing the pirates at sea."

"I had to avenge my late wife's memory."

She was filled with alarm. "What did they do to your late wife?"

Evelyn imagined the four frightening brigands as they had circled the bed. What would they have done to *her* if Adam hadn't been inside the room, too?

"The pirates once robbed me of a fob watch: a watch Teresa had gifted me."

Oh. After hearing the account, she was a bit more at ease. But she was still anxious to distance herself from the intimidating brood.

"I still don't want to go to the castle."

"Have I mistreated you, Evie? Have I given you any cause to be wary of me?"

He had not abused her. True. But she could not shake the nagging worry: *What if Adam was like all the others?* What if he had *yet* to hurt her?

"Trust me, Evie."

But that was the hardest thing in the world for her to do: trust. Betrayed so many times in her twenty years, Evelyn didn't think she could ever really trust someone again.

And yet Adam had come to the ball to save her from the prince. If it had not been for his help, she would still be locked inside the gruesome coffin. She was grateful for his assistance. But she had to wonder why he had risked his life to come for her.

Another dark thought entered her mind then.

"You know who I am, don't you?" she said quietly.

"I do, Lady Evelyn." His voice was low, a gruff whisper. "Why didn't you tell me your real name?"

"Why didn't you tell me yours?" she rejoined, suddenly aware of the fact that she was sitting in his *lap*. Very comfortably, too.

"I guess we both wanted to forget about the past."

What did he want to forget about? His late wife? His brother?

She closed her eyes, confused. Adam was at odds with his kin, he'd clashed with a band of pirates . . . and yet he was in league with both parties!

"I don't understand," she said. "What about the strife with your brother? The pirates? How did you all come together tonight?"

"I made a promise to protect you; thus I have a duty. And I will do whatever it takes to uphold it."

"Even join forces with your enemies?"

"That's right."

She took in a steady breath. Words about "duty" and "protection" were foreign words to her. Other than her sister, Ella, no one had ever looked after her. It was hard for Evelyn to imagine a man with so much chivalry.

The conflict inside her was wild. How could she inter herself within the castle walls with Adam and his notorious brother, the duke? And what about the band of brigands?!

Her heart thumped harder at the prospect. She was in a terrible fix. A wicked soul was irredeemable. She knew firsthand. And a man so sinful he was dubbed the "Duke of Rogues" did not just change his corrupt ways—nor did a seafaring brood of cutthroats. How was she supposed to trust Adam to safeguard her against so many villains?

How was she supposed to trust Adam?

"Evie."

The crushing pressure around her midriff startled her.

"Look at me, Evie."

She did, fierce panic in her blood, her breath.

"You will be safe at the castle."

Evelyn was sincerely dubious. Besides, he had said she'd be safe at the cottage, too. Yet the henchmen had found her there.

And they would look for her again.

She didn't doubt it. The prince would never give up the search for her. He would order the countryside ravished for word of her whereabouts. It was endless, his desire to obtain beauty and then destroy it. A sick and compulsive—and incurable—need to maim and kill.

"The prince will find me again," she said in a broken voice.

"How? No one in the seaside village knows my real name, and the cottage was destroyed by fire. There is nothing left to reveal my true identity. The prince or his men will never think to look for you at the duke's castle."

Talk about the quaint cottage had her feeling remorseful. "I'm sorry you lost your home, Adam."

"I don't mourn for the cottage. All that I cared for is lost at sea."

His wife.

Evelyn shifted in his lap. "What *if* the prince finds me?"

"Do not underestimate the duke. My brother might have changed, but society still fears him. You will be secure within the keep's walls."

No, she wouldn't. She was never going to be safe. The only haven left for her was the cold comfort of death. How many times was she going to learn that blasted lesson? There was no peace for her in this world. And she certainly wasn't going to find it behind the Duke of Wembury's chilling castle walls.

"Let me go, Adam." She scratched his hand at her waist. "Please!"

"I can't."

Tears welled in her eyes. "Why?"

"I know you're frightened, Evie, but I have a duty to safeguard you. I can't let you go. I can't leave you alone in the world."

There was a desperate need inside her heart to believe him—and a biting fear to mistrust him. And yet the need triumphed over the fear. Or perhaps fatigue encouraged her to surrender. Evelyn wasn't really sure. But she stopped struggling with Adam, slumped against him with a loud sigh.

"You'll see, Evie. No harm will come to you."

Evelyn prayed, rather than believed, he would keep his word.

Adam loosened his grip on her midriff and slowly moved his fingers across the silk of her skirt before he cupped her hand.

His touch.

His touch did not repulse her. She was awed by it every time he pressed his hands—or his lips—to her flesh. He brought her comfort with the whisk of a finger, disarmed her with the whisper of a word.

It unsettled her . . . yet she did not pull away.

She shivered at his tender caress. Her eyes absorbed the meaty strength of his palm. He fingered the dried blood smeared across her knuckles, where she'd struggled with the coffin.

"I won't let the prince hurt you again. I made a mistake thinking he would not find you at the cottage. But I won't make that mistake again."

There was a roughness to his voice. And yet when he lifted her hand and kissed her wounded fingers, there was a softness to his manner. A dual nature, indeed.

She closed her eyes and held her breath as he slipped another hand into her hair. His fingers brushed the knob of her spine at the base of her skull, drawing her closer.

Hot lips pressed against her throat. "I promise, Evie, no man will ever hurt you again."

Except for you.

She was stunned by the sudden and bleak thought. It filled her heart with despair to think that Adam, too, might betray her one day.

Not you.

Please not you.

Adam kissed her every wound and bruise, leaving his scent, his mark on her flesh. He wiped away the rough handling of the henchmen, the fear inside her with the oh-so-tender movements of his mouth.

She curled her fingers into his hair, searching for his sensual lips. And she found them readily.

He drew her bottom lip into his warm mouth, suckling. "Show me, Evie," he whispered between kisses. "Show me where it hurts."

Evelyn shuddered at his rough and commanding words. Her heart throbbed, the pressure fierce against her breast.

Slowly she touched her heart.

Adam followed the movement of her hand with his eyes before he lowered his lips to the tops of her breasts and bussed her breastbone with exquisite tenderness.

She swallowed the aching cry in her throat, fixed her fingers more firmly in his hair to keep him close.

Adam lingered over her heart, nuzzled the plump skin. She wanted to drop back against the cushioned squabs, feel the weight of his body cover her. She wanted to take him into her lonely soul with such a violent desire, she trembled in need.

After such a close encounter with death, her

heart begged for life. It pulsed in her breast, demanding sweet solace. A touch. A kiss. A mark to prove she was still alive—and not alone.

It was overwhelming, the loneliness, the intense isolation she had suffered since her sister's demise. The need to connect with someone preyed on her mind.

But the fear . . .

The fear of getting too close to a man and being hurt—again—always stormed its way to the forefront of her thoughts, dousing the burning sentiments in her belly. Adam's charming kisses wooed . . . to a place she was too afraid to go.

Evelyn grabbed his arm to bring the spicy encounter to a stop.

He winced.

She quickly let go of him. "I'm sorry."

He gathered her against him. He was breathless, filled with restless energy. She could feel the tension inside him, the thrumming muscles beneath her posterior.

"Don't say you're sorry," he rasped. The man's breath stirred the locks at her temples. She inhaled each breath he exhaled, as if his energy offered her life in return.

He kissed the dip between her neck and shoulder. The warmth of his words and the hot mark of his lips stirred her insides with frightening passion, making her shiver.

"But I hurt you," she said.

He embraced her tightly. "You didn't hurt me, Evie. Not you."

After a few more breathless moments, Adam placed her gently on the seat beside him.

She wanted to weep at the separation. She yearned so much to lose herself in his embrace, to let him crush the darkness in her soul. But she couldn't trust him to do such a thing. He was a man. And like all men, he searched for beauty and pleasure to consume and control. She didn't want to eventually find herself at the mercy of another tormenter. Her heart could not take the pain of more abuse.

Not from him.

Chapter 18

E velyn eyed the spacious bedchamber with white-paneled walls, furnished in cheerful shades of honey yellow and an indigo blue accent. "It this my room?"

"Yes," said Adam. "Do you like it?"

He set the candle on the nightstand, illuminating the large bed. She observed the ornate headboard with majestic lion paws carved at each corner, and imagined sleeping under the quilted covers, safe in dream.

"It's very pretty," she said. "Thank you."

She looked at Adam. He was a striking figure under the soft glow of candlelight. The shadows from the flickering flames rested across his features in billowing waves. The fiery reflection illuminated his eyes, too, aglow like two burning coals.

"You should thank the duke. He had the room prepared for you."

Thank the duke? She was too wary to do that.

She was surrounded by thick stone walls in an impregnable fortress, yet she did not feel wholly secure. Adam had ordered the vehicle and driver back to the engagement ball, and soon the passageways would be filled with the din of more notorious men. And then there was Adam. She was wary of him, too. He had an inexplicable pull over her. She craved his touch at times. Shied away from it at others. But there was always a restless storm inside her whenever he was near.

Adam moved toward the hearth, his steps sluggish. Servants had already prepared the chamber, for there was a small flame in the fireplace and other candles around the room.

"How long will I stay at the castle?" she wondered. "Adam?"

Very slowly he tipped to one side—and collapsed.

"Adam!"

She hastened to his side.

Brow moist with sweat, the man looked wretched, in agony. He grimaced and clutched his midriff.

"What did the henchmen do to you?"

That did it! Adam had rebuffed her quest for the truth long enough.

Fingers quivering, she reached for the buttons of his shirt.

He must have realized her intent, for he clasped

her fingers and hugged them against his chest. "Don't!"

She could feel the heat from his body, the robust life. It burned her fingertips to press her hand against him in such an intimate way.

"Let me help you, Adam."

She would not be swayed.

He eventually surrendered with a grunt, and she parted his coat first before she set to work on the buttons of his shirt.

Her cheeks warmed as the first tufts of hair appeared. She remembered how he had looked that day at the beach, near nude and wet and glorious. Her fingers trembled as she touched the wide expanse of muscles for the first time.

But soon her eyes lighted upon the rest of his exposed torso—and the bloody bandages.

Evelyn was sick. The blood seeping through the linen was a ghastly sight. She dreaded to meet the wounds beneath.

Footsteps light, she treaded over to the washstand and poured the water from the pitcher into a bowl. Carefully she carried the bowl back over to the hearth and set it on the ground before she reached down and split her skirt in two. Tearing makeshift bandages, she immersed the material in the cool tonic.

Adam covered his chest with his arm. "You shouldn't see this."

But she grabbed his hand to prevent him from concealing the pain. "I want to see it."

Adam observed her with steely regard. The firelight danced in his eyes, bewitching her. He looked to be imploring her not to take apart the soiled linen, but Evelyn would not be able to rest until she had witnessed the damage for herself. He must have suspected as much, for he didn't try to stop her as she pried apart the stained bandages.

Once she had uncovered him, she gasped.

She stared at the grisly injuries, entranced. The ugly swelling and blistered burns took her breath away.

"Oh Adam . . . I'm sorry."

He whispered roughly, "For what?"

"For your pain."

He sighed. "You didn't cause me pain, Evie."

She picked up the scrap of silk soaking in the dish and wrung out the moisture. With ginger taps, she dabbed at his bloodied flesh.

"I did cause you pain." She dipped the silk back into the bowl, the water turning a dark red. At the sight of the blood, her heart cramped. "This is all my fault."

"This is all *his* fault."

Again she rubbed the silk across his gnarled muscles, the torment inside her impossible to assuage.

"No, this is my fault," she whispered softly. "I should never have stayed with you at the cottage; I only put your life at risk. I should have drowned in the—"

He cupped her cheeks and lifted his head to press his nose to hers. "Do *not* finish that thought. What I do, I do of my own choosing. I suffer of my own will. Do you hear me?"

She blinked at him, stunned. "Yes."

"Good." He let go of her cheeks and rested against the cold stone hearth once more. "I don't want you to fret about me," he said with less heat in his voice. "It's my job to worry about you."

Bemused, she nodded and resumed her tender care.

It was his job to care about her? Why? Why did he keep insisting he had to look after her? He had already saved her from drowning, rescued her from the prince. He didn't have to do more; he had no real obligation toward her. So what did he want with her?

At length she finished washing the burns. "I need to dress the wounds."

Adam shifted to sit up. He was uncomfortable, she could tell. She helped him divest the coat and shirt before she ripped more of her skirt's lining and wrapped the strips of silk around his midriff.

She leaned forward to reach around his waist. The rich scent of seawater was still nestled in his hair, and she closed her eyes for a moment in memory of the night he had first kissed her at the cottage. The sea breeze and salt had lived in his hair then, too.

"You should rest," she said quietly, the binding complete.

She gathered the soiled linen, picked up the bowl of bloody water. But Adam took the articles from her hands and placed them aside.

He grabbed her wrists.

Evelyn gasped when he dragged her between his legs and tugged, forcing her to kneel again.

"What are you doing?" she demanded, breathless.

"Returning the favor."

She bristled as he brushed his thumb across her bruised throat. She was trapped—in more ways than one. His legs sheltered her, but his eyes ensnared her with equal strength.

"Do you need me to summon a physician?" he said.

"No."

He hesitated over his next words. "Did the prince ravish you?"

Her eyes rounded. "No!"

"Do you know what I mean by ravishment?"

She blinked. "Yes, I understand. Ella wrote me letters. I . . ."

He pressed his thumb to her lips, the aggressive touch making her heart flutter. "Did the henchmen hurt you in that way?"

"No!"

She had denied the injury twice, but still Adam appeared unsettled. "I should fetch the doctor."

"I'm fine."

"The prince buried you in a coffin, Evie!"

She shuddered at the chilling memory. "I know."

"He tried to kill you."

"No, he only wanted to punish me for deserting him."

Adam appeared murderous. She took comfort in his anger toward the prince on her behalf. The man's indignation riled her own sense of injustice: she was *not* supposed to suffer like this!

"What about the bruising, Evie?"

"It's gruesome to look at, I know. But I will recover."

He stroked the tender spot at her neck, his eyes intent upon the injury. The heat and pressure of his fingertips teased her already sensitive skin, and her flesh reacted to the man's enchanting touch by breaking out into goose pimples.

"Your voice is rough," he said.

At the sensuous roughness in *his* voice, her heart pulsed and the fine hairs on her limbs spiked. "It will heal."

"You're exhausted, Evie." He kissed her brow. "Go to sleep."

The simple gesture of a good-night kiss filled her with warmth, a balm for her tattered soul. She peered deep into his dark and shadowed eyes, stared at the reflection of the bed in the glossy pools.

Again her thoughts returned to the image of her asleep under the thick covers . . . only this time she imagined Adam beside her.

Shocked by the boldness of her own thoughts, Evelyn broke away from his mesmerizing gaze.

Adam appeared equally perturbed by their intense connection. He struggled to his feet with her assistance. Briskly he said, "Good night."

He picked up his clothes and slipped back into the garments before he departed.

Alone in the room, Evelyn was chilled. She gathered the soiled linen on the floor and placed it on a nearby table before she tossed the bloody water out the open window and approached the bed. She settled over the feather tick and inhaled a deep and soothing breath to banish the torment in her heart.

But then she heard it. The distant din of male voices.

They were home!

The duke and his piratical brothers-in-law had returned from the ball.

And she was alone.

Evelyn tossed the covers aside and sprinted for the door. She opened it, prepared to search the castle for Adam. But she didn't have to search very far for him.

He was sitting on the ground beside the door.

It appeared he didn't trust the brigands any more than she did.

"Come inside," she said. "You can take the bed. I'll sleep in the wingback chair."

"No."

She crouched beside him. He was hurt. He couldn't spend the night in the passageway. It was improper. "Since you intend to stand guard, you might as well come inside."

Adam looked uneasy at the suggestion. She wasn't entirely comfortable with it herself. But she couldn't leave him to suffer in the passageway, either. Not after what he had done for her.

"Come." She tugged at his arm. "Let's go."

She ushered him inside the room despite the man's growls of protest.

"I'll take the chair," he insisted. "You keep the bed."

He headed for the wingback chair positioned across the room and eased his battered body into the seat, propping his feet upon the ottoman. A hand draped over his belly, he closed his eyes and tried to appear comfortable.

She frowned. "Do *you* need a physician?"

"No."

He was curt. He tended to get that way whenever she challenged him.

"I'm not your lieutenant," she said.

He opened an eye to ogle her. "Pardon?"

She collected a blanket from the bed. "I don't take orders. I'm not a member of your crew."

Adam opened his other eye to peer at her.

Evelyn approached him with an unsteady gait. "I mean, I only want to help." She placed the blanket over his torso. "Are you sure you don't need a physician?"

She quivered slightly under the man's commanding stare. "I don't order you about, Evie."

He slowly pushed the blanket down to his waist. She was engaged by the almost teasing manner of his movements, and she realized she had covered him more to hide the breadth of his physique than to keep him warm. Hide the tempting parts of him from her eyes.

"Do you think I order you about, Evie?"

He kicked aside the ottoman and took her by the wrist. He pulled her closer to the chair—right between his legs!

Her pulse quickened.

"I don't want you to do my bidding." He folded his fingers around her hipbones. "I want you to tell me what you desire. What you need."

Ever so slowly he pressed his lips to her belly. She gasped and closed her eyes in bliss.

She didn't dare touch him. She sensed her own weakness when it came to Adam's hot kisses. He would lure her to a forbidden place if she wasn't careful.

And yet she couldn't resist the incredible movements of his mouth against her taut midriff. It was such a contrast to the agony she had endured, the delight now coursing through her. She was eager for more. But she was afraid to ask for it.

Adam, however, was not afraid to offer it as he warmed her belly with smoldering kisses. He nuzzled her midriff before he bussed it over and over again, making her quiver with a longing so great, she abandoned her fears for the pure pleasure he offered.

He tugged at her hips and demanded roughly, "Ask me."

The blood rushing through her limbs, her brain was making her dizzy. At last she folded her hands over his head in a silent command for more.

"Yes," he praised weakly and nipped at her through the ruffles in her skirt. "What else do you want?"

When his fingers curled around the backs of her legs, and he stroked the softness of her thighs, she whimpered and bit her bottom lip to stifle the improper request:

I want you.

Adam ended the kiss.

She trembled in frustration and longing, bunched her fingers together to keep from pressing him to her belly once more.

"When you are ready to ask," he said in a whisper, "I will give you whatever you want."

It sounded so tempting! What was he doing to her? What did he want with her? was perhaps the wiser question. Did he want to possess her? Hurt her?

He offered her protection. Yet he unsettled her with each look and touch . . . and kiss.

Flustered, she took a shaky step back.

Adam rested against the chair again. There was an unmistakable sparkle in his eyes from the candle flames. But the burning glow seemed almost sinfully inviting.

Evelyn swiftly clambered back onto the bed. She snuggled under the remaining covers and pretended to sleep. But she could feel Adam watching her closely.

There was little chance she would dream tonight.

Chapter 19

S unlight warmed the room. The brilliant rays danced across the furniture—and the sultry figure snoozing under the covers.

Adam observed the nymph, her thick black hair mussed and twisted to rest across one shoulder. With her dress askew, the soft curve of her other shoulder peeked through the frock, and Adam had to close his eyes to resist the tempting image of what else lay beneath her apparel.

Ask me.

He bowed his head and rubbed his brow at the memory of his heated words the other night. Shame came over him. Shame for his wild desires . . . his unfaithfulness to Tess.

How could he engage in such boorish behavior with Evelyn? He had promised to protect the woman, not seduce her . . . and yet there was nothing he'd rather do.

Adam silently lifted off the chair. He was careful not to wake Evelyn. She had suffered great hardship. She deserved the respite.

Slowly he headed for the washstand, the wounds at his breast still smarting. He dipped his palms into the cold water before he splashed the spray across his features, and combed the moisture through his hair to tame the curls.

A deep hunger was growing inside him: a carnal hunger. He closed his eyes to beat back the lustful beast—but it defied taming.

The reflection in the glass captured his attention: Evelyn watching him closely.

He picked up a nearby towel and patted his face dry. "I didn't mean to wake you."

She blinked, a somnolent look in her eyes. "Are you leaving?"

"I'll be back soon," he assured her. "I'm just going to fetch you some breakfast."

Another memory sparked:

"I'll be back soon, luv."

"Don't go, Adam. Stay here with me."

"It'll be all right, Tess. We've hit choppy waters, is all. I'm just going topside to see if the crew needs any help. I'll be back in a minute."

With a twitch of the head, Adam dismissed the haunting recollection—but a chill still resided in his heart, compounded by the look of uncertainty in Evelyn's eyes. The same look of uncertainty he had witnessed in Teresa's eyes the night the ship sank.

However, he would not fail Evelyn the way he had failed Teresa. He understood Vadik's ruthless and stubborn nature now. He understood the man was a powerful prince, wont to getting his way. But he would not get his hands on Evelyn. Not again.

"What's going to happen to me?" she said softly.

Such fire burned in her violet eyes, such pain.

Adam approached the bed and knelt beside it. He stroked her knuckles, the skin broken where she'd struggled with the coffin. "You're going to remain inside the castle for a time. The prince will eventually return home, and then I will find *you* a new home."

He admired her as she rested in bed, and was gripped by a profound desire to share other such intimacies with another being—and saddened by the knowledge that he never would.

"I'll return shortly, Evie. We'll talk more then."

He briskly quit the room, unable to maintain his firm composure.

Adam moved through the familiar castle causeways, insensible to his surroundings. Deep in thought, he reflected upon the enchanting woman . . . and his own desire to be near her. But he would not surrender to the desire. He would remain faithful to his late wife.

Another crisis pressed on Adam's mind. He had broken yet another vow: to apprehend the pirates. But Black Hawk and his brothers had settled their debt; they had helped him to save Evelyn. He could not in good conscience deliver the men into the hands of the magistrate. Hell, the cutthroats were *family*! Even if Adam still wanted to see the brigands hang, a public execution would cause his brother and sister-in-law a tremendous amount of pain and embarrassment. And Adam had already caused the couple enough grief.

After a long stroll through the keep's uncharacteristically cheerful tunnels—he noted the duke had renovated the castle, likely to be more appealing to his wife and child—Adam made his way down into the kitchen labyrinth.

He stood on the threshold, the air rife with freshly cooked fare. He was struck by the familiar furnishings, overwhelmed by a wealth of childhood memories. One in particular stood out from the rest:

"Shove over."

Adam scooted deeper beneath the table to make room for his elder brother. Damian crawled under the long structure and settled beside him, crossing his legs at the ankles. He opened the book.

"Let me read it," said Adam.

Damian swatted at his brother's hand. "You can't read."

He pouted. "I know my letters."

"Oh really?" Damian pointed to a word. "What does that say?"

Adam eyed the scratches. "F . . . rrr . . . i . . ."

"Friday," said Damian succinctly. "He's Crusoe's slave. And we're going to be here until Friday if you read the book, so don't pester me anymore."

Adam made a grimace in protest.

"Did you bring the food?" said Damian.

Adam reached behind his back for the satchel and pried apart the cords. "Two apples rolled in brown sugar."

He presented one candied fruit to his brother and savored the other for himself.

"Right then, where were we?" Damian scanned the marked page. "Aha! Crusoe and Friday are about to lay siege to the cannibals' camp."

Adam snuggled closer to his brother, munched on the apple, and eagerly listened to every word . . .

Adam spied the grand table, so lofty he could stretch out across it and still leave room for Cook to prepare the meals. He and the duke used to hide in the kitchen. Hide from their father . . . and it looked as if someone else was in hiding.

Adam narrowed his eyes on the little blond head peering out from under the wood table. She had the golden locks of her mother, but her eyes . . . she had the duke's eyes.

Gads, he must look a fright to her! His hair mussed, his clothes wrinkled. To offset his bedraggled appearance, Adam smiled. "You must be Alice."

Mother had often written to him about the young girl, his niece. She was a joy to the entire castle. And Adam could see why. She had a darling face with inquisitive blue eyes. A little imp, he sensed.

"My name is Adam."

Her pretty eyes rounded. "Uncle Adam?"

She had heard of him. There was a warm stirring in his heart at the thought that he was not a stranger to her. In name, anyway. And that she did not recoil in fear confirmed that tales of his monstrous behavior toward her father had never reached her innocent ears.

Alice closed her book, a burned and tattered copy of *Robinson Crusoe*. The very tome he and the duke had once read as children. It was the duke's favorite book. Father had tossed it into the fire many years ago in a furious fit, but Adam had rescued the pages from the flames and gifted the book back to his brother. He was glad to see Alice reading it—even if it was upside-down!

The quick taps of her feet danced lightly in his ears as she approached him, curious.

"You're tall," said the sprite.

"Am I?"

She dragged the burdensome book with her and stopped a short distance from him. "Very tall."

Adam stared down at her. "Is there something you need me to reach?"

Her pretty features brightened even more. "That."

She pointed to the wooden bowl perched high above the cupboard. He reached for the mysterious dish, covered with a napkin.

Adam flipped back the linen to reveal a square cut of chocolate.

He eyed the imp. "Is this chocolate for you?"

"Oh yes."

"Are you sure it doesn't belong to Cook?"

She blinked. "Oh no."

Adam was amused by the chit's blatant attempts at manipulation. She was spoiled rotten—and she had been waiting for just the right saphead to come along and do her bidding. Yet he didn't feel like denying her the treat.

A darkness entered Adam's heart, a tremendous regret. He remembered the night he had stabbed his brother. He had come so close to taking the duke away from this precious child!

And what of her mother? Adam had aimed a gun at her, too. For one brief and twisted moment he had contemplated ending her life to make the duke suffer. Had she carried Alice in her womb even then?

Overwhelmed by sickness at the morbid thought, Adam swallowed the fresh regret. He crouched and tried to ignore the pounding of his heart, as he offered the little girl her cherished sweet.

Alice was quick to swipe the sugary candy, her eyes round in great expectation. She was ready to bite into the chocolate when she peered at him with concern.

"Don't be sad," she said, and snapped a piece—a tiny piece—of chocolate. She handed him the candy. "We can share."

"Thank you."

Adam accepted the offering and tried to dismiss the misery from his features before Alice noticed even more distress. He was filled with bitter loathing for himself: a disgust that he had once come so close to devastating so many innocent lives.

Alice gnawed on the chocolate and smiled.

Adam, too, popped the treat into his mouth to coat the tart taste of bile in his belly.

The sound of firm footfalls resounded.

"Alice?"

At the ring of an authoritative voice, Alice quickly stuffed the rest of the chocolate into her mouth.

Adam was still crouched beside the little girl when the Duchess of Wembury entered the kitchen, her belly *very* swollen.

The woman was a fetching sight, her tawny gold locks in a soft chignon, a few loose tendrils caressing her regal cheeks and jaw. Eyes a soft gold, she wore a quiet, very complimentary, butter yellow frock.

She rested her eyes on Adam for an instant, fire flashing in the amber pools, before she quickly turned her attention to her daughter, and reproached, "Lady Alice Westmore, I warned you not to touch the chocolate. How is Cook going to make the frosting for the cake now?"

The little girl blinked.

The duchess eyed the empty bowl still in Adam's hands. "Alice, did you eat *all* the chocolate?"

Alice shook her head vehemently, her cheeks stuffed with the spoils.

Mirabelle narrowed her eyes. "The bowl is empty, Alice. Where is the rest of the chocolate?"

The treacherous sprite pointed her finger at Adam's round cheek.

The duchess lifted a delicate brow at her brother-in-law.

Overwhelmed by chagrin, Adam swallowed the chocolate.

Mirabelle pointed to the passageway behind her, where a shadow was seen. "Alice, return to the schoolroom with Nurse."

She mumbled, "Yes, Mama."

The imp pressed the old book against her chest and strutted from the room, showing no sign of remorse for having snitched on her uncle.

Adam put the empty bowl aside and lifted off his haunches. A tempest raged inside his breast. He had tried to kill the duchess and her husband at one time. Standing across from the woman was intimidating. He didn't know what to say, how to even express the shame burning inside him.

"I understand you dragged my husband and brothers away last night? To a ball?" Despite her swollen belly, she appeared very officious with her hands on her hips. "I also noticed I wasn't invited to come along."

Adam eyed her belly, thinking of the babe about to burst forth.

"It was dangerous," he said at length. "We didn't think it wise for you to come along."

She snorted. "I gathered that. My husband informed me of the goings-on—after he returned home, of course."

Her hands went to her belly as she stepped deeper into the kitchen.

Adam moved to fetch the woman a chair, but she waved him off.

"I prefer to stand." She paused a short distance away from him. "I understand I have a new houseguest."

"Yes, I—"

"Besides you."

Adam remembered the woman in his care. He was quick to insist, "Lady Evelyn is my responsibility."

The duchess laughed softly. "Lady Evelyn is a single woman, living under *my* roof and therefore under *my* protection. I will see to her needs."

Something sparked in Adam: a defensive posture. "I promised to protect her."

"And so you have; you've brought her here. Now I will take care of her. And I expect you to be on your best behavior."

Adam bristled at being mothered like a schoolboy. "I intend to be respectful toward Lady Evelyn."

"And the rest of the household?"

So that was her point of contention. Would he stab her husband again? Or perhaps her piratical brothers? "I'm not here to quarrel."

A curt bob of the head. "I'm glad to hear that." She eyed him closely. "I was beginning to think we would never see you again."

"I never expected to return." He searched for something more to say. At length he mentioned: "Thank you for your letters."

Along with his mother, the duchess had corresponded with him on a few occasions, encouraging him to reconcile with the duke. But Adam was immune to such a suggestion. There was no hope for absolution. His crime against the duke was unforgivable.

"You mean a great deal to my husband," she said.

I mean nothing to your husband, he wanted to clarify, but remained mum. The duchess was misguided in her belief that the duke cared one whit for him. It did her credit, though, her desire to make her husband content by doing what she thought would bring him happiness.

But Adam's prolonged presence at the castle would only displease the duke. Adam was just a bother, intruding upon their household. And just as soon as the prince returned to his home country, Adam would depart the castle to find Evelyn a proper home—and never trouble the duke and duchess again.

Mirabelle hugged her belly and moved toward

the door. "I think I will go and welcome my houseguest."

Adam wanted to protest that Evelyn was still *his* responsibility, but he sensed he was already on precarious ground with the duchess and so refrained from making the objection.

Chapter 20

Evelyn glanced down at her tattered dress. She had ripped the resplendent material the other night, to make bandages for Adam . . . but she had not ripped it nearly enough.

She reached down, clasped the hem of her skirt, and split it in two. With firm determination, she rent the rest of the silk fabric the prince had draped her in. She would take nothing from *him*—ever! The fabric hugged her flesh like a prison, reminding her of her royal gaoler. And she was eager to be rid of it; she wanted no memory of *him*.

She tore the brilliant skirt into more strips, then rived the lining. She battled with the fixed stitching, tearing the seams, tossing the bits of shiny fabric to the floor.

The corset proved troublesome, though, beaded with tiny pearls. She wrestled with the tight sewing, gnashed her teeth in dogged resolve, but her efforts proved fruitless. The quality-built garment was indestructible.

"Do you need any help?"

Evelyn blinked.

She turned around to confront the young—very enceinte—woman standing under the door frame.

The duchess!

Evelyn wanted to hide behind the wingback chair; she looked ghastly with her mussed hair and bruises and mangled frock. But she could not rebuff her hostess.

With a shaky step, Evelyn stepped forward, mustered some refinement, and curtsied. "Your Grace."

"Rubbish." The duchess flicked her fingers in the air. "My name is Mirabelle."

It had been a long time since Evelyn had mingled with members of the peerage. After her mother died and her father turned wild, respectable company had deserted her. She was accustomed to a solitary life. Now she was in the company of a duchess. Bashful, Evelyn gawked at the floor.

Faint footsteps treaded closer, and soon a head stooped and a pair of warm golden eyes peeked up at her.

"You have violet flower eyes," said the duchess. "Very pretty."

Evelyn slowly lifted her gaze; the duchess raised her head at a matching tempo.

"You must be Lady Evelyn," she said.

Evelyn nodded.

"Do you like your room, my lady?"

"Evie."

Mirabelle lifted a brow.

She finished softly, "You can call me Evie."

The duchess smiled again. "And you can call me Belle."

Evelyn spied the woman, a few years her senior, with careful appraisal. She was being very gracious, kind even. It was Evelyn's experience the peerage was quite formidable, vulgar at times. Once one lost fortune and respectability, the *ton* was unforgiving. So she didn't know what to make of the duchess.

And she was married to the "Duke of Rogues." How chilling! The poor woman must endure such hardship . . . and yet she appeared cheerful.

"That's a very beautiful necklace, Evie."

Evelyn reached for the heart-cast pendant in comfort. "It was a gift from my sister."

"You are fortunate to have a sister. I have *four* brothers."

The black-haired devils!

Evelyn observed the duchess. She could see why the duke wanted to possess the woman, even though she was sister to a band of pirates. The duchess was nothing like her intimidating kin in

looks or manner. She appeared beautiful in countenance and spirit alike.

"I understand," said Evelyn. "With four brothers who are . . ."

She quirked a brow. "Pirates?"

Evelyn rushed to mutter, "I would be frightened, too."

"Adam told you about my brothers?"

"Yes . . . I'm sorry."

"For what?"

"For the terrible things you must suffer with
such men in your life."

The duchess let out a husky laugh. "I need to
confide something in you, Evie."

She nodded meekly. "You can trust me. I have
no one with whom to betray your confidence."

"I love my brothers, scoundrels that they are,"
she whispered. Then, with more energy: "It's
just such a bother sometimes, to have four very
protective males interfering in my life. I often
wish I had a sister, too, to confide my secrets and
troubles."

A sadness welled in Evelyn's breast. "Yes, it's
wonderful to have a sister . . . I miss my sister."

"I'm sorry, Evie." Mirabelle's features fell, and
she glanced around the room. "Are you in mourning for your sister?"

Evelyn dropped her eyes once more. "No."

"Then why have you covered all the mirrors?"

Evelyn had stripped the bedding to hide the reflective glass. But it was not an easy matter for her to confess, her distaste for mirrors.

"I . . . um . . ."

A finger touched Evelyn's chin, gentle, yet forceful, hoisting her head. "Do you want to hide from the bruising?"

That and her eyes and her cursed face.

"Who hurt you, Evie?"

Evelyn reached for her throat to conceal the ugly abuse, but a firm hand gripped her wrist. "Do not hide from me. I won't judge you. Tell me, who did this to you? Was it Adam?"

Evelyn gasped. "No!"

But it alarmed her to think the duchess suspected Adam. Her old qualms that she was not safe at the castle returned. Was Adam a dangerous man? She had only suspected it; he had such a devastating pull on her heart, it was hard for her to think clearly about the man. But now she had another source to confirm her misgiving: the duchess.

"Then who hurt you, Evie? The prince?"

Evelyn quietly stared at the affable woman.

"My husband told me about the prince, that you are being forced to marry against your will." She cupped her hand. "You will be safe here at the castle."

Adam had said the same thing, but now Evelyn was even more perturbed. The duchess seemed wary of Adam. Why? Because he had once quarreled with her husband?

"How did you meet Adam?" said the duchess.

Evelyn swallowed a deep breath. "He saved me."

"From whom?"

"Death."

The older woman eyed her with great curiosity. "Do you need a physician?"

"No," she said, her voice still a rasp. "I will be all right."

"As you wish." Mirabelle did not look convinced, but acquiesced. She eyed the pile of rags on the floor. "Why did you destroy the dress?"

"I don't want to wear the prince's offerings."

"I see," she said sagely. "I'll find you something else to wear."

"Thank you, Your Grace."

The duchess cleared her throat.

"Thank you, Mirabelle."

A blond brow arched.

Evelyn said quietly, "Thank you, Belle."

Mirabelle smiled despite Evelyn's discomfort at such an informal appellation. "If you need anything, Evie, I want you to come to me."

Evelyn nodded.

The duchess squeezed her hand. "There is no formality between us, do you understand? You are *my* guest. If you are in trouble with Adam—"

Evelyn opened her mouth to inquire.

"—or with anyone else, you may come to me for help."

What was she to make of the woman's offer? wondered Evelyn. And why was the duchess so adamant that Adam might hurt her? What about the duke and the pirates? Surely Evelyn should be wary of them, too?

"And I will have the mirrors in the room removed if you'd like," said the duchess.

"Thank you . . . Belle."

Chapter 21

The warm and brilliant rays of the setting sun painted the room in a fiery glow. Curled in a ball and sitting on the comfortable divan, Evelyn worshipped the dazzling mesh of colors with the appreciation of a liberated prisoner.

She was draped in fresh fabric, the fine linen so much more soothing against her skin. She had been offered toiletries for her hair and a lovely opal white scarf to wrap around her throat, the soft silk cool against the burning bruises.

With the mirrors in the room removed, there was nothing to distract Evelyn from observing the glorious sunset—but for thoughts of Adam.

The harmony in her breast faded as she delved into memory, reminiscing about the duchess's words. That the woman should find rogues and brigands amiable, yet Adam a threat, was disquieting.

It plagued Evelyn, the need to understand Adam's true character. He wanted to protect her from the prince. But could she trust him to do so? Was he noble at heart, as he'd claimed? Or was he secretly a villain?

A knock at the door.

Startled, Evelyn glanced at the wood barrier. It was almost time for supper. A maid had bobbed in and out of the room a short while ago to inform her she was expected to dine with the family. Such an odd family! She dearly hoped the duchess would be dining with them, too. She was the only other sensible soul in the castle.

With that last wishful thought in mind, Evelyn slipped off the divan and approached the door.

But it was not a servant who'd come to escort her to the dining hall—it was Adam.

"Good evening, Evie."

The low timbre of his voice tickled her flesh, arousing goose bumps. She was disarmed by the handsome and respectable sight of him decked in dapper garb. There was also a sudden pang in her heart at the obvious transformation, for Adam was not a simple cottager anymore—he was a duke's brother. And she realized she didn't know the man standing in front of her at all.

"Did the duchess welcome you?" he wondered.

"She did." Evelyn pointed to the soft blue fabric strapped across her midriff. "She even offered me this dress to wear."

"It's lovely." He eyed her closely. "You're lovely."

Her heart quickened.

"How do you feel, Evie?"

Before she could respond to the question, he lifted a forefinger and brushed the silk scarf that was hiding the swelling at her throat.

The feather touch made her tremble.

Her voice quivered, too. "I feel better."

He whisked his thumb across the length of her jaw before he withdrew his hand. For an instant, she mourned the loss of his strong yet tender touch.

"Allow me to escort you to the dining hall."

She eyed the sturdy arm he offered. A whiff of panic curled in her breast, a familiar bout of mistrust.

"It's getting late," he said. "You will never find the hall in the dark . . . but I know the castle very well in the dark."

She spied him, curious. There was no threat underlining his voice. Rather a firm sadness. Why did he know the castle so well in the dark?

Despite her lingering misgiving, she placed her palm on his arm. There was an instant spark. It filled her belly; the flurry of warmth seeped into her blood. She inhaled the scent of him, the essence. So masculine. So robust.

Her first step was shaky.

He cupped her elbow. "Are you all right?"

"I'm fine," she whispered, her throat still parched.

"Come." He maneuvered her through the gray darkness. "This way."

A few minutes later, Evelyn was ensconced in an ornate chair under the bright glow of candlelight—and the bright and curious stares of rogues and brigands.

She picked at the warm morsels of lamb and roasted carrots on her plate, trying to ignore the scrutiny. At length she lost her appetite.

The Duke of Wembury was seated at the head of the long table, a true rogue with his dashing looks and suave manner. But Evelyn sensed an underlying darkness in the man. She suspected that, if provoked, he would crush an adversary's throat. Fortunately the duchess was seated at the other end of the dining table to offset her husband's intimidating façade.

But then there were the pirates. Retired pirates, she should say. According to Adam, the brood had renounced their sinister ways once their sister had ascended to the lofty position of duchess. A pity the brood hadn't renounced their sinister looks, too. Evelyn quailed under the close examination of the rest of the brigands seated around the candlelit table.

She was surrounded by frightening company indeed.

An elf suddenly stormed the room, causing Evelyn to drop her fork in surprise.

Dressed in a fluffy white nightshirt, the tiny creature rounded the table and tossed herself into the affectionate embrace of the youngest pirate, Quincy. He very loudly smacked the chit's cheek with a kiss before he passed her over to his brother.

Down the table the child rolled, from uncle to uncle, before she landed, giggling, in her father's lap.

Breathless, the little girl shouted, "Again!"

However, the duchess was not amused. "Lady Alice Westmore, why aren't you in bed?"

The little girl grimaced. "The sun's still out!"

"The sun has set."

The chit looked out the window to observe the last lingering rays. "There's still a little bit peeking."

Under the chortle of her uncles, the child beamed. But soon her attention was snagged by another guest.

"Oooh," said Alice, blinking at Evelyn. "You have pretty eyes."

Evelyn blushed.

"Alice, go back to bed at once," ordered the duchess.

The elf quickly twisted her neck to stare up at the duke. "Papa, can I stay up with you?"

The duke glanced from his daughter to his wife in a clear fix.

Evelyn watched the entire spectacle unfold with awe. The notorious duke at the beck and call of a mere babe? The brutish pirates doting uncles? Something wasn't right.

The duke sighed. "I think it best if you go back to bed, squirt."

"Oh, Papa!"

The duchess bobbed her head in approval and summoned a maid into the room. "Please escort Lady Alice back to the nursery."

"At once, Your Grace."

The servant approached the duke.

The elf scrambled down her father's lap. She took the maid by the hand and stomped the length of the room before she quit the hall with a huff.

"You all spoil her rotten," said the duchess.

Quincy grinned. "It's our duty as uncles."

"You're too hard on her, Belle," said another pirate, William.

The duchess pinched her brow. "If I don't offer the girl some sort of discipline and structure, she'll grow up to be wild."

Quincy made a wretched face at the words "discipline" and "structure."

The duchess ignored her youngest kin to glare at her husband. "And what's your excuse?"

The duke eyed his wife. "My excuse?"

"For spoiling Alice?"

"Do I need an excuse?"

She offered him a pointed look. "The girl is going to make a spectacle of herself one of these days."

"Belle's right." The pirate captain, James Hawkins, glared at the duke with dark intent. "Our father didn't restrict Belle's behavior growing up, and look what happened . . . she married you."

The duke sliced the cutlet of lamb, seemingly unperturbed. "You see, my dear. Alice will turn out to be just fine—like you."

Apparently the blasé retort was not the sort of response the pirate captain had hoped to hear from the duke, for the man appeared cantankerous.

"Let's not quarrel at the dinner table," said the duchess with warning. "We have guests, remember?"

Quincy looked straight at Evelyn. "So what *are* we going to do with you?"

The ring of porcelain resounded as the duchess hit the plate with her knife.

Quincy glanced at his sister. "What?"

"Lady Evelyn will remain in hiding until the prince returns to his homeland."

Adam had announced the plan with confident resolve. He had been quiet for most of the dinner conversation, but he was first to speak on her behalf when the matter of her fate was addressed.

"And once the prince leaves England?" said the duke. "What will happen to Lady Evelyn?"

Yes, what would happen to her? She didn't want to find herself in another position of weakness. She wanted the freedom to determine her own destiny. Imprisoned by a derelict father and a monstrous fiancé, she was tired of her thoughts and wishes always being put asunder.

"I will find her a new home," returned Adam.

Unfortunately Adam didn't think to confer with her about the matter.

"Even if the prince returns home, he isn't likely to give up the search for Lady Evelyn." The pirate captain took a swig of wine. "Vadik is not the sort of man to bear humiliation humbly, I suspect. He will likely order the henchmen to continue the search for her."

Evelyn had suspected the very same thing. The prince was a dominant beast. He would not permit her, mere property, to best him. She knew the prince well enough to believe that.

The duchess looked at her brother in alarm. "But there must be somewhere Lady Evelyn can live in security?"

The duke suggested, "We can hide her in the country."

"In Scotland," said the duchess in accord. "The prince will never think to look for her so far north."

"No." Adam interrupted the scheme to impress, "I will find Lady Evelyn a proper home."

Evelyn noted frown lines crease the brow of her hostess. She also noted the rising tension in the room and despised being the cause of it.

"I thank you for your hospitality, Your Grace." Adam was firm. "But Lady Evelyn's security is my responsibility."

More interested in the well-cooked fare than the heated conversation, Edmund, the last of the brigands, piped up to suggest, "She can always go to America."

Quincy beamed. "Oh, that's right. We're going to America in a few weeks on business." He looked at Evelyn and winked. "You can come with us."

A boat trip with the four devils sounded disagreeable . . . but America? America sounded safe and far from the prince's brutal hand.

"It's not a poor idea," said William in support. "There are many well-to-do families there, so she won't be starved of company. And she can change her name to start a fresh life."

"Then we'll go to America."

The table fell quiet at Adam's announcement.

The duke looked at his brother. "You're going, too?"

"So long as Prince Vadik lives, Evelyn is in danger," said Adam. "Someone must look after her welfare."

Evelyn was seated next to Adam. Sharing the intimate space with him made it difficult for her to forget their cozy encounter the other night. Her belly still burned with the memory of his hot lips. He was going to travel with her to the New World? She was going to be susceptible to his dark and sensuous kisses forever?

"But to leave England?" said the duke.

Adam shrugged. "It's better this way . . . Besides, I don't have anything keeping me in England."

The very thought was distressing; her and Adam alone in America? Evelyn preferred him to accompany her on the boat trip; she didn't want to be alone with the infamous brigands. But then it was better for them both to part ways. Adam had a family in England, and she wanted to start a fresh life without the distraction he imposed upon her senses. So how to convince him of that truth?

Adam stood at the mouth of the pond, skipping stones.

He could see the castle from his vantage point, a silhouette in the moonlight. The crescent-shaped moon was tipped upside-down. It would rain soon, according to folklore.

The stone hopped across the lambent surface of the water, the ripples distorting the castle's reflection.

The matter was settled. Evelyn would live in America, and he would go with her to make sure she was safe. It was a sound plan. The pirate captain was right; the prince would never give up the search for Evelyn. He might return home, but he would keep the henchmen in England to look for her . . . to punish her for deserting him.

Adam was stiff with fury at the thought of Evelyn interred in a coffin. She would never find herself—alive!—in such a ghastly place again. He would see to it.

"Am I disturbing you?"

She disturbed his every waking thought. And un-waking thought. He had to struggle to repress the passion he had for her. She was everything his dark and lonely soul was missing . . . and she was everything he couldn't have.

"It's late." Another stone stroked across the lake. "What are you doing here, Evie?"

Each light step she took warmed his body until a fire was raging in his belly.

She stopped near him; her long, dark hair swatted his arm in the tender breeze. "I need to speak with you."

The gentle taps of her hair against his sleeve distracted him from his sport, and the stone dropped into the water with a loud plop.

He sighed.

Evelyn stepped closer to the pond and picked up a small rock. She flicked her arm and sent the pebble flying.

Adam listened to the audible slaps of water as the stone skipped over the surface twice, thrice . . . five times.

He lifted a brow. "Impressive."

"As children, my sister and I used to skip rocks by the lake where we lived."

He imagined her as a little girl, running beside the lakeshore with her sister . . . joyful.

"What is it you need to speak to me about, Evie?"

She turned toward him with a solemn expression. "I don't want you to stay with me in America."

Adam's heart dropped like a stone in the water. "What?"

"You have a family here in England. I don't want you to be estranged from your kin. It's a terrible feeling, I know. And I don't want to be the cause of it. I can look after myself in America. I will work as a governess. You don't have to remain with me."

The idea that she did not need him, that she

did not *want* him, had a profound effect on Adam, making the blood pound in his breast and resound in his ears. "Are you mad?!"

She started. "I beg your pardon?"

"You can't reside in America alone. What about the prince?"

"He won't think to look for me in America. He knows I have no money with which to buy passage aboard a ship. It will never occur to him I might travel across the ocean with a band of pirates. He will never think to look for me so far."

To hell with her reasonable point!

"No!"

She appeared startled by his curt rebuttal, but after a moment she said, "Do you remember what you promised me the other night?"

Adam bristled at the erotic memory of the woman pressed between his legs as he'd bussed her trim midriff.

"You promised to give me whatever I asked for."

Blast her for using *that* vow against him!

"And I'm asking you to return to England after I'm settled in America."

Every muscle in Adam's body was taut. He glared at the woman with a desire to shake sense into her.

"You are not living in the New World without me," he said tightly.

"Be reasonable, Adam."

"Me? How can you even suggest I abandon you in a strange country?"

"I told you; you have a family."

"If you failed to notice at dinner, I am *not* on good terms with my family."

"But you can reconcile with your kin if you return to England."

Adam stalked away from her. Why the devil was she so eager to be rid of him all of a sudden?

"It's improper for you to live with me in America." She sighed. "It was different at the cottage; we were alone. But in America I hope to begin a new life, to get acquainted with a family of respectable means in need of a governess."

Yet another excuse as to why he should sail back to England. How many more did she have? What was the *real* reason behind her antagonism?

"I will hire a female companion," he said. "We will not be alone together."

"I've made up my mind, Adam. I want you to return to England."

He headed for her with brisk strides. He lowered his lips a hairbreadth from hers and gritted, "And I've made up mine. I'm staying with you in America."

For a moment he thought he might have persuaded her to submit to good sense, but then he observed a defiant spark in her eyes.

"You are not my husband or my father. You have no clout over my life."

He wanted to argue the point; he had a duty. He had promised to protect her. But he sensed the woman would only rebuff that argument, too.

Pushed too hard, she was combative. He was glad to see the hot-tempered streak in her. But did she have to argue with *him*? He was not the enemy, didn't she realize that?

"It's settled then?"

She mistook his quiet indignation for begrudging agreement. He didn't disabuse her of the misconception, though. Let her believe him in accord. It offered him time to find some other way to convince the woman he had every intention of remaining with her in the New World.

Chapter 22

"Are you ready?"
Evelyn dropped the comb, startled. With no mirror in the bedroom, she had not noticed Adam's approach.

She turned around to confront him—and suppressed a shiver.

Adam was dressed in black breeches; the material hugged his legs. It also illustrated the brawn pulsing through his muscles. Her own pulse quickened at the sight of him, her heart throbbing faster as she skimmed her eyes over the rest of his robust form.

Draped in a crisp white shirt with no vest or coat or neck cloth to tidy his rugged appearance, he reminded her of their lazy days at the cottage by the seashore. He had dressed in rural attire then, too. And she was gripped by a profound desire to return to those dreamy days before the dark cloud of uncertainty and mistrust had cast a shadow over them.

She peeked through the bedroom window. It was early morning and she had to wonder, "Ready to do what at this hour?"

"To continue with our lessons."

Evelyn had had very little sleep, overwhelmed by restlessness after her heated talk with Adam the other night. Her brain a bit foggy, she said, "What lessons?"

Adam took her by the hand and dragged her from the vanity. "You must learn to defend yourself, remember?"

Evelyn tossed the comb aside, his meaning clear. "But I don't want to fight with swords!"

"Very well." He pulled her from the room. "You will learn to fight with your hands instead."

Some minutes later, Evelyn was sheltered beneath a cluster of trees in the garden with Adam.

"Let's begin," he said, "before the sun rises too high and the heat drives us to seek shelter indoors."

"What about your injuries?"

She eyed him closely as he pushed up his sleeves and exposed his stalwart forearms. It baffled her, the energy he possessed. He had strength enough to crush bones, yet he was tender at times, too.

"I'm fine, Evie. You must learn to protect yourself." There was a dark glow in his eyes. "I won't always be beside you."

Adam sounded displeased by the remark. Clearly he was still vexed with her for foiling his plan to be her guardian. But she'd had to do it. The thought of being ruled by another man, especially one who made her yearn for kisses, was frightening. He had power over her, like her father and the prince. It was only in a different form. But it would bring her the same heartache.

"Are you ready, Evie?"

Slowly he circled her.

Evelyn shivered under his assessing stare. He prowled around her like a predator about to pounce.

"Yes, I'm ready," she said.

But she was having a deuced hard time ignoring the jitters in her belly and concentrating on the session at hand. Rapt by the man's hard stare, she started to feel like real prey.

Evelyn gasped as a hard set of arms circled her from behind and clinched her waist. She could feel the man's muscles as he pressed against her back, feel the flex of his weight. He was so tight against her, so firm. His strength confused her . . . comforted her . . . alarmed her.

"Break away, Evie."

Lost in reflection, she quickly composed herself and struggled. But her thrashing proved ineffectual; he maintained his hold. And the more she battled, the more frustrated she became.

At length she stilled. "It's hopeless."

"It's not hopeless," he said deeply by her ear, making her quiver with delight. "After years of physical work, you have the strength to resist. You only need to learn how to do it properly."

He let her go.

The cool morning air whooshed across her back, moist with sweat, washing away the heat of Adam's touch.

She shuddered once more, this time at the chill of being let loose.

"If trapped from behind," he said, "use your feet as a weapon." He demonstrated. "Kick back against your assailant's shin; you'll throw your attacker off balance."

Evelyn eyed his every move.

"Try again, Evie."

He approached her, moved behind her, and wrapped his arms around her.

"Are you sure you want me to do this?" she said.

"Just don't break my leg."

For a moment she didn't budge; she just let the heat from his torso warm and invigorate her spirit.

But then his arms pinched her waist, reminding her to fight. She did. She raised her foot and sent it back. She didn't strike with force; she didn't want to crack his shin, but keeping her locked in his embrace, he allowed her to practice her aim until she nailed him right below the knee.

"Well done, Evie."

There it was again, that familiar joy at being praised.

"You can also use your elbow as a weapon." He let her go. "Put your arms around me."

She balked. "What?"

"I want you to pretend you're the assailant." He crooked his hand to encourage her. "Come."

Her heart thumping loudly in her ears, Evelyn opened her arms wide and slowly reached around either side of his waist.

Goodness, he was big. Her fingers just touched at the apex of his chest . . . and the fire that burned in her belly quickly spread through the rest of her, too.

She pressed her cheek against his back and inhaled the spicy scent of his musk. Prickles of nervous delight danced across her fingertips as she hugged him with all her might.

Adam was quiet. He had stilled under her embrace, and for a short while she sensed his steady breathing and nothing more.

There was a quiet roughness to his voice when at last he said, "With your elbow aim for the ribs." He slowly demonstrated the movements against her. "Now you try."

Once more Evelyn was cocooned in his arms.

And once more she resisted the impulse to sigh in contentment.

She trained her eyes on the tree for balance, and then curled her body to slowly mimic the attack postures.

"Good." He let go of her midriff and faced her again. "Now in a frontal attack, use your knee." He shot his knee upward to demonstrate. "Aim for the most sensitive part of a man."

Heat touched her cheeks as her eyes inadvertently fixed to the said muscle between his legs.

Quickly she focused on the well-hewn ground instead, but she sensed her straying eyes had not gone unnoticed by Adam, for he said gruffly, "Why don't we practice with our hands next?"

She prayed the earth would shake and crack and swallow her whole. How mortifying! If only her instructor weren't so captivating. A boorish toad would be ideal, she thought. Such a teacher would spare her from further embarrassment.

"If your hands are free, strike at the throat." He made a quick chopping movement. "But make sure to put considerable pressure on the target or you won't do any harm."

Choking back her discomfiture, she followed suit.

Adam pointed toward her eyes. "Or poke your finger into the villain's eye."

She grimaced.

"It will disarm him, Evie, and give you a chance to run away."

"What if my hands aren't free?"

"Bite!"

"I don't know if I can do this. It's so . . . bloody."

"If your life depends upon it, you *will* do it. Get angry, Evie. It will give you the inner strength to fight."

His conviction was infectious. Resolute to conquer her qualms, she followed his direction and practiced the movements.

As the morning progressed and the sun burned brighter, Evelyn sighed.

"Are you tired?" He gestured to a tree. "Do you want to rest in the shade?"

Her limbs aching, she readily assented and crouched beside the tree, the gnarled root an ideal stool. Adam joined her beneath the canopy of leaves and pressed his back against the rough bark in respite.

"You're doing well," he said.

"Thank you."

She observed her slippered feet, stained with grass. As the conversation lulled, her thoughts returned to Adam, her instructor. The man was skilled with a sword, with his fists. That he could so easily render an enemy senseless offered her comfort. However, it also disturbed her, for she had to wonder if he would ever turn his fists against her . . . as the duchess had subtly suggested.

"Is something the matter, Evie?"

She poked the grass with the tip of her shoe. "I was just thinking."

"About?"

"About veiled dangers."

He crouched beside her. She peered into his soft blue eyes. Once she had found truth and kindness in the pair. Now she looked upon him with apprehension.

"Do you still fear being in the castle, Evie?"

She formed her words carefully. "The duchess thinks I might still be in danger."

He frowned. "The duke will *not* harm you."

"It is not the duke she thinks will harm me."

Quietly Evelyn stared at him.

"Oh." Adam glanced away. He moved away, too. Restless energy thrummed through his muscles. It was evident in the way he bristled. "I admit, I'm not surprised."

She pinched her brows together. "Why not?"

"The duchess and I parted on very poor terms four years ago."

"Because you quarreled with her husband? And is the woman still angry with you?"

"I think she is afraid."

"Of you?"

"Of what I might do."

Evelyn regarded his inscrutable features, masked by the shade of leaves. "And what might you do?"

Adam looked at his hands. "I hurt my brother once."

"How?" she whispered.

"I stabbed him."

Evelyn grabbed the locket at her throat for comfort and support. Terrible thoughts beset her: thoughts of Adam attacking the duke in a feral rage . . . attacking her.

"You . . . you stabbed him?" she stammered. "But why?"

"Evie, listen to me."

He reached out to clasp her hand, but she jerked her fingers away.

Adam stepped back, his eyes cloudy, stormy. "I was a very angry man many years ago. I blamed my brother for my wife's death."

Evelyn stilled the rampant beats of her heart, shushed the blood in her ears. "The duke killed your wife? I thought she drowned at sea?"

"She did. Six years ago, Tess and I curtailed our wedding tour to return to England and help the duke. He was still a wicked man then, the 'Duke of Rogues.' But he was also my brother. I thought I could save him from his wickedness." Adam sounded tortured. "There was a brutal storm one night. Tess drowned, but I survived. After the sinking, I was filled with grief . . . rage. I blamed the duke for my wife's drowning. I reasoned if he wasn't such a villain, Tess and I would still be on our wedding tour. We would not have had to sail home to save the duke from sin—and Tess would still be alive."

"So you tried to kill him?"

"I wanted to avenge Teresa's death."

"Why didn't you?"

He bowed his head. "I realized my mistake."

She could hear the shame in his voice, the regret. Her thoughts whirled, danced together in a mad rush. She searched her brain for comfort, for words to soothe the turmoil, the agitation in her breast. "Why *is* the duke so wicked?"

"He *was* wicked. And it was all my father's doing. The late duke was a villain." The man's voice was hard. "Always drunk, he hurt my mother . . . and my brother."

Evelyn gasped softly. Something sparked within her: an instant comprehension and sympathy, for she, too, had suffered under the wild rantings of a foxed father.

"I escaped the beatings," said Adam, "only because I was second born and Father didn't care much for me. He was obsessed with making his heir, my brother, a rogue—just like him."

The light of knowledge filled the dark pockets of her imagination. "And so Damian became the 'Duke of Rogues'?"

Slowly Adam nodded. "As boys, Damian and I had gathered in secret for many years. Father didn't want us to be friends or even brothers."

"Why?"

"He didn't want a positive influence to distort his wicked protégé."

"I see."

"But once Damian was older and Father's clout started to take its hold, I lost my brother." Adam pointed to his chest. "Damian didn't exist in here anymore. I tried to help him, to drag him away from the terrible vice that consumed his life . . . but I couldn't save him."

"I understand. Your father's hold was too great."

"Father died more than a decade ago, but still Damian reigned as the 'Duke of Rogues' until . . ."

"Until?"

"Until he met his wife. She offered him strength: the strength he needed to heal."

Evelyn was struck by the truth of his words. Adam was teaching her to fight with swords and fists, but she still lacked strength: the inner strength to defeat the prince in her mind. Adam had suggested she get angry; it would help her find that missing strength. But how could she get past the *fear* to get to the anger?

"Why did you bring me here, Adam?"

He spoke with uncanny conviction. "Because you will be safe here."

"You are at odds with your brother. Why would I be safe here?"

"He will not hurt you, Evie."

"But he might . . . to avenge himself on you."

"He won't."

"How do you know that?"

"My mother lives in London. She writes to me often. I know my brother has changed. He is not the 'Duke of Rogues' anymore."

A mother's fondest hope, Evelyn mused. But it did not negate the fact that both Adam and his mother might be wrong about the duke. Four years was a long time for a temper to rankle. Perhaps the duke was filled with bitter hate toward his brother after all.

And what about Adam? Was his anger toward the duke really gone? The duchess wasn't so sure. She believed Adam capable of violence.

Evelyn *really* wasn't safe inside the castle.

"You are still frightened?" he said. "Of me?"

She was overwhelmed with uncertainty—about everything. "Is that why you are so skilled in swordplay? And fisticuffs?"

Adam approached her. "I spent a long time preparing my revenge against the duke. After the ship's sinking, I washed up on an island off the coast of Wales. I was delirious with grief and a fever, and I lost my memory for almost a year. I lived with a group of monks who took care of me. Once my memory returned I spent another year learning how to fight . . . to kill before I confronted my brother. But I think it's time I put that training to better use."

She eyed him curiously. "How?"

"Let me teach you all that I know."

"About death?"

"Use the knowledge to live, Evie."

She inhaled a shaky breath. Her heart was thumping, her pulse tapping. She was confused. Who was the real villain here?

She stepped away from the tree, away from Adam. "I want to return to the castle."

Chapter 23

Evelyn stood beside the window in the parlor. Ever since her escape from the coffin, warm light was intoxicating to her. She needed to bathe in it for comfort.

But still a darkness dwelled in her heart.

I stabbed him.

Even the memory of the words chilled her to the bone. No wonder the duchess feared Adam. He had stabbed the duke! He *was* a dangerous man. She had always suspected it . . . but Adam claimed he wasn't filled with hatred anymore, that the strife with his brother was over; he had changed.

She wasn't so sure, though. A violent man was always violent. He might bury his feral inclinations, act a gentleman at times, but beneath the thick exterior of grace and charm was a beast ready to pounce.

She knew firsthand.

She shivered at the morbid thought. It was a good thing Adam wasn't going to stay with her in America. She didn't want to spend the rest of her days wondering: *Will he hurt me as he hurt his brother?*

Evelyn lifted her head at the sound of heavy footfalls.

A chill enveloped her spirit at the sight of the Duke of Wembury. He stood under the door frame in a lazy manner, regarding her with an intense curiosity that was hard to ignore.

Beads of sweat pooled between her fingers at the intimidating sight. She noted there was no other door for her to escape through. Trapped inside the room with the rogue, she swallowed to moisten her dry throat.

"Good morning, Your Grace."

He did not respond. Instead he continued to stare at her with inquisitive blue eyes.

She prattled onward: "Thank you for your hospitality."

The duke stepped deeper into the room, but still said nothing.

Did the devil have his tongue?

Her heart quickened as he approached her slowly.

At length he said, "What do you think of my brother?"

Lightly her hands trembled. After Adam's

shocking confession, she truly didn't know what to think of him.

"He saved my life." It was not a direct answer, but Evelyn was filled with uncertainty and didn't know how to respond. Adam *had* saved her life. He had a noble side. But he had a dark nature, too. It shadowed the tender soul she had come to know at the cottage. The only real question was: How much of the darkness in his heart still ruled his senses?

The duke stilled a short distance away from her and crossed his hands behind his back. "That isn't a proper answer."

Her tremors worsened. She sensed the duke was searching for something: an answer to a question he was too uncomfortable to ask outright. "What else is there to say?"

"He is going with you to America . . . Do you enjoy his company?"

She enjoyed his kisses . . . the feel of his crushing hold . . . the rough timbre of his voice.

Distressed to admit the truth, she ignored the duke's question to clarify instead, "Your brother is going to escort me to America, but then he will return to England."

The duke's dark brow creased. "That isn't the impression my brother made the other night."

Now her voice quivered, too. "I asked him not to stay with me in America."

"Why?"

She twisted her fingers together. "Adam belongs here in England with his family."

Away from me.

The duke appeared genuinely glum. "I don't think Adam wants to be here with us."

Evelyn observed the man closely. The quiet sadness in his voice disarmed her. Slowly the tight knot in her belly unraveled, and she looked upon the duke with a newfound light.

He was not the frightening reprobate anymore. Rather he was a simple man mourning the loss of his brother's friendship. It occurred to her then that Adam had been right: the "Duke of Rogues" had retired his epithet.

It also occurred to her that between the two brothers, it was Adam who concealed the greater darkness.

"I've taken up enough of your time, Lady Evelyn." He composed his features. "I'm here on an errand. My wife requests your company in the drawing room."

"Thank you for inviting me to tea, Belle."

"Think nothing of it, my dear." The duchess tried to set her cup and saucer on the low round table, but couldn't quite reach it, so she set the china across her round belly instead. "We ladies have to band together in a castle overrun with men."

Evelyn sipped her tea with pleasure. She had been deprived of the afternoon ritual after many years of poverty. "I don't know how you've managed so far with so many men afoot."

"Oh, I'm used to it." Mirabelle waved a hand. "I grew up in a household full of men: a father and four brothers."

"What happened to your mother?"

"She died in childbirth to Quincy." Her voice softened. "I was four at the time so I don't remember her very well. Although my older brothers assure me I look very much like her."

Evelyn said quietly, "I lost my mother at a young age, too."

"Then we are kindred spirits, you and I."

A warmth touched Evelyn's heart at the tender sentiment. It had been a long time since she'd known the comforts of a sisterly bond.

The duchess took a sip of tea. "There was another reason I asked you to tea, Evie."

"Yes?"

"We should organize some belongings for you. To take with you on your trip to America."

"You don't have to do that, Belle."

"I want to do it. Besides you can't travel with just one dress." She patted her round belly. "And if it wasn't for the babe, *I'd* be the one accompanying you to America as chaperone, not Adam."

Thoughts of Adam set her pulse pounding, and she blurted: "I know Adam stabbed your husband."

The other woman shifted slightly. "I see Adam confessed his past to you."

To quiet the mad rush of emotion in her breast, Evelyn took in a deep breath before she said with more grace, "I understand why you fear him, Belle. I would, too."

"Yes, about that . . . I don't fear him anymore, Evie."

She blinked. "You don't?"

"I wouldn't allow him inside the castle if I really believed he might hurt the duke again."

"What changed your mind about Adam?"

"I understand the man better. Four years ago, Adam was angry and distraught. He blamed the duke for his wife's death. Wrongly, of course. But I can see he's changed."

Evelyn's thoughts returned to Adam and the grisly confession he had made earlier in the day. "Do you think a violent man can change, Belle?"

"No. But I think an angry man can find peace." She winked. "I know my husband did."

Then was it possible Adam really *had* mended his ways? Evelyn was overwhelmed by the thought. If the man had changed, she needn't fear him. And yet he still possessed a mighty pull over her senses. Surely *that* was something she should still fear?

"You are very good to forgive Adam for what he did to the duke."

The duchess snorted. "The duke would like to reconcile with his brother. And I do have a particular fondness for my husband." Then in a whisper, she said, "There's just something about His Grace that's so attractive; I can't seem to deny him his fondest wish."

"I don't think your brothers see the charm."

The duchess laughed heartily. "No, I don't suppose they do. In truth, I didn't see the *charm* in Damian at first, either . . . or perhaps I did, but I just didn't want to admit it to myself?"

"How do you mean?"

The duchess appeared deep in thought. "Well, my feelings for the duke were frightening at first. I suppose I just didn't want to acknowledge them for that very reason: I was too afraid."

"And now?" Evelyn asked boldly.

"Now I can't live without the feelings—or the man."

Evelyn pondered the idea: being unable to live without someone. At one time she had thought her life void without Ella. And yet gradually she had learned to exist without her.

Oh, she had desperately missed her sister: the pain of separation still smarted in her breast. But she had lived. Evelyn did not understand the sort of bond the duchess was referring to: one where even the will to survive depended upon another.

"The duke has a very strong hold over you, doesn't he?" said Evelyn. And not without a hint of resentment, for there was always a man in her life with a hold over her.

"And I have one over him . . . or so I like to think."

"You have a hold over the duke?"

She smiled with mischief. "Any woman can have power over a man, Evie."

Evelyn was bewitched by the idea. She wondered what it would feel like to have power over a man. Power*less* most of her life, she found it an attractive thought.

"How does one have power over a man, Belle?"

"You must make him fall madly in love with you."

Her heart fluttered. "Really?"

"Oh yes. The more he loves you, the more power you have over him. Unfortunately, the deuced sentiment works both ways, for I fell madly in love with the duke."

Evelyn rubbed the rim of her teacup in somber thought. "So you're still powerless in the end?"

The duchess eyed her guest with quiet scrutiny.

"You know, I was only teasing, Evie. Love isn't a power struggle. Or it shouldn't be."

"But you *are* powerless in the affair?"

Mirabelle sighed. "I lost some of my power, I suppose: the power to be in complete control of my emotions, for love makes one feel many different things."

"It sounds so frightening . . . so why love at all?"

"I don't think one really has a choice in the matter, Evie."

Evelyn disagreed. She had no intention of placing herself in a position of weakness again. "I would rather live without love."

The duchess eyed her with tender regard. "You sound like one of my brothers."

"There's no Mrs. Pirate?"

She chuckled. "I'm afraid not." Then, with more gravity: "Are you sure you'd rather live without love, Evie?"

"Yes." Her fingers tightened around the china. "I'm sure. I don't want to give a man power over me—in any way."

"You might change your mind one day."

"No, I won't."

"The right man might come along and inspire you to take a chance at love. He might even steal your heart without you realizing it."

"Is that what happened to you, Belle?"

"Yes, in a manner," she said dryly. "I should have robbed *his* heart, the blackguard. I was the bloody pirate."

Evelyn choked on the tea. "*You're* a pirate, too?"

"Was, my dear. Well, I had a short-lived career at it, unlike my brothers, who took to it for years."

Quickly Evelyn patted her chin with a napkin to mop the dribble. "The duke married a pirate?"

"Scandalous, I know . . . but the poor devil couldn't live without me. Ouch!"

Swiftly Evelyn set the cup and saucer on the table and rushed to kneel beside the duchess. She took the china, ringing in the woman's shaky grip, and set it aside, too.

"Are you all right, Belle?"

"I'm fine." She clutched her belly. "The babe just kicked, is all." She looked down at her swollen midriff. "Anxious to come into the world, aren't you?" She then muttered, "I bloody hope it's a boy. I don't think I can raise another girl like Alice."

"Do you want me to summon the duke?"

"No, he'll only fuss. The babe's not due till the end of the month."

"Why don't I help you to your room so you can rest?"

"No, really, I'm fine."

"You're not fine, Belle. You have to rest."

The duchess regarded her with surprise. "You've become more headstrong, haven't you, Evie?"

"I insist, Belle."

"Yes, I gathered that." She sighed in discontent. "Oh, very well. If *you* insist."

Chapter 24

Adam hoped she would come.

He had penned a note and slipped it under her door. Now he stood beside the pond and waited, listening to the soft and lyrical chirp of night critters, observing the hazy reflection of the castle in the smooth surface of the water.

It was dark out, the warm air brimming with the scent of wildflowers. He closed his eyes and inhaled the fragrant summer breeze.

Slowly he divested his clothes. In a pair of flannel drawers, he stepped closer to the water's edge and immersed his foot in the cool pool before he waded through the tranquil waves. Making his way deeper toward the center of the pond, he arched his body forward and stroked across the healing waters.

A good swim always put his mind, his muscles to right.

Adam made a few laps before he sensed a pair of eyes watching him from the darkness.

"Good evening, Evie."

Her shadow stirred beside a tree, and he shifted his eyes to capture the movement.

"How good of you to join me," he said.

"Why did you summon me here?"

He stilled, waist-deep in water. "I have something more to teach you."

"What?

"Take off your clothes and come into the water."

She fell quiet.

"You don't have to remove all your clothes, Evie. Just strip down to your shift."

"I'd rather not."

"Are you still afraid of me?"

Silence.

He sighed. "I might have made a mistake many years ago, an unforgivable transgression against my brother. But I won't hurt you. Besides, if you want to go to America, you will do as I say. I won't let you board that pirate ship before I teach you how to swim."

She moved away from the tree and slowly approached. "Why do I need to learn how to swim?"

"Any number of things could happen aboard a ship: you might slip and fall overboard, for one. I want to make sure you don't drown during the voyage."

"What if I promise not to leave my cabin?"

The ship might sink, he thought in morbid reflection.

"That's not good enough, Evie. You need to know how to swim. Come." He stretched out his hand to encourage her. "It's dark. No one will see you, I promise."

She let out a huff in protest before she reached for the buttons of her dress.

Adam turned around to offer her privacy.

After a few moments, he heard her tepid steps sink into the pond. Slowly he turned around.

His heart shuddered at the sensual sight. Draped in a chemise, she waded through the still water, her trim figure cast in the milky white glow of the moon. The ghostly light bounced off her sooty locks, too, the tendrils twisted into a knot atop her head. She was a vision of loveliness—and he was having a devilishly hard time keeping his thoughts chaste.

"It's cold," she griped.

It was indeed. He noted the hard points of her nipples pushing against the immodest shift. The impulse to cup her bountiful breasts and chase away the chill gripped him.

"Your body will adjust to the water," he said roughly.

Her skirt ballooned around her waist the deeper she entered the water, and she quickly tried to drown the garment by pressing her palms against it.

He imagined lifting the feckless shift up over her shoulders and pressing his lips to every part of her body.

Swiftly he smothered the thought.

"I want you to lie across the water on your back, Evie."

"Why?"

"So you can float. I want you to get a feel for the water."

She was uneasy; he could sense it.

"You won't sink. I'll place my hand under your back to keep you buoyant."

At length she acquiesced and eased her torso backward.

She gripped him for support. The muscles in his arm capered under her tight, almost clinging hold.

He pressed his palms against the curve of her spine. "Stretch out your legs."

She did. The water rushed over her chest, filled the space between her breasts, soaking the shift.

Adam's body hardened. The diaphanous material hugged her every delicious curve, exposing each dip and groove and smooth expanse to his avid eyes.

"Close your eyes, Evie. Feel the water."

Her lashes fluttered before she shut her eyes.

"Now take a deep breath," he said.

Air filled her lungs, the sharp sound too audible to miss. He noted the quick rise of her breasts, too.

The sultry image of her bare and plump breasts bobbing in the water came to play in his mind. He lingered over the wanton thought, imagined the tender way he would widen, then peel back the wet layer of her bodice to expose the heavy mounds of flesh. The raw joy he would take in parting his lips and taking the hard nub of her nipple into his mouth and sucking.

The ache in his body pulsed with such vigor, he removed his hands from her back.

She flapped her arms and disappeared beneath the surface of the water for a moment before he fished her out and propped her back on her toes.

"I lost my grip," he said tightly.

My grip on reason.

She sputtered and wiped the moisture from her eyes, her locks an adorable slop of curls around her head. "You tutor in swordplay and fisticuffs with more ease," she charged.

He was chagrined. "Why don't we try it another way?"

"Why don't I go inside and dry off?"

"You have to learn how to swim." And he *would*

teach her, despite the wild cravings in his heart. "Lie on your front this time."

He reckoned if she rested across her midriff, he wouldn't see her swollen and tempting breasts. Perhaps *then* he could keep a cap on his wits.

She let out a short huff before she shakily stretched out across the water.

Adam maintained a firm hold of her belly as she dipped forward. But he stiffened at the sight of her plump arse, the round flesh so incredibly erotic. Blood hastened through his veins, pounded in his groin.

He stifled a curse.

"Stretch your legs and kick, Evie."

Lightly the water splashed.

"Good," he praised. "Move your arms now. Paddle."

She stopped kicking and stroked across the water instead.

"Evie, you must do *both* movements at the same time."

She started to kick again.

"Much better." He moved beside her as she practiced, keeping her afloat. "Get accustomed to the rhythm. I'm going to let you go soon."

"No!"

She wavered and dunked beneath the waves again.

"I've got you." He curled his arms around her waist and hoisted her back to her feet. Pressed against him in such an intimate embrace, she stirred the embers of desire in his belly. "You have to learn how to swim without my help."

"I can't do this, Adam."

"It will take time to learn," he assured her. "But we'll practice in secret every night until the ship sets sail."

She appeared dubious. "Every night?"

"Yes, you must learn to swim with confidence. Now let's try again."

Shakily she assumed the position, and Adam once more supported her underside as she rehearsed the movements—and once more he was distracted by her plump behind.

He forced himself to focus on the swimming lesson. "Turn your head from side to side."

She followed instruction . . . but then she screamed.

Evelyn reared up and grabbed ahold of him, clinging to him like an iron shackle. She was shivering, and his instinct was to keep her warm, so he slipped his arms around her midriff.

He wondered, "What the devil . . . ?"

A thin shadow slithered across the surface of the pond.

"It's just a snake, Evie."

"I hate snakes!"

He gathered that. The prince was akin to a serpent in many ways, so Adam suspected the woman's distaste for the reptile a more subtle phobia.

Her quivering limbs vibrated against him, making him warm. He closed his eyes to better enjoy the comforting feel of her feminine body crushed against him.

He was starved for closeness, and Evelyn's healing touch aroused him from a deep and lonely sleep.

Once the snake had slinked away, Evelyn loosened her hold on his neck. She appeared sheepish after her outburst. And he found her discomfiture endearing.

A gruesome pang gripped his heart at the thought of parting from her. He was determined not to abandon her in America. He had only to convince the woman it was wise for them *both* to remain in the New World.

She lifted her sweeping lashes to look at him.

Moonbeams filled her eyes with enchanting light.

He tried to beat back the fierce desire growing in his belly, but he was bewitched by her haunting expression, her plump lips swollen with blood, so inviting . . .

Adam dropped his head and pressed his mouth over hers with savage hunger. When she didn't protest, he deepened the kiss, claimed the sweet balm she offered him with her heady lips.

Tremors wracked her body; she weakened.

"Hold me, Evie," he said roughly. "Don't let me go."

She shuddered, her every quiver a visceral spark of energy that danced along his rigid body.

Adam scooped her in his arms and carried her toward a nearby boulder. He pressed her against the smooth surface of the rock, hooked his hands under her knees, and forced her legs apart.

He needed to feel her arms, her thighs wrapped tight around him. He needed to sink inside her, to be one with her. It burned in his blood, the wild desire.

"Evie," he breathed, and kissed her throat, her bust. "I need you."

Hard with passion, Adam reached between his legs and unfastened the buttons of his drawers.

Evelyn's moist flesh was opened to him, and he slipped inside her dewy cleft with a hoarse cry.

Evelyn was mesmerized.

The swift passion unleashed inside her was overwhelming. She squeezed Adam's neck, pinched her legs together to keep him close.

This was not the vile experience her sister had written about in her letters. Every sense inside Evelyn danced with life. The heat, the energy, the sheer thickness and strength invading her body filled her with indescribable warmth, chased away the lonely darkness.

Hot blood rushed through her limbs, giving her vigor. Her heart pounded in rhythm to the desperate swell of Adam's movements.

She could hear the water lap against his buttocks as he thrust into her deep, yet with a measure of tenderness. It confounded her, the very thought of being *part* of someone else.

The sultry coupling dazzled her wits. Each stroke disarmed her, whittled the fear inside her to a nub. Only one dangerous desire consumed her: the yearning to share her heart, her soul, her body with another being.

Evelyn groaned at the sweet pleasure of Adam's teasing touch. She was so sensitive, her core throbbing, aching with life. Tears filled her eyes, and she gasped at the intense fire burning between her legs: a heat so profound, she cried out at the crushing pressure that swelled in her veins before a surge of relief washed the tightness away.

Life drained from her limbs; she was weak. She relaxed her arms, her legs, though she still hugged Adam close.

Tears spilled from her eyes as she searched for breath. Her thoughts drifted to the man snug in her embrace. Lightly she stroked the moist curls at his head, appeased her curiosity to better know the texture of him. All the while she mused about the unearthly experience she had just shared with the man.

Adam lifted his head from her bust. She was arched over the curve of the rock and turned her eyes downward to better see his handsome expression.

For a moment neither said a word to the other, the experience so intense. But after a brief lull, Adam lifted a hand to brush the tears from her eyes.

"Did I hurt you?"

"No," she said, her voice a rough whisper.

Her body still trembled in the aftermath of the passionate tussle. He must have construed her shivers for pain, for he said, "I didn't mean to hurt you."

Hurt her? He had done everything *but* hurt her. Renewed life pulsed through her. Awareness. Shut away in a quiet room in her mind, she had been asleep for a long time.

But Adam had awakened her. And for the first time in many years, she felt alive.

As Adam tried to pull away from her, she panicked. She wanted to hold on to the feeling of closeness for a while longer, and she pinched his neck. "Don't let me go."

She had echoed his words. He blinked at her, bemused. Soon, though, he eased his robust body back against her.

She sighed with contentment when he fingered the curve of her throat, the swell of her bosom. Her heart ballooned with delight.

Don't stop.

Don't stop touching me! But she was too timid to express her desire aloud.

Adam must have sensed her thoughts, though, for he added his sweet lips to the mix of his tender touch.

Her pulse throbbed at her throat as he pressed his hot mouth against the hollow of her neck.

Both liberated from the feral need to join flesh, their subsequent intimacy was less urgent and wild.

Evelyn dropped her head backward to rest on the rock. She stared up at the brilliant heavens, the blinking stars and crescent moon. Overwhelmed by the beauty around her, she was even more entranced by Adam's sultry kisses, his seductive touch.

And he seemed equally engaged by the moment. He was slow to caress her, careful to taste every part of her. At length his lips, his fingers moved lower to brush across her breasts.

She shuddered.

He fingered apart the laces of her bodice.

Breasts exposed, her skin erupted with goose pimples, her nipples firming. She heard one low moan before he dropped his head and captured her breast in his mouth.

The feeling was exquisite. Her muscles flexed each time he sucked and pulled her nipple deeper into his mouth.

Glorious!

She moved her hands across the wide breadth of his back, searching for every twisted muscle to commit to memory. She wouldn't have him to chase away the loneliness once she was settled in America. She needed to feel every part of him now. To know him in detail, so she could summon the man's image in her mind whenever the desire arose.

But she didn't want to think about parting from him.

Not now.

Adam shifted his mouth to her other breast and offered it the same wondrous care.

She twisted her legs around his waist to match the twisting desire once more growing inside her.

When his fingers slipped between her legs to ease her need, she whimpered at the startling pleasure of his deft strokes, gasped for breath to ease the thunder of her heartbeat.

The pulsing need inside her ballooned, each solid thrust against her thrilling. Her muscles flexed, her blood burned before the sweet pleasure of release dazzled her senses again.

In time, each frantic heartbeat cooled, and she welcomed the serenity of satisfaction.

Evelyn blinked to brush away the moisture from her eyes. The stars cleared, and she looked upon the heavens with newfound pleasure and delight.

Adam rested against her breasts. She stroked his hair in laziness, content to feel the warmth of his flesh, the beat of his heart against her.

His muscles flexed.

Evelyn sensed the shift in him, the sudden stiffness. "Is something the matter?"

Adam pushed away from her.

Startled, Evelyn slipped down the smooth surface of the rock, and pressed her skirt against her legs to cover herself.

"We should return to the castle," he said hoarsely.

His eyes masked by shadows, she couldn't make out his expression. But the physical distance he maintained indicated he wanted to keep away from her.

Something cold, something ugly settled in her heart. The sentiment of rejection . . . of abuse.

Had he used her for sex? Did he want to toss

her aside now that he had fulfilled his lustful cravings?

She shivered as her blood turned cold, and she bit her bottom lip to keep the tears of humiliation and betrayal at bay.

She was such a fool.

Chapter 25

A dam stood beside the window and observed the breaking dawn. Restless with insomnia, he was sheltered inside the bedroom, thinking of Evelyn.

A memory gripped his imagination: a sea nymph with her legs wrapped tight around his hips.

Adam suppressed a groan, the image too erotic to bear. Blood pounded in his head, making him dizzy.

More intoxicating memories came flooding forth. He remembered Evelyn's gasps, her cries of delight. He closed his eyes to *feel* the tight spasms of her flesh grip him in ecstasy.

Adam opened his eyes to vanquish the incredible recollection from his mind. He pressed his palm against the wall to support his quietly shuddering legs.

He rested his gaze on a faraway hilltop. A short distance away was his late wife's childhood home.

He thought about his earlier days with Teresa, the playmate and confidante of his youth. He recollected his vow later in life to honor and cherish her until his death.

And he recollected breaking that vow by seeking companionship with another woman . . . and enjoying it so immensely.

Guilt raged in Adam's soul, the oppressive weight crippling. He stepped away from the window and grabbed the first article in reach—a bowl—and smashed it against the wall.

"You remind me of your father."

Adam reared his head up.

Under the door frame stood his mother: Emily, the Dowager Duchess of Wembury. A small woman of over fifty years, she had dark and sooty locks streaked with gray, and maintained a traditional style of dress befitting her age and station.

But her words disarmed him . . . enraged him.

"How can you compare me to *him*?" he cried.

Unperturbed by the outburst, Emily stepped deeper into the room and outstretched her arms.

So accustomed to the violent outcries of her late husband, the dowager duchess didn't seem all that distressed by her son's behavior. In truth, she seemed very delighted to see him again.

Adam was forced to swallow his indignation and return the woman's embrace. He hadn't seen his mother in four years, and an invective was not the proper way to greet her.

She smiled up at him. "It's your temper that reminds me of the late duke."

Adam was gripped by the sudden urge to eat his tongue. The idea that he was remotely like his father outraged him . . . terrified him.

Adam had struggled hard over the years to maintain a distance from depravity. He wanted so very much to be nothing like his father. But according to the dowager duchess, a part of the late duke was inside him. Was there really no way to escape the blood in his veins?

His mother's soft features and pleasing countenance cooled his passionate anger, though, and he said with less bite, "I've missed you."

"I've missed you, too." She stepped back from the embrace. "Your brother wrote to me in London, informing me of your return."

Adam stroked his brow, temples throbbing. He was in poor condition, mood sour. But he sensed his mother wanted to talk about his outburst. Perhaps he could postpone the inevitable discussion for a later time?

"You must be tired after your journey, Mother."

The dowager duchess moved toward a chair and settled in the seat. "Not a'tall. I napped in the chaise."

Or perhaps not.

Adam sat down on the edge of the bed and sighed.

"Why are you so distressed?" she demanded. "Is it the woman, Lady Evelyn?"

"I see Damian wrote to you about more than my return home," he said dryly.

"Your brother doesn't hide anything from me anymore."

The former "Duke of Rogues" was once a notorious debaucher with a tendency to disappear for weeks at a time into dens of sin. During those troublesome years, Damian had rarely spoken two words of civility toward their mother. But the estrangement appeared to be at an end.

"You and Damian are close then?" he wondered.

"We are."

"Good . . . I'm glad you're a family at last."

Even if he wasn't a part of it.

"You're not going to wriggle out of my question so easily." She offered him a pointed look. "Why are you breaking bowls?"

Adam glanced at the shattered pieces of pottery on the floor and tried to suppress the guilt inside him. "I've made a mistake."

"What sort of mistake?"

"I broke a vow . . . a sacred vow."

"And now you hate yourself for it? I understand. I suffered with the sentiment for many years myself."

Adam lifted his eyes. "How so?"

"I failed your brother." Her features turned melancholy. "I failed to keep him safe from the late duke."

Thinking about the late duke turned Adam's blood hot. "Why *did* you marry Father?"

"I was young and headstrong—and in love. The former duke was so charming and handsome; I was flattered by his attention. Unfortunately, I learned too late his true nature. Once I was wed, I belonged to him. And it was then he removed his mask. The dashing suitor was no more: a monster in his place."

"I'm sorry, Mother."

"Stuff." She sniffed. "It's not your place to be contrite. You did nothing wrong. It was I who failed myself—and your brother. I was able to keep you away from the late duke, but I wasn't able to save Damian. It haunted me for years, the failure to help him."

"Does it haunt you still?"

"No, not anymore."

Adam was curious to know: "How did you get over the guilt?"

"I asked your brother to forgive me. He did. But it took me a little longer to forgive myself."

"How much longer?"

"Oh, a few years. But I daresay I've made peace with the past at last."

"I'm glad. You deserve to be happy."

She leaned forward to emphasize, "So do you, Adam."

His heart cramped at the thought. Happiness? It was an idea he had not dwelled upon since his wife's death . . . since Evelyn had entered his life and stirred his passions.

The older woman said coyly, "Tell me about Lady Evelyn?"

"The woman is under my protection."

"Yes, your brother mentioned that in his letter."

He gritted, "What else did Damian say in his letter?"

"Don't growl, Adam. Your brother isn't a gossip." But then she smiled. "I understand Lady Evelyn is very beautiful."

Adam moved away from the bed and stalked across the room in agitated strides. He stopped beside the window. "She is very lovely."

In every way, he thought. Her touch, her voice, her lips washed away years of pain. She filled his heart with a warm and familiar light.

"Do you care for her?" said the dowager duchess.

"No. She is in danger, and I've offered to protect her," he said again. "There is nothing more between us."

He had found comfort in her arms for a brief time. Perhaps she had found comfort in his, too. If so, their encounter had served a mutual purpose and was of mutual benefit. There was nothing more between them.

"Are you sure you don't care for Lady Evelyn?"

The casual inquiry belied a more wily intent. He suspected his mother intended to do a little matchmaking. She likely believed it would do him good to marry again—it would make him happy.

But she didn't understand how deep the darkness reached in his heart. Marriage would fix nothing, and he was quick to quash her groundless hope.

"I don't care for Lady Evelyn."

But she didn't appear moved by the negative sentiment. "You went to a great deal of trouble to rescue her from the prince."

"I had no choice."

"Didn't you?"

"You don't understand, Mother. Lady Evelyn needs help."

"And you are a gentleman, so you offered the help?"

"Precisely. I don't care for the woman."

Not in the way his mother was suggesting. He

had vowed to protect the woman from the prince, and he would. He need only convince Evelyn to let him stay with her in America, and then everything would be fine.

What if she's pregnant?

Adam started.

"Adam, are you all right?"

He stared at the blank stone wall, so cold and hard. He, too, was cold and hard inside, the very thought of a babe so disquieting. After the death of his wife, he had believed he would never be a father; he had resolved not to be with another woman . . . but now?

Adam quickly walked across the room.

"Where are you going, Adam?"

He paused, kissed his mother on the brow, then continued to march toward the door.

Adam strutted through the corridor in agitated strides. Evelyn might be pregnant. He had to protect her *and* the babe. She wouldn't fight him now, surely. Not with a child at risk. She could not live alone with a babe under the threat of the prince. He would *have* to stay with her in America!

"Adam!"

The commanding voice bit into his step, and he stilled. "Yes, Your Grace?"

"What's this rubbish?" The duchess advanced with a look of reproach in her eyes. "You know you can call me Belle."

He knew no such thing, but refrained from making the remark aloud. Rather he dismissed the informality of address to inquire, "Is there something I can do for you?"

"There most certainly is." Her hands went to her belly in a motherly gesture. "I'd like an accounting from you."

"About what?"

"About Evelyn."

His heart cramped. "What's the matter with Evelyn?"

"I was hoping you'd enlighten me about that very thing. The woman is despondent." Her eyes narrowed. "I don't suppose you know the reason for her melancholy?"

Images of last night filled his head. Melancholy? He didn't remember the experience being melancholy. Unless . . .

Had he hurt Evie?

Adam didn't have much experience with women. Other than his late wife and Evie, he had not been with another woman. Had he harmed Evelyn in some way during their hasty love making?

"I'll go and speak with Lady Evelyn," he said.

"I'd rather you didn't."

"And why is that?" he said with clear irritability.

"You've caused enough trouble, I think. What

happened between the two of you? Tell me so I can speak with Evie about it."

Adam growled, "*I* will take care of her."

"Not while she lives under my roof."

"Damn it, Belle, I—"

"Bloody hell!"

Mirabelle squeezed her belly and doubled over.

In a moment of profound regret for his sharp temper, Adam dropped to his knees and cradled the distressed duchess.

"Belle, I'm sorry," he quickly expressed. "I didn't mean to snap at you."

She hugged her midriff and gritted, "It's not you . . . it's the babe."

Adam's heart fell.

In one swift movement, he scooped the duchess in his arms and rushed her through the passageway, shouting for the duke.

Chapter 26

The room was quiet. Candles softly burned beside the bed, the dance of shadows quick under the flickering glow.

With a moist towel Evelyn cooled the duchess's fevered brow. Mirabelle had birthed a healthy boy many hours ago. The babe was secure in another room under the care of the nurse.

Unfortunately the afterbirth had yet to manifest.

The midwife, unable to deal with such a complicated condition, prepared clean linens in expectation of the doctor's arrival and imminent needs. Evelyn, too, was ignorant in the medical matter; she offered the duchess solace with her company and tender hand.

Mirabelle gasped for air, each breath a struggle. Her otherwise rosy cheeks ashen, she appeared a wraith. And it took all of Evelyn's inner strength to swallow the knot of tears pressed deep in her throat.

"Alice," the duchess whispered weakly. "I want to see Alice."

Evelyn glanced at the duke, requesting the man's silent approval. But Damian stood quietly beside the window, seemingly unmoved by his dying wife's appeal.

However, Evelyn knew better. The duke's stone façade was a thin mask holding back a torrent of grief ready to spill forth the moment the duchess breathed her last breath.

Evelyn shivered. She was about to witness the birth of a monster; she recognized the signs well. Her father had slipped into a similar bout of misery upon the death of her mother . . . although she suspected the duke's bereavement altogether more passionate.

The door opened.

A gentleman entered the room, senior in years. Escorted by the Dowager Duchess of Wembury, he approached the bedside with a leather bag in hand.

Evelyn wanted to weep, her relief was so great. She quickly stepped aside to grant the doctor intimate counsel with the duchess.

Curt and efficient, the physician eyed the dying woman prostrated under the covers and said, "I would like everyone to leave the room."

The duke remained rooted; he offered no indication he had heard the doctor's order. Only

Evelyn quietly approached the door, the midwife and dowager duchess determined to stay behind to assist the practitioner.

With a heaviness pressed on her breast, Evelyn quit the room.

Stepping out of the chamber of death did not lessen the load on her heart, though. One look at the sullen countenances of four bereft pirates, and she was filled with overwhelming sympathy.

The dark and brooding figures lined the stone wall, their woe stifled under a misleading mask of forbearance. Only the youngest brigand appeared glassy-eyed with tears.

Evelyn commiserated with the youthful Quincy. Although one year her senior, he appeared a lost child under the pressure of grief.

"How is she?" said James.

Evelyn shifted her eyes to the pirate captain. She parted her lips to betray her misgiving, but sorrow snatched her voice away.

The silence was answer enough, though, for the men's long features fell even more.

She took in a deep breath. "The duchess wishes to see Alice."

"I'll go and fetch the child."

Evelyn watched the pirate captain's lonely figure wade through the dark passageway before it disappeared.

"How's Damian?"

Adam was grouped with the rest of the mourning pirates. United under a parasol of misery, the men behaved with uncharacteristic civility. There was no outward ill-will to indicate their former strife.

She stepped closer to Adam. "The duke is somber, but . . ."

"Yes?"

"But I fear for his mind," she confessed softly. "Should the duchess die . . ."

"I understand."

Adam's eyes filled with despair. She peered deep into the wet pools and witnessed grief, even . . . guilt?

"Adam, what is it?"

He pressed the back of his head against the stone wall. "I know my brother's heart."

"How do you mean?"

"I can feel the cold, unimaginable shock of watching a wife die . . . and being unable to help her."

It struck Evelyn, clear as water: Adam blamed himself for his late wife's death!

Memory of the other night filled her head. Adam had pushed away from her, so cool and abrupt. She had believed it brutality, but now she wondered if guilt had provoked his curt behavior. Did he feel he had betrayed his late wife's memory by being with her? A wife he had failed to save from drowning?

The grief fixed across the man's features was plain to read. He was reliving the death of his wife through the duchess. And it appeared to cause him as much agony now as it had then, which meant . . .

He was still in love with Teresa.

So he will never love you.

Evelyn was startled by the thought. Confused. Where had the baffling sentiment come from? She didn't search for love. In truth, she was determined to stay away from it—and the dangerous power it could wield over the heart.

Within a few minutes the pirate captain had returned with a sleepy elf bundled in his arms.

Alice rolled her fists in her eyes and yawned, blissfully unaware of the trauma unfolding just beyond the bedroom door.

"Is he here?" the child demanded.

James wondered, "Is who here, squirt?"

"My baby brother."

"Yes, he's here."

The elf pouted in distress to hear she was not the baby of the family anymore. At length she huffed. "Where is he?"

"In another room."

"But I'm still squirt, right?"

Her uncle ruffled her curly hair. "You'll always be squirt."

She appeared mollified. "Can I see him?"

"He's sleeping," said James. "You can meet him in the morning . . . but Mama wants a word with you."

"I didn't do anything!"

"Mama isn't going to scold you, I promise."

The child looked at her uncle, dubious.

James eyed Evelyn with silent instructions. The captain was accustomed to giving orders with just a look, she suspected. He certainly made his wishes clear.

Her footfalls light, Evelyn approached the door and quietly slipped back inside the bedchamber.

"Did you hear me, Your Grace?" The doctor stood beside the duke. "I recommend we wait another few hours. If the afterbirth still does not manifest, I will remove it by hand."

Slowly the duke nodded, his expression blank. But his eyes were red. Red from tears he had not shed—yet.

Evelyn swallowed her own tears and knelt beside the duchess. "Alice is here."

The duchess inhaled a heavy breath. "Open the window."

"Your Grace, I must protest!" the doctor exclaimed to the duke. "In her condition, it's highly improper."

Slowly the duchess insisted, "I don't want Alice to sense the scent of death. Open the window."

The doctor looked at the duke. "Your Grace?"

"Do as she says." The characteristic dark timbre to the duke's voice was nothing more than a hoarse whisper. "Do anything she asks."

The midwife whisked across the room to part the glass. Meanwhile the dowager duchess dabbed at her eyes with a napkin and settled in a nearby chair.

The room quiet, the air fresh, Evelyn opened the door once more and motioned for James to bring the elf inside.

Alice was a quick-witted sprite. She took one look at all the grave faces and demanded, "What's wrong?"

James hushed her and crouched beside the bed so mother and daughter might meet face-to-face.

Mirabelle smiled at the child, her lips shaky. She was trying not to weep, and it pierced Evelyn's heart to witness the tragic exchange.

"Alice, you have a baby brother," said the duchess.

"But I'm still squirt."

"Yes, you're still squirt . . . Bring her closer, James."

The pirate captain rested the child near her mother, and Mirabelle wrapped her arms around the small figure.

"I want you to take care of your brother, Alice."

The elf screwed up her face. "Why, Mama?"

"Because that's what big sisters do."

"I thought that's what nurses do?"

"I'd like you to help Nurse. Can you do that for me?"

The elf sighed. "Yes."

The duchess took in another shaky breath.

"What's wrong, Mama?"

"Nothing's the matter, squirt. I'm just tired."

"It's late," Alice quipped wisely.

"It is. I'm sorry Uncle James had to wake you, but I needed to tell you something . . . I love you, Alice."

The sprite regarded her mother with suspicion. "I love you, too, Mama . . . Are you mad at me?"

"No." The duchess stroked the little girl's hair, her lips trembling. "I'm not mad at you. I'm sorry I've been so cross with you lately. I didn't mean it."

Now the sprite looked worried.

"Give me a hug and a kiss, squirt."

Obediently Alice leaned forward and pecked her mother's lips.

Her eyes filled with grief, the duchess quickly asked her brother to take the child back to the nursery.

James collected the elf and headed for the door.

He paused.

Evelyn watched as the pirate captain retraced his steps and pressed a kiss to his sister's brow before he quit the room, moisture glistening in his eyes.

Once the door was sealed, Mirabelle let out a wretched sob and brought her hands to her face to cover her tears.

The immovable duke was pressed to dash across the room, and to the near outrage of the physician, settled beside his wife on the bed and cradled her in his arms.

Evelyn was gripped by a profound sense of injustice. The couple, intertwined in each other's arms, let loose the sorrow that pervaded the room, leaving Evelyn to gasp and tremble at the horrific sight. Her heart ready to burst, she darted from the room and went straight into Adam's arms.

Adam embraced the sobbing woman, crushed her against his breast. She trembled in his arms, and he squeezed her tight to banish her suffering.

But he, too, suffered under the desperate cries of the duchess. The haunting howls coming from the bedroom made his heart cramp.

Had Teresa cried with such vehemence during her death?

He shuddered to think so.

"I think I understand my father better," said Evelyn.

He looked down at the woman in his arms, her cheeks stained with tears. He hated to see her tears, and brushed the drops away.

"I think I understand you better, too," she said in an unsteady voice.

"Do you?" he rasped.

"Is this how it was when your wife died?"

Slowly he nodded.

Lightning flashed in Adam's eyes. He was transported to the stormy sea. The black waves swelled, ready to swallow the fiery wreckage of the *Hercules*. He beat his arms against the robust current, screamed for his wife. But he was a poor swimmer. Strength and voice eventually deserted him. The ship slipped beneath the churning waters—he had let her die.

"You still love Tess, don't you? You always will?"

Yes, he always would . . . but something else stirred in his heart. Like infant foliage breaking through a charred layer of debris after a fire, a tender sentiment bloomed in Adam's breast. He was disarmed by it, confident for so long that nothing could ever grow in the bareness of his heart. And yet something did.

Evelyn sniffed. "I can't believe Ella might die."

"You mean Belle?"

"Yes, of course." She appeared sheepish. "I was starting to think of her as a sister."

Adam was all tangled up inside, too. He grieved for his brother, for the duchess. He grieved for his late wife. And then he looked upon the woman in his arms with a sense of hope. Longing, even.

Longing for what?

He was too baffled by the sentiments inside him to think clearly, though. He only prayed his brother wouldn't have to live through the horror of losing a cherished wife.

It was a grief he was sure the duke could not endure.

Chapter 27

Adam lifted the lamp, illuminating the stairwell. He ignored the chill biting his spine and descended the spiral steps—into hell.

A musty smell greeted him, an overwhelming blackness, too. Childhood memories surfaced. The echo of sobs filled his ears.

Adam remembered listening to the cries as a child: his brother's cries.

At the bottom of the abyss, Adam once more lifted the lamp and searched the abandoned cells, looking for the duke. At the end of the passageway, he spotted the man's lone figure squatting in a dark room with his back braced against a wall.

Adam was not surprised to find his kin in the dungeon; the duke was very familiar with the grisly surroundings.

"Would you like some company?"

Adam did not wait for an invitation to sit. Instead he crouched beside his brother and set the lamp on the icy floor.

Once settled, Adam glanced at the slimy walls and the faint scratches embedded in the stone. The juvenile script spelled out a name: Damian.

The duke had endured many a wretched stay in the dungeon. As a child, he had suffered under their father's cruelty. Chained in the dank dungeon as a form of punishment for any minor grievance, Damian had grown accustomed to the forbidding abyss. He had sobbed less and less with each imprisonment. And eventually he had not sobbed at all.

Adam still remembered those ghastly childhood days. He had not been able to help his brother then, but perhaps now . . .

Eyes fixed forward, Damian said with a rough voice, faint with stress and exhaustion, "How did you do it?"

Adam eyed his kin and wondered, "Do what?"

"Live . . . after Teresa died."

Adam looked away. He pressed his head against the damp wall and breathed deep to still the hard thumps of his heart. "I have you to thank for that."

"Me?"

"I wanted to kill myself after Tess drowned . . . but I hated you even more than I craved death."

Fortunately, Damian wouldn't have to confront such a fate. The duchess would live. She had eventually delivered the afterbirth, as the doctor had predicted. Her fever had broken shortly thereafter. Now she appeared to be doing better.

But her near death had devastated the duke. So much so, he now searched for comfort in the one place that had caused him so much pain in the past: the dungeon.

Adam understood the reason, however. The dungeon's dark surroundings mirrored the duke's dark heart.

Damian was quiet for a moment before he said, "Do you still hate me?"

There was a sharp pain in Adam's breast, a phantom knife twisting into his heart. "No, I don't hate you anymore." He had not hated the duke for a long time. "But I used to feed off the hate. Once I stopped loathing you, though, I thought my soul would starve."

"What happened?"

"I started hating pirates."

The duke snorted. "It's good to know someone else in the castle resents them as much as I do."

Adam grinned. "I despised Black Hawk for stealing the fob watch Tess had given me. I chased him for years, seeking vengeance . . . and he was here the whole time."

"Tormenting me."

"But I can't hate Black Hawk anymore, either," said Adam. "I can't hate any of the pirates. Without their help, Evelyn might still be suffering under the prince's cruelty."

There was another short pause before the duke said, "Evelyn will leave for America soon."

"I know."

"And I understand you won't be living with her in the New World?"

"Did she tell you that?"

"Yes."

Adam had yet to speak with Evelyn about the matter of her possible pregnancy. Once he did, though, he was confident the woman would change her mind about letting him stay with her in America.

"The matter isn't decided yet," said Adam. "Evelyn and I have more to discuss."

"Will you marry her?"

Blood pounded in Adam's ears. "No."

"You could be happy with her. Teresa was the joy of your past. Evelyn could be the joy of your future."

Adam dismissed the frighteningly tempting idea with a succinct: "I will never marry again."

"Why not?"

"I made a vow to honor Tess forever."

"The vow was broken upon her death."

"Death is not a barrier."

Besides, Adam did not deserve to be happy.

Lightning cracked . . . fire raged . . . screams filled the stormy night.

Adam closed his eyes to shut out the dreadful memory. He had failed Tess; he had let her die . . . He deserved to be alone.

"How will you live then?" said the duke. "Who will you hate now?"

"Prince Vadik."

It filled Adam's heart with dark energy, the thought of the prince. He was determined to keep the fiend away from Evelyn; she would not meet the same fate as her hapless sister.

"But the prince is Evelyn's demon, not yours," said Damian.

"No, he's mine!"

"Your demon is guilt. I know you, Adam; I know you feel guilty for Teresa's death. It's just easier to fight Evelyn's demon instead of your own."

Adam bristled at the suggestion, for it implied he was chasing the wrong villain. And yet how could that be? Vadik was evil. Adam was *not* misguided in his efforts to combat the devil.

"Trust me, Adam. I learned that truth the hard way. I, too, chased pirates for years. I wanted to destroy them for destroying you."

Adam wasn't surprised to hear his brother's assertion. The whole of England believed pirates had destroyed the *Hercules* in a raid, for it had been in all the papers.

The story had reached the public by way of the captain's cabin boy. The poor chap had survived the wreckage a mere few hours by clinging to a piece of debris before he was rescued by a passing ship. Although a fever took his life, the boy related the tale of the sinking before his passing—the wrong tale. The kid must have confused the pirate attack with the storm, thinking the thunder and fire aboard ship cannon blasts. It was a simple mistake to make in a delirious state of mind; the two events had been but hours apart. And there had been no one to challenge the boy's account—until Adam had re-entered society—so pirates had taken the blame for the sinking.

"It was easier to loathe the brigands rather than face the loathing I had for myself," said Damian. "I first met Belle while hunting for her brothers. And I almost lost her because of it; I almost killed her kin."

"What stopped you?"

"I loved Belle more than I hated her brothers . . . a good thing, too, since they didn't kill you."

Adam chuckled. "She really turned your life upside-down, didn't she?"

"Yes, she did . . . and I'm very grateful to her for it."

Adam thought about Evelyn, and how she had turned *his* life upside-down, too.

"Damian?"

"Yes?"

He paused before he said, "I'm sorry I stabbed you."

"I forgive you."

"Why?"

"Because we used to be friends," said the duke. "Because it wasn't supposed to be like this, and I want to make it right."

"You're a better man than I." And it was true. There was a time when the very thought would have seemed preposterous, but sitting in the dungeon after all the recent turmoil, Adam knew the words were true.

"You're not a bad man, Adam. I think it's time you learn to forgive yourself for Teresa's death."

But Adam didn't think such a thing was possible.

Chapter 28

Evelyn tiptoed through the dark castle, deep in thought.

Two days ago the duchess had come close to death. Now she rested, recovering her strength.

Tears welled in Evelyn's eyes at the memory of Mirabelle's sobs, her fierce battle to survive and not abandon her husband and children. The moving encounter would stay with her forever.

But Evelyn spilled tears for another reason, too.

The sound of frothy waves stirring against a ragged coastline filled her ears. She reminisced about the salty smell of the ocean, the sight of dark and heavy storm clouds rolling across the heavens. At one time she had been willing to throw her life away, to surrender to her grief . . . to welcome death. But no more. After she had witnessed the duchess struggle for survival with every breath, Evelyn was more determined than ever to fight for her life, too.

She stopped beside a closed bedroom door. The fine mahogany wood gleamed under the luster of a vigorous polish and warm candlelight.

It was late; most of the household was asleep. She was careful to keep quiet. She didn't want to rouse a maid or a footman; she didn't want anyone to see her standing before *this* particular door.

Evelyn took in a deep breath and wiped the tears from her eyes. She knocked lightly on the door.

Silence.

She knocked again.

More quiet.

Someone might discover her if she continued to rap on the door and make noise, she thought, so she lifted the latch and stepped inside the room—uninvited.

The bedchamber was poorly lit, and she squinted to make out the shadows.

"Adam?" she whispered. "Where are you?"

She heard the bedsheets rustle.

"What are you doing here?" he said gruffly.

"I'm sorry to wake you, but I . . . I want to learn."

"Learn what?" he rasped.

The man's heavy frame shifted from the feather tick. As he tweaked the low-burning oil lamp beside the bed, the more vibrant glow illuminated the room—and the bed.

Her heart fluttered.

Adam was dressed in breeches—only breeches—and resting atop the covers. It was impossible to ignore the wide breadth of his shoulders in the smoldering light. Chest nude, it was impossible to ignore the solid build of the man's muscles, too. Nor could she disregard the wounds at his breast.

He had done so much for her, struggled for *her* life when she was too weak to do it for herself. But no more.

As he stared at her with those somnolent eyes, a shiver tickled her spine. She briefly lost her voice before she gathered her senses and remarked, "I want to learn how to swim and use a sword and engage in fisticuffs."

She was ready now to learn all he had offered to teach her before. She was tired of cowering at the prince's feet. She was determined not to let the royal devil torment her anymore, the way he had tormented her sister.

"And you came here to tell me this now?" Adam rubbed his brow slowly. "This couldn't have waited until morning?"

"I didn't want to waste time," she said, her words shaky. *Or lose courage.* "I'll be leaving for America in a fortnight."

He looked at her with hard eyes. She marked the shift in his lazy manner. He was stiffer, his lips pressed firmly together. Was he still angry with her for refusing his protection? She supposed so.

She sniffed the air.

Brandy?

She spotted the empty spirits bottle beside the bed. "Are you foxed?"

"I hope so." There was heat in his eyes—aimed straight for her. "You shouldn't be in here, Evie."

Tremors moved along the curve of her back. "No, I suppose I shouldn't be in here if you're foxed. I'll go."

She hastened to leave the room. Her hand was on the latch when Adam was suddenly behind her. He braced an arm against the door to prevent her from opening it.

His cheek brushed her hair softly. "Why did you *really* come here?"

Her eyes seemed heavy, and she fluttered her lashes closed at his sensual touch. The spicy scent of his musk teased her senses with equal passion. "I told you—"

"I don't believe you." Lips beside her ear, he was curt—but his breath stirred the sensitive skin at her neck, arousing her and making her muscles flex in expectation of more. "I think you came here looking for a bedding."

She gasped. "I most certainly did *not*!"

But perhaps *he* was hoping for a bedding. She'd experienced firsthand from her father that an inebriated man had a loose tongue—and often expressed his most honest thoughts.

Swiftly Evelyn raised her heel—and stomped on Adam's bare foot.

He cursed and hopped backward before he landed on his rump with wicked force.

She winced and quickly knelt beside him. "I didn't mean to hurt you."

He was massaging his foot and glaring at her, more sober now. "So what *did* you mean to do?"

"I want you to know I'm determined to learn how to defend myself. I won't shirk from my lessons anymore."

He humphed and struggled to stand.

She helped him to his feet.

He hobbled toward the bed and sat down on the edge. "We'll continue the lessons in the morning. I'll meet you in the garden."

"Thank you, Adam." Again she moved toward the door, but this time she stopped herself from leaving. "Did you drink the whole bottle of brandy?"

He sighed and stretched back across the feather tick. "I think so."

"Why did you drink it?"

"I had a very revealing chat with my brother today, and I came to a very depressing conclusion."

"Which is?"

"I will never be happy."

Evelyn moved away from the door and approached the bed. For a long time she had suspected a darkness in Adam's heart. She had not been mistaken in that regard, but she had failed to realize the true nature of that darkness. She had feared Adam. Falsely. Believed him to be a violent man. But he was not filled with hate or anger anymore. He was filled with guilt. Guilt over the death of his wife.

She picked up the coverlet folded at the foot of the bed and draped it across his frame. "Good night, Adam."

A robust hand grabbed her wrist. "Are you sure you didn't come in here looking for a bedding?"

"I'm sure!"

He sighed and let go of her wrist. "Pity."

"You're confused, Adam." She took a shaky step back from the bed. "You're drunk."

"Not that drunk, Evie."

A tight knot formed in her belly at his sultry words. He was sober enough to know he wanted her, and just foxed enough to admit the truth aloud.

Under the warm glow of candlelight, Evelyn stared at the sharp folds of muscle across his firm chest. She listened to the heavy, yet lyrical sound of his breathing, and tried to tamp the wild thumps of her heart at the sensual sight of him.

"Are you still here, Evie?"

She started at the rough way he said her name—
and blushed to be caught admiring him.

Mortification swallowed her whole, and she
skirted from the bedside.

But she was able to take only two steps before a
set of sturdy arms circled her waist and dragged
her back to the bed.

Evelyn gasped as she found herself embraced
by the soft feather tick—and Adam's hard chest.

"Adam, what are you doing?!"

"Bedding you."

Her fingers tingled, her toes curled at the man's
hot words. Oh, and his touch! It stirred her senses
to sweet life, making her heart ache for him in the
most critical way.

"You taste good, Evie."

He kissed a tender spot of skin below her ear,
as he moved his hips to press against the swell of
her bottom.

Evelyn closed her eyes in quiet ecstasy, too
abashed to voice the dark cravings brewing inside
her.

But Adam sensed her desire.

He clinched her waist with one arm, holding
her snug, and caressed her throat, her bustline
with his other hand, stirring the flames of want
in her belly.

Evelyn opened her eyes. She stared across the

room at the groping shadows on the wall, aroused by the spectacle. With Adam behind her, she didn't need to look into his eyes, to blush or feel awkward, to betray her impolite yearnings to his face. She could just enjoy the sensuous experience, take pleasure in his warm kisses and wanton caresses.

Adam's large hand slipped along the peak of her hip, fingered its way to the bend in her knee, then started up again—dragging her skirt along the way.

Evelyn bit back a sigh at his fiery touch; it burned through the fabric of her dress, making her sweat.

"You feel good, too, Evie."

She shivered as the soft material of her frock rubbed against her flesh and gathered at her waist.

She was nude from the waist down, and Adam was quick to stroke her bare bottom, to knead the plump flesh, which she undulated into his cupped hand.

"So good," he whispered roughly.

Adam slipped his fingers between her buttocks, rubbed the tender and damp flesh between her legs.

Evelyn heaved the deep sigh she was holding back, each gasp a soft cry of bliss, urging him to work harder, faster to give her release.

He did as she bade.

After a brief surcease to relax the buttons of his trousers, Adam positioned himself behind her again and lifted her leg.

Evelyn seized, aware of his intent.

"Let me in, Evie." He rocked his hips against her backside, disarming her. "Let me fill you completely."

She couldn't hold back the groan anymore—or resist his sweet demand.

Adam slipped inside her, so deep. She cried out to feel the thick muscle throbbing between her legs, teasing her already pulsing arousal.

Evelyn reached back to grab his hips as he thrust against her buttocks. She needed the support, the intimacy of his touch.

He filled her again and again; moved with hunger, quick and hard.

Her heart pounded as the desire inside her ballooned and stretched. She was dizzy with delight. The most sensitive part of her aching for satisfaction.

Evelyn gasped as piercing pleasure poured through her veins. Adam groaned with release soon thereafter.

Breathless and content, they both remained on the bed, trapped in an embrace.

Evelyn eyed the shadows on the wall again, now subdued. She smiled. She couldn't help it. There was something about the closeness, the thrill of intimacy that always lifted her spirits.

"Marry me, Evie."

Her smile fell. The heat quickly cooled from her limbs, and she struggled to gather her lazy thoughts.

"What did you say, Adam?"

He said into her hair, "I want you to be my wife."

"Why?"

She blurted out the request without thinking. Rather uncouth, but it *was* the most pressing matter on her mind. He couldn't possibly care for her. She had witnessed the devotion he still had for his late wife firsthand. So why did he want to wed her?

"Because you might be pregnant, Evie."

Yes, of course. His duty.

Evelyn wriggled in the man's arms. "Let me go, Adam."

He did without protest.

She sat up and smoothed her dress over her legs. "I think it's best if I return to my room."

"I'll announce our engagement in the morning."

"Don't bother."

She headed for the door, her toes still twinkling after their heated tumble in bed.

Adam was on his feet, too. "We must make the announcement before we leave for America."

She opened the door. "I'm not going to marry you, Adam."

He closed the door with his hand and then blocked it with his body. "And why the devil not?"

There was a dark look in his eyes, almost threatening. But Evelyn was used to seeing that look whenever she challenged the man. She wasn't intimidated by it anymore.

"I don't want to marry you, Adam."

"Why?"

Because you don't love me!

"I want to have control over my own life," she said.

"Did you hear me?" He crossed his thick arms over his chest. "You might be pregnant."

"I heard you." She mimicked his posture. "But I will deal with the babe—if I have one—alone."

His features darkened even more. "The hell you will."

"I beg your pardon?"

"That's my babe." He pointed to her midriff. "And it's my responsibility to take care of you both."

"You don't know that I'm even going to have a babe."

"I'll know for sure by the time we reach America."

"And then?"

"And then we'll get married."

"No, we won't."

"Damn it, Evie! Don't be foolish!"

She was more disturbed by the man than the outburst. If she married him to protect the babe, she would have to live with the knowledge that he did not care for her; that he never would. But she would one day care for him, she was sure. It was just another form of ownership in the end. He would own her heart, but never love her in return. And what sort of a life was that?

"I won't marry you, Adam. It's my final word."

"Evie, I *can't* abandon you."

"I know you feel a sense of duty to protect me, but I release you—"

"Damn it, you can't release me from my duty! It's *my* duty. And I won't release myself from it!"

She huffed. "Then I suppose you'll have to find some other damsel in distress to comfort, because I won't be a substitute for your late wife!"

Adam looked at her aghast. "What?"

She was quick to group her features together in quiet repose. "I know you regret Teresa's drowning. I know you feel guilty for her loss. But you don't need to be beside me always to keep me safe, to keep what happened to Teresa from happening to me."

His every breath was uneven, his eyes stormy.

Evelyn rallied her strength. "You've already helped me, Adam. You took me away from the prince. And I thank you for it. But to follow me around all the rest of my days, to protect me from potential threats is fruitless. It won't bring Teresa back."

Adam moved away from the door.

Cleary she'd struck him with greater might than she'd anticipated. "You're trapped in the past, Adam. I understand the grief, the guilt you feel. But I don't want to live in the past. My own past is so dreary. I want to look toward the future. And I can't do that with you."

Quietly she walked out of the room.

Chapter 29

Adam wandered through the castle cause-ways.

He had just ended his morning training session with Evelyn. Over the past two weeks she had much improved in both skill and confidence, for with each ability she mastered, she grew surer of herself. But the pleasure he had found in watching her progress was tempered by an unsettling thought.

I won't be a substitute for your late wife!

He stilled, knocked insensible by the memory of her provoking words. What did she mean by the accusation? He wasn't like the dastardly prince, seeking a replacement for his late wife. Evelyn was nothing like Teresa in manner or appearance, so the argument was rubbish. Besides, one cannot recapture the past.

You're trapped in the past, Adam.

Once more the memory of Evelyn's words disarmed him. He rubbed the back of his neck to ease the stiff muscles. He was haunted by the past; that much was true. And rightly so: he had failed to save Teresa from drowning. The weight of guilt was his penance. However, his desire to make Evelyn his wife had nothing to do with the past. He only wanted to do the right thing by marrying her. She might still have a babe.

It haunted him; the image of Evelyn alone and struggling in America with his child. And the stubborn woman wouldn't even think of wedding him for her own protection.

Adam moved through the keep with brisk strides. He intended to convince her of the soundness of his proposal. Perhaps after a few days in a strange new world, she might reconsider her avowed independence? He certainly hoped so.

"My lord."

Adam stopped and eyed the butler as he approached. "Yes, Jenkins?"

"There is someone here to see the duke—about you."

The prince!

"Who is it, Jenkins?"

"He would not give his name."

Adam's thoughts danced. "Where is he?"

"I bade him to wait by the door; I posted a footman to guard him."

"And Lady Evelyn?"

"She is secure upstairs with the duchess."

Adam nodded. "I'll deal with him, Jenkins. Don't trouble the duke."

"Very good, my lord."

Adam marched toward the entranceway, fisting his palms. His temples pounded. A hazy darkness came over his eyes, a thrumming desire for blood filled him.

"Capt'n! You're alive!"

Lieutenant Eric Faraday greeted him at the door.

Slowly Adam uncurled his fingers and stretched out his hand. "It's good to see you again, Lieutenant."

Adam dismissed the footman. A part of him was relieved to see the loyal lieutenant again. Yet another part of him was disappointed, for thrashing the repulsive prince was a very attractive thought.

Faraday grasped his hand in a hearty handshake. "When I found the cottage destroyed, I searched for you to no avail. I resolved to contact His Grace about your disappearance. But I didn't think to find you here. I thought you were estranged from your brother."

"We've had a reconciliation."

"I'm glad to hear it, sir. But what happened to the cottage?"

Adam said with considerable ire, "There was a quarrel."

"Why didn't you come to me for help?"

"It wasn't something you could help me with, Lieutenant."

"Well, I'm glad you're safe." The lieutenant lowered his voice. "I have news about Black Hawk."

Once more the pressure in Adam's head spiked. "What about the cutthroat?"

"He's been spotted, sir."

"Where?"

"South Africa."

The pressure in Adam's head diminished. Black Hawk's whereabouts and identity had not truly been revealed. Adam was grateful for that. He didn't need a scandal on his hands just before he set sail with Evelyn for America. And there would surely be one if word ever spread that the duke's brother-in-law was the most dreaded pirate captain on the high seas.

"Africa?" Bemused, Adam said, "How did you hear about him in Africa?"

"After the debacle at Raven's Cross, the men and I returned to the ship as ordered. Another vessel had moored not two hours before, the crew fresh from Africa and telling tales of a corsair with the heart of a devil."

"More ghost stories," said Adam dryly.

"Aye, sir, but I still thought you should hear it. We've had no luck hunting the rogue in English waters."

"So perhaps we should try African waters, is that it?"

"I don't see the harm, Capt'n."

Adam sighed. He had to feign frustration to keep the lieutenant in ignorance. "I'm tired of chasing shadows, Faraday."

"I understand, sir, but it's reasonable to think the pirate might be near South Africa."

"How so?"

"Well, it's been four years since we've heard a credible account of Black Hawk's whereabouts. Most folks believe the villain's dead, but perhaps he's just raiding distant waters. There is the lucrative slave trade in America to consider. It might tempt a roving buccaneer."

Ever the soldier, Faraday. Once committed to a mission, he would see it through to completion. It was one of the traits Adam had found so admirable in the man.

But it was time to stop hounding ghosts.

"We're not going to hunt Black Hawk anymore, Lieutenant."

The older man paled. "But why?"

"I want you to pay the crew, Lieutenant. Tell the men to settle down and be happy. The search for the pirate captain is over; I have another duty on my hands."

Faraday eyed the stack of crates by the door. "Are you leaving England?"

"For a time, yes."

For forever, in truth—if he could convince a certain headstrong woman to be his bride.

"Is it the woman?" said Faraday. "Your ward?"

Adam didn't want to talk about his "ward," but he trusted the lieutenant enough to admit, "Yes, it is."

The color returned to the senior man's features, red-hot at that. "Begging your pardon, sir, but what about your duty to justice? To the crew? We've been with you for years. We've chased the pirate Black Hawk like he was the devil himself. And now we're going to let the scoundrel go free?"

"You can sell the ship, Faraday. Or captain it yourself, if you'd like." Then, thinking of Black Hawk: "Turn the rig into a merchant vessel."

"But Capt'n, these men aren't merchants, they're men of war!"

"The war with Black Hawk is over."

Faraday glared at him. "You'll forsake your loyal crew for a woman? I didn't think you so ignoble."

The pressure in Adam's head started to mount again. "It's not that simple, Lieutenant."

He didn't want to disappoint the lieutenant or the crew, but it was impossible to apprehend Black Hawk. And to travel the world in search of a ghost or a fraud like Hagley was fruitless. The men would never find satisfaction in justice, for the men would never arrest the corsair. It was better for them all—even if they didn't know it now—to give up the empty pursuit and search for contentment elsewhere.

The lieutenant demanded, "*How* can you surrender and allow Black Hawk to plunder the seas?"

Blast it! How to reveal the truth to the lieutenant without revealing the *truth*?

"Black Hawk is dead."

Faraday appeared stunned. "What?"

"I discovered the notorious rogue is dead." And it was true in a way. The Hawkins brothers had retired from piracy. "Now do you understand why the search for the brigand is futile?"

"How did he die? When?"

"You must trust me, Lieutenant. I have the news on very good authority."

"But the report from Africa—"

"Is wrong." Adam offered his hand once more. "You've been a good and faithful lieutenant—and friend. I thank you. Pay the men well; I will cover all expenses. And express my gratitude to them, too."

The older man stared at Adam's hand, a departing gesture. "Aye, Capt'n."

* * *

Evelyn cradled the baby in her arms. Henry Westmore, the heir to the dukedom, was sound asleep, sweet as a sugar plum.

"You got your wish, Belle. It's a boy."

The duchess smiled. She was still bedridden. Ordered to rest by both the doctor and her husband, she wasn't permitted visitors. However, Evelyn was departing for America tonight, so an exception was made to allow the women to say farewell.

"He is a darling, isn't he?" said Mirabelle. "So quiet, too."

Evelyn chuckled softly. "Why the name Henry?"

"In honor of a dear friend."

With care Evelyn returned the tiny creature to the cradle. She then looked at the duchess and struggled to keep her composure.

"I suppose it's time to say good-bye," said Mirabelle. She, too, appeared woebegone. "Do you have everything you need for your trip?"

"Yes, I'm prepared."

"Are you sure? You seem preoccupied. Is there something on your mind?"

"No, I'm fine."

"Is it Adam?"

Even the pangs of childbirth and a fever had not dampened the woman's sharp eye.

Evelyn approached the bed. "Adam asked me to marry him."

However, she neglected to confess the reason for the man's proposal: a babe. And while Evelyn wasn't even sure she was going to have a babe, she was determined not to marry Adam even if she was enceinte. She would not fix one mistake by making another.

"How did you answer Adam?"

"I said no."

"Why?"

Evelyn shrugged. "He doesn't care for me."

He still loves his late wife.

"Are you sure?" said Mirabelle.

"He only wants to control me. He believes he failed to keep his late wife safe, so now he wants to keep me safe in her stead."

"I see." The duchess touched her hand. "Do you love him?"

"No!"

"You seem very determined to convince me of that. Are you sure you don't love him?"

Evelyn's heart pulsed. "Are you suggesting I accept his proposal?"

"I don't want to meddle; it's not my place. I only want to be sure you make the right choice. Don't let fear decide your fate."

She looked at the duchess, confused. "What do you mean?"

"You don't want a man to control you, right?"

Evelyn nodded with confidence.

"You want freedom? The right to make your own decisions?"

"Yes," said Evelyn. "I want all of that."

"Then don't let *fear* control you. Make sure you decline Adam's offer because you do not love him, and not because you are afraid to love him."

Chapter 30

"**W**elcome aboard the *Bonny Meg*, Lady Evelyn."

Evelyn took the pirate captain's hand and stepped onto the deck. "Thank you, Captain."

The dark devil wasn't so intimidating anymore. After a few weeks in James Hawkins's company she had learned he was a caring brother and a devoted uncle. He was a surly brigand, too, but that character trait wasn't the *only* one she saw when she looked at him now.

In truth, she had come to understand each brother's true nature. And with the insight, the fear inside her had vanished. She now accepted that not all men were like her father and the prince and the henchmen. That there were kind men in the world, too.

"What do you think of the ship?" Quincy approached her, beaming. "She's named after our mother."

The bright and ghostly blue light of a full moon

pierced the white canvas stretched high above Evelyn's head, illuminating the sails like clouds before a storm. "She's a lovely vessel."

"That she is," James was quick to affirm. "There's not a bonnier ship on the high seas."

"I beg to differ."

There was a flutter in Evelyn's belly at the sound of Adam's voice. The familiar low tone always stirred her senses, made her warm, too.

Adam boarded the schooner, the Duke of Wembury at his heels.

"The last time I saw this ship," said Adam, "she was sailing away—with my fob watch!"

The pirate captain appeared indifferent, but Evelyn heard the humor in his voice. "You got the watch back, didn't you?"

Adam frowned. "Why *did* you keep it all those years?"

He shrugged. "I liked it; it reminded me of someone."

And with that enigmatic remark, James offered her a curt nod. "If you'll excuse me, Lady Evelyn."

The pirate captain strutted off, shouting orders to the crew. Quincy followed—but not before he offered her another charming grin, the scalawag.

Alone with the Westmore brothers, Evelyn looked from one towering figure to the other.

The duke was the first to approach her. "Lady Evelyn, I bid you farewell."

"Good-bye, Your Grace." Cloaked in a fine linen mantle to hide her features from the crowd in port, she removed the hood now that she was secure aboard ship, and smiled in return. "Thank you for your kindness."

The duke then turned toward his brother. Damian had accompanied the party to port at the behest of the duchess, who wished to know if the *Bonny Meg* had set sail with good winds and smooth tides.

But now it was time to part company, and Evelyn suspected the duke wanted a private word with his kin.

"I think I'll go to explore the ship," she said.

Quietly Evelyn moved across the deck of the *Bonny Meg* toward the prow of the ship. She stopped near the jibs, and looked out to sea.

She inhaled the rich, briny air. A storm was coming; she could tell by the smell of the water. Clouds drifted across the night sky and covered the proud full moon, casting the ship in even greater shadow.

She heard the distant holler for lamplight and closed her eyes to the disorder. Instead her thoughts returned to the tang of the salty sea. The scent reminded her of Adam and their time together in the quaint country cottage by the beach.

She had adored the charming abode. But it was no more, destroyed by fire. So much of Evelyn's past was the same: in ashes. She hoped her future would be different.

But she wondered if perhaps her fate would go up in smoke, too. The duchess believed her ruled by fear. Was she right? Had Evelyn displaced the authority of a man in her life with that of fear?

Yet even if the duchess was right and she was afraid to love Adam, it was with reason. The man still cared for his late wife. He could never care for her, too . . . could he?

"Good evening, Lady Evelyn."

A cold hand clamped over her mouth; a thick arm clinched her waist.

Evelyn's heart pounded. She recognized the voice . . . Dmitri!

A henchman!

Evelyn struggled with her captor in the shadows, screamed against the palm pressed to her lips. But the bustle of passengers in port, the movement of the crew loading crates of supplies and cargo all proved a sound distraction; she couldn't flag down help.

Evelyn tried to remember Adam's teaching; she kicked and thrashed and bit . . . but panic in her breast stifled her movements, made them erratic and ineffectual. She was dragged overboard, down a rope ladder, and into a waiting rowboat.

* * *

The duke outstretched his palm. "Safe journey, Adam."

Adam reached for his brother's hand. "Thank you."

"You are welcome to come home, you know?" said Damian. "If you decide not to stay in America."

America.

A new world.

It could also be the start of a new life for him—and Evelyn.

Could he really be happy with Evelyn? She filled him with a pulsing warmth. If he dared to think too much on the matter, his heart cramped at the thought of being apart from her. But whether he deserved to be happy was perhaps a better question. With all the mistakes he had made in the past, did he merit forgiveness?

Can you ever forgive me, Tess, for failing you?

"I should go," said the duke.

His quiet prayer interrupted, Adam escorted his brother off the *Bonny Meg* and over to the waiting coach stationed dockside. "Take care of Mother."

"I will," said the duke. "And if you have the opportunity to push one of the Hawkins brothers overboard during the voyage . . . please do."

Adam smiled. "I'll see what I can do."

Adam then spotted a figure with a familiar limp.

He blinked. The crowd was thick and the character vanished.

"What is it, Adam?"

"I thought I saw"—once more a pocket in the crowd appeared, and Adam observed the same proverbial shuffle of—"Lieutenant Faraday."

"Who?"

But Adam was already cutting through the masses toward his comrade. "Lieutenant!"

Lieutenant Eric Faraday glanced over his shoulder—and took off at an uncharacteristic speed.

Adam was swift to catch up with the man and seized him by the arm.

"Lieutenant, what are you doing here?"

Faraday resisted the arrest. But when he noticed the ominous approach of the Duke of Wembury, he must have realized he was cornered, for he cooled his heels.

"Taking care of business, Capt'n."

"Don't call me Captain, Faraday. I'm not your captain anymore."

The lieutenant did not even try to hide his rancor. "Therein lies the trouble, sir."

"Answer me, Faraday." Adam glared at his comrade. "What are you doing here?"

"I'm here with the crew, sir. I had come looking for you, but it was a wasted effort, I see that now . . . Or perhaps it wasn't an entire waste."

"What do you mean?"

"I happened upon a group of men. They were searching the countryside, asking travelers about a woman."

Adam bristled. "What woman?"

"Your ward, sir."

Adam reached for the lieutenant's throat—and squeezed. It was the duke who disentangled the couple, forced Adam to back away.

"How could you betray me, Faraday?!"

It churned in Adam's belly, the incomparable disloyalty. The vile hurt crushed the very breath from his lungs.

"Betray *you*?" Faraday sputtered and rubbed his tender throat. "You betrayed me, Capt'n. You betrayed the entire crew!"

"How?"

"You abandoned our righteous mission to apprehend Black Hawk for a woman. You surrendered to lust!"

"I told you, Black Hawk is dead."

"I don't believe it! You just want to be rid of your obligation, so you can cavort with another man's woman." Faraday paused for breath. "I know the truth. I was informed of your treachery. How could you steal another man's bride? A royal bride?"

"You son of a bitch!"

Adam again reached for his former friend's throat—and again he was curtailed by the duke.

The lieutenant was unabashed. "Perhaps now—with her out of the way—you will come to your senses and fulfill the mission you're honor-bound to meet."

"What did you tell them, Faraday?"

"I think you had best confess the truth," admonished the duke.

"I'm not ashamed of anything I've done," said Faraday. "I'll gladly reveal the truth . . . I told them you had the prince's fiancée."

Adam and Damian exchanged quick glances before both charged back toward the *Bonny Meg*.

"Evie!"

Adam shouted her name over and over again, zigzagged across the deck in a desperate search for the woman.

"What the devil are you bellowing about?" demanded Black Hawk. He approached Adam from behind, expression dark.

"Where's Evie?"

"Belowdecks, I'm sure," said the pirate captain. "There's no reason to disrupt my—"

The duke was quick to advance. "The prince knows we have Evelyn."

Black Hawk faltered.

But within two seconds the pirate captain roared: "Search the ship! Find the woman!"

The men scrambled to obey.

A frightful image stormed Adam's brain: Evelyn accosted by the henchmen, throttled by the prince. Her lifeless body . . .

He shoved the dread, the wretched sickness back down into the bowel of his belly.

Be strong, Evie.

Fight!

Curse the blackness! A fierce storm brewed in the distance, the thick clouds hiding the precious moonlight, making their search for Evelyn all the more difficult.

"Over here, Captain!"

Black Hawk thundered across the deck, Adam and Damian quick on his heels. The men gathered at the starboard rail and looked out to sea.

The tar lifted the lamplight higher. "Do you see her, Captain? The boat?"

The men peered into the darkness.

Every so often a flicker of torchlight reflected off a pair of wet oars, as a small rowboat moved across the waters toward the much larger rig moored a league away.

That alone was not suspicious enough—but for the figure struggling *in* the rowboat.

"Oh God!" cried Adam. *"Evie!"*

Black Hawk rounded the deck. "Weigh anchor! And ready the cannons!"

The pirates followed instructions without a moment's pause. The deck was thrust into organized chaos as each brigand headed for his appointed station.

"Gentlemen." Black Hawk returned a minute later with two shiny pistols. He handed one to Adam and the other to Damian. "You'll be needing these."

Chapter 31

Evelyn was alone in the cabin with Prince Vadik.

As soon as she had been dragged aboard the royal vessel, the prince had ordered the captain to weigh anchor.

She was trapped.

There was a table wedged between them, dotted with sumptuous dishes. She didn't care for a bite, though, her belly twisted with nausea. And it was not the undulating waves making her queasy. It was *him*.

"You look so much like your sister." He said the words with pleasure. "I miss your sister very much."

Evelyn was damp with sweat. If she lifted her eyes to look at the prince, she might faint. Did he have a coffin aboard ship? How long would he keep her interred this time?

Her heart pumped madly. She was grateful for

the support of a chair, for without it she would surely collapse.

Tears welled in her eyes. Hopeless tears. Adam had trained her to fight with fists and swords. He had demonstrated kicks and punches. Where had all that knowledge gone? She sat quiet, trembling.

Dead.

It was useless to fight the prince. One thought—one look—at him and her mind panicked, her fingers froze.

"I suppose it's too much for me to hope my fiancée is still a virgin?"

She remained silent, but took small pleasure in the thought she had aggrieved him in that matter at least.

"You disappoint me, Lady Evelyn. I believed you less rebellious than your sister. But I broke her spirit. I will break yours, too."

Evelyn was resigned to her wretched fate—but she had yet to resign herself to her sister's death.

"You killed Ella."

The prince poured himself a glass of red wine. "My late wife died in a terrible riding accident."

Evelyn was willful. "You killed Ella."

After a measured sip of the spirits, the devil smiled. "It's better to let the matter rest, Lady Evelyn."

She clutched the heart-shaped pendant at her throat. "How did Ella die?"

"Too rebellious, Lady Evelyn. I warned you." The prince set the glass aside before he slipped the silk cravat off his throat. "Do you see this?"

She stared at the crisp white fabric through her tears. "You choked her?"

Her own words choked as ghastly images stormed her brain.

"I did." The prince caressed the silk cravat in fond memory, it appeared. "I choked her . . . while I was inside her."

Evelyn's hands trembled. She couldn't feel her fingers anymore, the nerves numb.

"What can I say? I'm fascinated by the beauty of death." He gracefully fastened the cravat around his neck once more. "It all happened so long ago. I saw my mother's corpse laid out as a child. She was so exquisitely lovely in the coffin. I'm afraid it's been an obsession ever since. I cannot help myself."

Years of misery and aloneness and fear gathered inside her, and in one brilliant burst, the sentiments twisted together into pulsing, feral—

"You son of a bitch!" She pounced on top of the table and lunged for the prince. "I will *kill* you, Vadik!"

Spooked, Vadik cried, "Men!"

The door burst open and the cabin filled with henchmen.

Hunkered near the prince at the other end of the table, Evelyn snatched the cravat from his throat and wound the silk around her knuckles. He would take no more pleasure from her sister's brutal death.

The henchmen approached.

Evelyn stood and kicked the plates of food across the room, the henchmen her target.

Red-hot anger strangled her fear. There was a wild need inside her to fight. And she tossed the silver-plated chargers around the cabin like a mighty windstorm.

In the confusion the door was left open. Evelyn jumped off the table and dashed out of the cabin.

An uproar resounded behind her.

"Bring her back to me!" cried the prince.

Filled with energy, Evelyn sprinted through the corridor and scrambled up the steep steps leading topside.

A tempest raged.

She was soaked within seconds. But Evelyn didn't care about the wild winds or the crashing waves.

She wanted off the ship.

She snatched ratlines for support, making her way toward the stern. In the distance lightning charged, the bright blue light sparking quickly, illuminating another ship.

The *Bonny Meg*.

Evelyn grabbed hold of the portside rail and started to climb overboard.

"Light the cannons!"

"No!" Adam grabbed Black Hawk by the arm. "If you sink her, you'll kill Evie."

"I'm not going to sink her!" the pirate captain shouted in return. "Just send her—and the prince—a warning." He then ordered, "Aim off her portside rail!"

"Aye, Captain."

The tar rushed to impart the command to the gunners belowdecks.

Adam grabbed a thick rope and wrapped it around his hand to keep steady. Another tempest raged in his breast. It scrubbed and polished and washed away all the years of guilt and confusion. Truth lighted. For years he had lived under the pressure of pain, imposed a sentence of solitude upon himself as a form of punishment. But there was nothing he could have done to save Tess. He realized that now. She was gone. But he was alive. And somewhere in the deepest part of his soul, he could hear her sweet voice:

Be happy, Adam.

The sea churned with angry might. The wind pushed the rain across the night sky in thick and blinding sheets.

Adam now looked out with anxious expectation to the furious sea for that very happiness: he looked for Evelyn.

She had stroked his heart back to life from their first meeting at the beach. And she had been stroking it ever since, bringing him hope and joy and peace.

"Adam!"

He looked at his brother. Damian pointed across the deck of the *Bonny Meg*, toward the other vessel.

Adam stared in the same direction—and chilled.

Lightning flickered across the stormy heavens. For a brief moment he recognized Evelyn crawling over the portside rail.

And then she was gone.

The sea black once more.

"Evie!"

But it was an unheard scream, swallowed by the roar of thunder and the lashing waves.

Adam moved closer to the ship's edge. Heartbeat wild, he gripped the sturdy rail and peered into the darkness, willing to see Evelyn again.

Another distant crack of electric light.

It illuminated the other rig—and revealed a gruesome sight.

Evelyn was struggling with the prince!

A blast roared from the *Bonny Meg*.

"No!" Adam cried.

The cannonball streaked the skies and exploded in the waters off the other ship's portside rail.

Both Evelyn and the prince tumbled into the churning sea.

Without another thought, Adam vaulted off the side of the *Bonny Meg* and into the swirling waters.

"Adam, no!"

Damian charged after his brother, but Black Hawk grabbed him by the arm. "You can't go after him, Damian!"

The duke struggled. "I won't lose him again!"

"Adam belongs in the sea with Evie. *You* belong on land with Belle."

The pirate captain was right. Curse it all to hell! Damian slammed his fist against the ship's rail in defeat.

Once he was sure the duke would not follow his brother into the ocean, Black Hawk shouted, "Man overboard!"

Evelyn struggled with the long hem of her skirt, trying to make her way over the rail and into the sea.

She had to get to the *Bonny Meg*.

She had to get to Adam!

After her duel with the prince and the henchmen, the years of murky uncertainty and dread had washed away. Her mind was clear now. And for the first time, she could see what was truly in her heart.

"You little bitch!" The prince snatched her ankle and yanked her roughly. "Come back here. You belong to me!"

Evelyn kicked and thrashed.

The prince grabbed her by the waist and tried to haul her back onto the deck. He maintained a firm hold, and she scratched and slapped him to get him to let go.

The low and heavy boom of a cannon blast pierced the stormy night.

Evelyn glanced sidelong in time to catch the explosion rock the already tempestuous waves.

The ship rolled.

She and Vadik plunged into the ocean, tangled together.

The water cut like ice, so cold and sharp. It embraced her. Strangled her.

Evelyn kicked and kicked. She surfaced and gasped for air. A comber crashed over her head. She drowned—and surfaced again.

Thank God for her swimming lessons with Adam! Now if only she could get to the *Bonny Meg*.

A desperate Evelyn stroked across the turbulent waters—but something snagged her foot.

Vadik surfaced. "Help me!"

There was chaos aboard the other ship; the henchmen tossed ropes overboard. But the prince was too far away from the vessel to grab hold of the rigging.

"I can't swim!" cried the prince.

He latched on to Evelyn like a lifeline. She drowned under the pressure of his hold, but the will to live surged through her blood, and she cast off the prince's death grip.

Vadik seized her again. "You're mine!"

"I'm *not* yours!" Evelyn sputtered, the waves pounding her, the prince suffocating her. "You have no power over me!"

She summoned a surge of strength, and with all her might crashed her elbow into Vadik's nose.

The blow disarmed an already confused and panicked prince, and he released his hold.

Evelyn quickly swam off, leaving the shrieking prince to sink under the thrashing waves.

She was exhausted. Pure will was keeping her afloat. She eyed the *Bonny Meg*. It was so close— and yet so far.

Her strength was slowly slipping away from her, the sea too brutal to combat.

She was going to die.

She was going to die without telling him.

A set of hard arms circled her waist.

Adam!

"I've got you, Evie! Now kick!"

Her heart shuddered with delight. She kicked.

"Now swim!"

She started to swim. Adam's presence offered her enough strength to keep fighting.

But the furious waves seemed set against their reaching the *Bonny Meg*. The combers swelled and smashed over them with livid purpose.

Adam put his arms around her, and together they treaded water.

"I love you, Evie!"

Evelyn laughed.

Weeks ago she had searched for death. Now she had *finally* found life—yet it was going to be snatched away from her.

But she would die free of her fears. She would die knowing the prince had no hold over her mind anymore. She would die knowing she could trust Adam, that she didn't have to be afraid to give her heart away.

"And I love you, Adam!"

He kissed her hard. "We're not going to make it back to the ship, Evie."

"I know!"

"Don't be afraid! I'm here with you."

"I'm not afraid." Her heart was filled with joy. The joy of letting go of crippling fear and welcoming the love she had searched for for so long. "I'm not afraid of anything anymore!"

The comber surged and crashed over the entangled couple with savage force.

Adam and Evelyn slipped beneath the wild winds and rolling waves . . . and slowly started to sink.

Epilogue

I t was a crisp fall morning.

Evelyn split the log with an axe. There was a lot of work to be done before the winter winds set in and the snow started to fall.

The brisk sea breeze carried with it memories, and she neglected her chore for a moment to look out across the gray water.

"Are we dead?"

Adam spit seaweed. "I think so."

She touched herself to feel the aches and fatigue and . . . "Then why are we wet?"

The waves still crashed and the winds beat, but the brutal summer tempest was dying; the ocean was righting itself.

Adam rolled across the rough sand to be beside her. "Maybe we're not dead?"

Had the sea taken mercy upon them and tossed them back out onto land? She looked into the distance to see the faint flicker of lights in port.

Evelyn grinned despite the hurt in her jaw. "I think you're right, Adam."

Another grin touched Evelyn's lips at the fond recollection. It had surprised her and Adam both, their survival. The sea had offered them a second chance.

The clip-clop of hooves resounded.

Evelyn searched the beach for Adam with her eyes. "You're late!"

He steered the horse over the embankment and toward the sturdy cottage. With an easy grin, he dismounted—and kissed her passionately on the lips. "It's good to see you, too, my dear."

Content with her husband's atonement, she said, "What took you so long in the village?"

Adam fingered the fob watch in his pocket and checked the time. "I was detained at the post." He then handed her the letter. "It's a note from the duke and duchess."

Evelyn set the axe aside and snatched the missive. She broke the red wax seal and scanned the elegant script. "We're invited to a wedding."

Adam unpacked the household supplies strapped to the animal's back. "For whom?"

"For Captain James Hawkins."

Adam balked. "Black Hawk? You're not serious?"

Evelyn giggled with equal astonishment. "I'm afraid it's true."

"But who the devil would marry *him*?"

"I don't know . . . but I can't wait to find out."

Adam whistled in disbelief. "I suppose splitting wood will have to wait, then." He nudged his head toward the pile of kindling. "You really should let the servants do that."

"We don't have any servants."

"We really should get some servants to do that."

She laughed heartily. "Maybe when the babe comes."

Evelyn patted her belly. Although she wasn't showing yet, she had missed her menses, so it was natural to assume she was enceinte.

"I purchased some more of that blue fabric you like so much, Evie."

She eyed the bundle of material. "It's perfect. I'll get started on the drapes tonight."

She and Adam had never made it to America. Instead they had both decided to remain in England now that she was forever safe from the prince. Their new seaside home was reminiscent of Adam's quaint country cottage—only bigger. Her husband had insisted their new abode have room for a growing family. And she was quite in accord.

"There's strawberry jam in the cottage; fresh baked scones, too," she said. "If you're hungry."

"I'm famished."

"Adam!"

But Evelyn's protest turned to laughter as he wrapped his arms around her and nibbled her neck.

"I have work to do," she charged.

"It can wait," he said in that sensual and robust tone.

Evelyn closed her eyes, susceptible to his charm. "And you can't?"

"Not a minute more, I'm afraid." He scooped her in his arms and headed for the cottage. "We really should hire servants, so you and I can better spend our time."

"I want *us* to work on the cottage together."

He set her on the bed with care. "Then I'm afraid we're going to work at a rather slow pace." He kissed her soundly. "The distractions, you know?"

She smiled. "I don't mind the distractions."

Not one bit. She looked forward to every distracting moment with her husband—and all the lazy days of happiness that stretched before them both.

Unforgettable, enthralling love stories, sparkling with passion and adventure from Romance's bestselling authors

AVON

978-0-06-133535-8

978-0-06-144589-7

978-0-06-137452-4

978-0-06-134024-6

978-0-06-134039-0

978-0-06-111886-9

At Avon Books, we know your passion for romance—once you finish one of our novels, you find yourself wanting more.

May we tempt you with . . .

- **Excerpts** from our upcoming releases.

- Entertaining **extras**, including authors' personal photo albums and book lists.

- Behind-the-scenes **scoop** on your favorite characters and series.

- **Sweepstakes** for the chance to win free books, romantic getaways, and other fun prizes.

- Writing **tips** from our authors and editors.

- **Blog** with our authors and find out why they love to write romance.

- **Exclusive content** that's not contained within the pages of our novels.

Join us at
www.avonbooks.com

AVON

An Imprint of HarperCollins*Publishers*
www.avonromance.com

Available wherever books are sold or please call 1-800-331-3761 to order.

FTH 0708